OF ICE AND DEMONS

THE EXORCIST CHRONICLES, VOL. 1

Of Ice And Demons

The Exorcist Chronicles, Vol. 1

Erin Evans

First Edition: November 2021

Editing and Interior Design
Preserving the Author's Voice
www.ravendodd.com

Cover Design by Jenn Smith
Glass Onion Publishing

ISBN: 979-8-9854647-1-9

Dedication

To Patrick, without you this book would remain but a dream.

To Betsy, you inject my life with something of the marvelous.

One

"This is a very strange place for a demon to roost," Micah said to himself. He stared at the hillside off to his left, back to his compass, and back to the hill. It was an isolated patch of high ground amidst the flat desert landscape. Its steep sides were covered in broken red rock, gray sage, and dust. A few old Joshua trees, their branches twisted and full of spines, dotted the gentler lower slopes while the last twenty feet rose to the crown as a nearly vertical fortress of red rock.

There was no doubt a demon was present. Micah's gaze drifted to the compass again. This side of the small device resembled a watch with its two moving needles. The red needle pointed straight toward the hill without a waver while the silver pointed down the long road ahead. Micah never doubted his compass. He never shook it, opened and closed it to doublecheck, or ignored it. The beautiful steel device had been with him for nearly two decades.

Ever since the International Witch's Council had presented it to him for services rendered, survival primarily, it had never been out of arm's reach, and it had never been wrong. His finger traced the fine and discreet silver inlay along the reverse side of the case while he thought. *Why would there be a demon here? There are no people nearby to influence. The closest portal is four miles away in Canyon Town, and there are plenty of people there. Still…*Micah sighed, clicked the lid closed, and placed the compass back in his waistcoat pocket. With its fine steel chain and traditional case, it looked like a pocket watch. The reverse side was, but he rarely used it.

He left the road to begin his investigation. Micah had been hunting demons for nearly thirty years. He'd started seeing them as a child when his brother was overpowered by one and attempted to throttle Micah in his sleep. Luckily, he'd put up enough of a fight to wake their parents. Micah had not seen his brother since, but he would never forget the sight of the grinning monster leering at him from his brother's shoulder. That night set the course for the rest of his life.

At the bottom of the hill, he paused to consider his gear. He was drastically low on purification potions. All wounds inflicted by demon claws and fangs became infected. So purifying them was essential to survival. "Ah, shit," he muttered. He only had three enchanted bolts left for his hand crossbow. His oiled daggers, however, slid out of their sheaths soundlessly and gleamed in the cold sunlight.

Micah started to climb. He kept his long dagger in his left and dominant hand. Then, sheathing his short blade, he used his right hand to push aside the grey-green sage bushes. His long legs ate up the ground until he stood near the vertical cliff face. He heard it snarl a second before it pounced.

The only thing that kept Micah from becoming another gruesome and bloody cautionary tale for future generations was that leopard demons, like all cats, play with their prey. The demon could have launched itself directly at Micah and fastened its five-inch fangs deep into his throat, but it didn't. Instead, it flashed above his left shoulder, and its claws scored deep cuts through his shirt, his waistcoat, and along his pectoral and neck muscles. Micah swore and dove away from the demon, rolling down the hill in a storm of sharp rock chippings, dust, and blood.

The leopard demon did not immediately chase after him. Demons like that did not go careening down hillsides. It preened itself then began stalking down the hill on all fours. Its double-jointed hips and accordion-like spine meant it could stalk, crawl, creep, or walk at will. Its orange eyes, their pupils flickering like flames, were fixed on Micah, and he felt a surge of fear as he scrambled free of the small landslide he'd created. His chest and shoulder burned, but the protection charms stitched into his clothing had absorbed a lot of the blow.

What the flying fuck is a leopard demon doing here? he thought, plunging his long dagger back into its sheath and madly reaching for his crossbow. Massively powerful demons like this were usually sequestered in isolation in hell. They rarely escaped, and it was nearly unheard of for them to make it to the human world. He watched it stalk nearer as he locked one of his enchanted bolts into his crossbow. Fresh, long, pink scars marred its body. Whatever it had done to make it out of hell hadn't been easy.

A throaty hissing laugh made him scowl in anger. The demon had reached the bottom of the hill and was raising itself to walk on two legs. Its yellow teeth were bared in a malicious grin as it flexed front paws that looked closer to deformed human hands. Micah brought his crossbow to bear and fired. The demon, thinking he'd aimed for its head, dropped to all fours again. In fact, he'd aimed at its waist. A scream of fury and pain rent the air as the bolt buried itself deep into the demon's shoulder with a satisfying *crunch.*

The leopard demon leaped forward—ignoring the wound—the fires in its eyes dancing insanely as it charged. Micah fired off another bolt, missed, then launched himself sideways. He landed on his injured shoulder and couldn't contain the cry of pain as the demon's outstretched front claws cut through his boot and into his right calf.

From the ground, Micah grabbed his final enchanted bolt as the demon skidded to a halt. If it came down to pure hand-to-hand, the odds were drastically not in his favor. The leopard demon turned and, seeing him down on his back, began to laugh again. Clearly, it thought the injury to his ankle was devastating. Sauntering forward on two legs, it prepared to kill him. Micah aimed carefully as he simultaneously unsheathed his right-hand dagger, just in case, and fired.

The bolt caught the leopard demon low on the abdomen. It wasn't a lethal shot. Few things short of decapitation were fatal to a demon that powerful, but it was painful. The demon's roar became a high-pitched screech of pain as it doubled over. Then, clumsily, it wrapped one of its paws around the bolt and began trying to pull it out. Micah didn't hesitate. He had nothing on him powerful enough to defeat the leopard demon, so the only way to live was to run.

Ignoring his injuries, which were already starting to burn with infection, he ran for the road. His damaged boot flopped about his ankle at every step. The only thought in his head was to get to Canyon Town before the demon recovered and gave chase. Demons drew power from isolation, and injured as it was, the leopard demon wouldn't pursue him into a populated area.

Reaching the road and seeing the demon hadn't followed, Micah paused long enough to pour one of his two remaining purification potions on his ankle. It stung and itched fiercely before numbing the area. The bloody tatters of his boot swayed and scraped against the injury as he started running again.

Despite the pain, Micah didn't use his last potion on his shoulder. He was in a race against time to get to town before the infection overwhelmed him. He'd risk his shoulder to use both small potions on his ankle but just had to make it to Canyon Town before the infection incapacitated him. In Canyon Town, he knew, he could find professional help. The silver arrow guaranteed it.

The potions wore off far more rapidly than he would have liked, and he knew he was feverish as he stumbled past the gates onto the main street of Canyon Town. His eyes felt heavy, and his tongue swollen as he fumbled for his compass. Luckily, the silver arrow spun around once and pointed dead center at the third shop on the left.

He was too exhausted from the fight, the injuries, the four-mile race, and the adrenaline crash to notice what kind of shop it was as he stumbled inside. All he knew, thanks to his compass, was a powerful witch was here.

"Micah? What happened?" a familiar female voice said.

His eyes snapped up, and he blearily saw a woman with stunning red hair and green eyes wearing a dark, long-sleeved dress.

"Caroline," he mumbled. Relief surged through him as he tried to take a step forward, but his injured ankle refused to take his weight, and he fell, facedown hard! Glasses rattled on a shelf as he hit the wooden floor. Caroline sprinted over to Micah and struggled to turn him over. Her hand came away from his chest bloody as her agile mind noted several things at once: Ripped shirt. Flushed face. Injured ankle. The smell of blood, dust, and sweat.

She sat back on her heels and reached up for the hairpin she always wore. Caroline's fingertips deftly navigated her way through the mass of curls and encountered the rounded end of a large steel pin. She swiftly drew it free and, holding it in her right hand, raised her left hand and angled her fingers to see the inside edge of the middle one.

Faded against her skin and running the entire length of her finger was a pattern of scars. Caroline pricked her skin near the edge of her nail and dabbed the pin into the resulting drop of blood. She took a deep breath and traced the pattern of scars with the fresh blood. Her vision began to swim, and she shut her eyes while muttering, "I will see."

Opening her eyes, she gritted her teeth against the staggering rush of technicolor now swimming through the scene. She shut out everything except Micah and studied him. He was the only man she'd ever met who had a two-layer aura.

Close to his body, it flickered like blue-grey lightning, each bolt flashing with power before channeling the energy elsewhere. It was always contained, always controlled. Over that lay a gossamer web of shining silver energy. It glittered under her gaze like a cage over the lightning, but today it was besieged by a demonic infection.

Micah's aura fought valiantly against the toxin, but it was fading, the silvery sheen becoming leaden. Caroline wondered how long ago he had been injured as she looked him over. Orange and sickly-green strands extended from his neck down into his chest and rose from his ankle to his knee. A mere second of analysis told Caroline everything she needed to know.

Dashing to the sales counter in the corner of the store, she retrieved her emergency kit and had it open before she was back at Micah's side. She pulled out an extra-large, notched needle, a small copper hoop, white and silver thread, and a small vial of purified water. Quickly clicking the hoop into the notch on the needle, she attached the thread and began braiding it as fast as her fingers would allow.

"Two white, one silver," she muttered. "Two silvers would be overwhelmed by the infection." Once the braid was done, she dipped it into the vial of purified water. Then, Caroline expertly tied and attached it to the hoop at both ends. Turning to Micah, she ripped his shirt open and studied his chest closely. *There*, she thought, then positioned the tip of the needle above the point where his aura was starting to fail. One quick tap on the needle and the charm stood out of his chest like a flag. His eyes fluttered slightly, but he gave no other physical response.

Caroline watched the effects of her charm as she rapidly created a second one. It had halted the spread of the infection at Micah's chest but had not defeated the demonic energy. She scrambled around, straightened Micah's right leg, and pushed his pants up to the knee. After quickly analyzing her spot, she drove the second charm into his shin.

Letting out a pent-up breath, she began a third identical charm. Its placement would be crucial. Her stomach rolled, and she felt a headache starting at the base of her skull. Seeing the technicolor world of energy was taxing, and she was already feeling the side effects. "Hold on," she told herself. "For him, you have to hold on."

The last charm was ready, and she swayed slightly as she leaned over Micah's motionless form and set it into his neck just below the ear. The demonic energy immediately began to recede, and Micah sighed.

Relief coupled with anxiety, overstimulation, and nausea made Caroline feel sick. She smeared the blood on her finger, and the world returned to its "normal" muted colors of blue and grey, but it was too late. She made it to her hands and knees, turned away from Micah, and started dry heaving. Tears pricked the corners of her eyes when she felt his fingertips gently touch her leg.

Once the nausea spell passed, Caroline grabbed two squares of white cloth from her emergency kit and soaked them with the remainder of the purified water in the vial. The first, she wrapped around Micah's injured ankle and was relieved to see all traces of infection were gone. The second she gently dabbed over the wounds on his neck and chest. He flinched, but his coloring was back to normal.

He let out a groan of relief after a minute. "That was the good stuff?" he asked, slurring the words slightly.

Caroline rolled her eyes to hide that they were still teary. "That was the best I have, and you know it. Like I'd really go for bottom shelf purifications when it's you." Micah managed a crooked smile and tried to move. "No way," she said firmly. "You do not move until you tell me what from hell did that to you."

"It was a leopard demon," Micah muttered.

"WHAT?" Caroline exploded.

Micah winced and rubbed a weary hand over his eyes.

"A leopard demon? One of those hasn't made it to our world in nearly two centuries. How did it get here?" she demanded.

"No clue. The *hard way* is all I can tell you," Micah replied. He went on to describe the horrendous scarring across the demon's back and shoulders.

"It must have forced its way through a small portal then," Caroline mused as she plucked the needle charms out of Micah's skin. The white thread had turned grey while the silver was dull and smoky looking. "Maybe that is what's going on here."

The statement piqued Micah's interest. He maneuvered slowly into a sitting position, despite Caroline's protests, and awkwardly began dismantling his shredded boot with his right arm. He sighed in relief as his injuries appeared normal with no signs of demonic influence. "What's happening?"

"The demons are way more active," Caroline replied. "I've noticed a drop in business as they don't want their people coming anywhere near this clean space, and at least half the townspeople have one or more riding them around."

Micah brooded on this. Humans fell into one of two categories when it came to demons. Either they saw them, or they didn't. For those who didn't see them, the demons couldn't physically hurt them. It was a strange cosmic glitch. Instead, the demons would burrow into their auras, whisper, and try to influence those people to do horrendous things. The specifics depended entirely on the type of demon. People could overcome the whispers, decide not to listen, and eventually, the demon would have to leave; however, achieving this required real strength of character, the force of will to persevere—and help.

The second category contained those who could see demons, mostly witches and monks with a few exorcists. Demons rarely tried to influence these kinds of people because they wouldn't listen. Instead, the demons tried to lure them to isolated

11

places and kill them or turn public opinion against them and run them out.

"Think I'm safe here?" Micah asked, looking up at Caroline. She was still so beautiful even now that she was nearly fifty. Her fiery hair had some fine streaks of silver, and there were laugh lines and crow's feet around her eyes. The edges of scars peeked out around her neck and from the right cuff of her dress.

She looked him over thoughtfully. "I don't know. There are precautions in this building, but the demons might still try something if they get wind of who you are. We can deal with that later. Right now, you need to explain why you took on a damned leopard demon with nothing."

"Not nothing," Micah protested.

Caroline raised an eyebrow and stared at him with infinite patience.

"Fine, a couple of crossbow bolts were all I had," he admitted and grimaced. "I've been out of touch for the last few weeks. An entire nest of hate and rage demons tried to take over an isolated village about forty miles from here. It was the first time on record a portal had opened there, and I don't think the place even shows up on most maps."

Caroline's lip curled in disgust, and Micah knew why. Demons like that combined all the worst traits of feral cats and cockroaches. They could slip through the smallest portals and were intensely difficult to kill. And they were intelligent. They only emerged when there was a clear advantage and lured their hunters into traps. Being social demons, they planned and schemed together and attacked in force.

"I finally got them all and closed the portal," Micah continued, "but it took about everything I had on me. They caught me out the first night. I should have seen it coming. It was dark of the moon, and I was walking down a small side street. Anyway, enough about me, what brought you here?"

"Melanie," Caroline said shortly. Micah remembered her friend very well. A pasty and sickly-looking woman, she always seemed distracted. It was as if she wanted to focus on what was going on around her but could not. Something else always demanded a portion of her attention. It was easy to guess what that was. Melanie was a seer. Her gaze pierced the present and, at the same time, saw into the probabilities and possibilities of the future.

"What's she seen?"

"That's just it," Caroline said with some exasperation. "She doesn't know. It was dark and ugly, whatever it was. There were no details to the vision save the main bridge over the canyon outside and a feeling of horror." She gestured out the front windows of her shop, where the edge of the canyon was just visible. "So, of course, the Council didn't listen. They said that there is always something happening here. The portal at the bottom of the canyon is one of the most active in the world. They had other priorities."

"So why are you here then? If I remember correctly, you hate the desert in wintertime."

"Melanie came to me directly," Caroline said, refusing to rise to the bait but clearly glad Micah was feeling well enough to banter. "Her expression told me everything I needed to know. She was terrified. So, I packed up and came here about three months ago. I had to lease this place from the normal witch that runs it, out of my own pocket too," she grumbled.

Micah looked out the window to hide his grin as he finished taking off his ruined boot. Canyon Town was always a sight to see. The red sands, green cactus, and grey sage formed the backdrop for the stunning orange and gold canyon walls. The walls stretched down into darkness only sixty feet apart, joined by three arched, stone bridges and several informal rope ones. The town sprawled on both sides of the narrow fissure. It was the only place with reliable and safe crossings for the enormous canyon and one of the few places to stop for supplies and comforts while traveling through the desert.

Pulling himself from his reverie, Micah pulled out his compass.

"Don't bother," Caroline said, "too much interference." She was right. The silver arrow pointed directly at her while the red arrow swung in a lazy arc encompassing the entire town.

Instead of commenting, Micah looked around at his immediate surroundings. The shop was filled with furniture arrangements, knickknacks, and décor items. Here and there were touches of Caroline's personality. Her custom-made satchel lay rolled out on the floor next to him, and small charms hung around the windows and doors. The colors didn't match well, which was normal for her. Micah frowned as he realized the space did not feel like it was hers.

Putting it from his mind, he asked, "What kind of shop is this?"

"Interior goods," Caroline responded promptly, "furniture, dishes, bedding—that kind of thing."

"That all?" Micah asked with a smirk.

"Of course not. Let's get you upstairs and have a look at the rest of what happened." She paused before adding, "I'll fix that shirt too."

Micah laughed and tried to stand. He swayed slightly as a wave of lightheadedness washed over him and grabbed at the nearest shelf. Unfortunately, it was in a slim cabinet full of precarious glassware. Two teacups wobbled off the shelf to shatter on the ground, and a small saucer landed on his bare foot. Micah jumped in surprised pain and swore, then swore louder as the motion jerked his injured shoulder. Failing to regain his balance, he sat down heavily and gave into several minutes of fluent cursing.

"Are you finished?" Caroline asked, nearly succeeding in keeping laughter out of her voice.

Three more curses answered her before Micah grumbled, "Yes." He pulled himself up carefully and let Caroline drape his uninjured arm over her shoulders. The difference in their heights made him lean awkwardly to one side as she helped him.

Unsteadily, they made their way to the back of the store and up the stairs to the small flat where Caroline lived. Micah took a deep breath as she swung the door open and let the scents of hazel, cardamom, and orange blossom overwhelm him. He always associated hazel and orange blossom with her, and she usually combined them with whatever spice she was on a kick for.

The main room contained a small loveseat on the right wall with a circular coffee table. To the left, there was room for a square four-seater table and chairs. In the back left corner was the kitchen area: stovetop, sink, cabinets, and icebox. On the counter near the sink was an apparatus for making purification potions. Just past the icebox and in the corner behind the loveseat was the only other door. Micah assumed it led to a master suite.

Caroline heard Micah sigh and felt some of the tension drain out of his tall frame. She deposited him on her tiny, two-person couch and started rummaging through her icebox. "I know I have one," she muttered as she searched to the very back.

Micah reclined back. With his head on one armrest, his legs were far too long to fit on the couch. Instead, he bent one leg and rested his foot flat against the other armrest while his injured leg got stretched out on the floor. Then, he twisted his shoulders to keep his weight off his injured side and laid that arm across his chest. He didn't look very comfortable, but he was flat-out exhausted.

"Here," Caroline said, marching back over and extending a small chocolate bar toward him.

"I'm fine," Micah muttered, his eyes closed.

"When was the last time you ate?"

He thought about that. "Yesterday? No, that's not right. This morning, I did have something this morning while I was walking."

"It's nearly dark," Caroline said, purposefully patronizing him. "You will eat this while I knock something up." When Micah still didn't take the chocolate, she added, "It's filled with salted caramel and toffee chips."

He held out a few seconds more before grabbing the candy and tearing open the wrapper with his teeth. "Cheers," he muttered around a large bite.

Caroline rolled her eyes as she turned to her cupboards. She couldn't stand salted caramel and toffee chocolate, and they both knew it, but it was Micah's favorite, and she always kept a couple of bars around. She heard the chocolate wrapper hit the floor and turned to see him throw his uninjured arm across his eyes and relax. His presence seeped gently through the room and brought with it a feeling of familiar safety.

Placing several vegetables, but no onions as he was allergic to them, on the counter along with some flatbread she'd baked yesterday, Caroline started her prep work. She angled herself so she could study her long-time friend while her fingers neatly maneuvered the cutting board, cutting some vegetables, peeling others, and slicing the bread. Once everything was ready, she tossed some oil in a pan and started heating it with a large spoonful of pickled garlic. The vegetables quickly followed, and she cast covert glances at Micah while she sauteed everything together.

His long frame looked leaner than when she'd last seen him two years ago, and he hadn't had any extra weight to lose back then. He still wore his hair long in the current fashion but braided it across his scalp and shaved the back of his neck to stay cool.

She felt the flicker of an old memory stir and for a moment smiled. He always used to plunk down next to her, regardless of where she was sitting, and say, "Head scratches?" Her smile faded. That had been many years ago before he had any white in his black hair or grey in his beard. Now, his hands were covered in scars, his voice was gravelly from lack of use, and his whole body looked tired.

"I can feel you staring," Micah said without removing his arm.

"Just debating how much stir fry to make," Caroline said blithely.

"All of it," he said as he yawned.

"I can't believe it's been two years since I sat at your table," Micah said later as he tore into his sixth piece of bread covered in melted cheese. He shoveled a heaping spoonful of peppers and zucchini into his mouth and chewed with evident pleasure.

"You should come by more often," Caroline remarked dryly. "It'll help get some meat on your scrawny frame."

Micah laughed and finally began to slow down eating. Almost immediately, his eyelids began to droop. "That's it," Caroline said decisively. "You need rest. You've got two injuries to heal from, and that shoulder looked bad. Give me your shirt first, though. I'll mend it."

"Where am I sleeping?" he asked. "There's no way this place is big enough to have a guest suite."

"You're sleeping in my room." Micah opened his mouth to protest, but Caroline overrode him. "If you dare complain about it, I'll knock you upside the head with my best frying pan and dump your unconscious ass in the bed anyway."

They stared at each other before Micah finally relented. "I'll skip the headache then."

"Smart man."

He stretched carefully, then rose and headed for the bedroom while undoing his remaining buttons. At the door he turned, removed his cufflinks, and tossed the shirt across the room to Caroline.

Two

Micah woke suddenly and sat bolt upright in the bed. The unfamiliar surroundings startled him, but then he breathed in the scent of witch hazel and cardamon. He exhaled slowly and stretched carefully, mindful of his injuries. Then taking a rare moment of ease, he lay down again and snuggled into the mattress and pillow, his body reminding him of the difference between sleeping on a bed and sleeping on the ground. He wondered how long he would get to enjoy the comfort of a mattress.

Micah let out a sigh and got up cautiously, testing his wounds and marveling at Caroline's healing mastery. The purification potions she turned out from that little countertop apparatus were without equal. He peeked out the bedroom door and saw Caroline curled up on the loveseat. Her face was buried in the crook of one arm, and her breathing was slow and steady. Smiling, Micah left the bedroom and strode carefully to the small, square table in the corner. His shirt hung off the edge of one of the chairs, and he examined it. Caroline had measured and cut a patch for the ruined material, and, he looked closer, she had hand-stitched protection charms over every inch of the fabric. From experience, Micah knew that such work took hours. She'd probably stayed up all night just doing that, and he wasn't surprised then to see she hadn't attached the patch yet.

A thought struck him, and he quietly stole back into the bedroom. If Caroline kept his favorite chocolate bars on hand, she might keep an old shirt or two. There had been a time where most of his clothing hung in her closet, and she wasn't the type to throw things away.

In the back of the closet, he found a small chest of drawers. The middle drawer on the left was labeled, "Micah." As he opened the drawer and rifled through it, Micah noted the other drawers weren't labeled. He flicked open a neatly folded long sleeve, buttoned shirt and smiled. He could wear this in the meantime, and he silently promised himself he would fight Caroline to finish the patch himself.

Additionally, vowing to make her take the bed the next night, Micah began quietly looking for his things. He decided to slip away for a few hours and let her sleep. His waistcoat was hanging on the back of another chair, but he decided to leave everything but his compass, boots, and wallet where it lay. Lastly, he scrounged up a scrap of paper and a pencil. *Sleep well. Back for dinner.* Micah placed the note on the counter and stole out of the apartment. Popping the lid off a small perfume bottle he kept in his pocket, he dripped some of the clear liquid onto his finger and touched it to his collar and handmade cufflinks before he left the building.

The sun had risen, but barely. There were still vestiges of a pink and gold sunrise in the east. Micah took a deep breath and considered his options. Finding a cobbler was highest on his list as he had one beautifully crafted boot that extended nearly to his knee and one with a ragged edge that barely passed his ankle. He knew there was one around but couldn't quite remember where. It had been years since he'd last set foot in Canyon Town. However, he was in no rush. He set off down the street slowly, favoring his injuries. Caroline was phenomenal with purification potions and charms, but no one could fully heal cuts and abrasions that fast. The cobbler wasn't among the row of shops lining the street, and none of them caught his interest to go in and ask.

So, he headed toward the closest bridge while the morning gleamed bright and cold around him. Townsfolk emerged to do their shopping and daily business. Caroline had been right. Many of them carried small demons about on their backs. Micah wasn't concerned. The demons weren't powerful enough to challenge him, even if they did recognize him for what he was. Injured, with the potion on his shirt, the series of aura suppression

Dorset buttons and cufflinks, and without his blades, he was easily overlooked as a threat.

Micah saw a small chocolate shop down the next street. Something about it piqued his interest, and he sauntered in. It was peaceful and quiet. At first, he thought the shop was empty and left unlocked by mistake. The lights were on, but no one seemed to be behind the counter. He decided to go in anyway. The place smelled heavenly. Rich aromas of cocoa, coffee, and butter filled the space while hints of toffee and cream teased his nose and made his mouth water. As he stepped inside, he felt relaxed and strangely comforted.

"Can I help you?"

Spinning around carefully, Micah saw a pretty woman in her twenties with bright blue eyes and shiny black hair smiling politely at him, having just straightened up from behind a small display of chocolate bars. She was slim and graceful, wearing a flattering bright turquoise shirt belted with a deep red, braided leather cord over a dark skirt. "Yes, I was hoping to purchase some truffles."

Her smile widened, and she beckoned him over to a display case in the corner. He noticed a strange chunky bracelet on her wrist. "Everything we have in stock now is displayed here. Can I help you look for something specific?"

"Bittersweet dark chocolate please with—"

She interrupted him. "I'm sorry we don't make bittersweet truffles."

"Would it be possible to special order them?"

"As a policy, we generally don't." She looked sincerely distraught and fiddled with the bracelet. "I'm sorry, is there anything else you might like?"

They were interrupted by a sandy-haired young man in his early teens. He entered the shop through a curtain at the back and stopped dead when he saw the two of them. "It's you!" he exclaimed, staring at Micah.

"I'm always me," Micah responded nonplussed. "Who else could I be?"

"Don't go anywhere," the young man said earnestly. "Just stay right there." He ran back through the curtain, and they heard him thundering up a set of stairs, yelling, "Mom!"

The young, dark-haired woman looked questioningly at Micah, but he just shrugged his good shoulder.

Less than two minutes later, the teenager was back, and he brought with him a woman that could only be his mother. They had the same hair color, the same dark brown eyes, and the same bright smile. Everything fell into place, further clarified by the small pin the woman was wearing.

"Elaine!" Micah cried. The woman swept toward him, ignored his outstretched hand, and gave him a warm hug. He hid the pain the embrace caused his shoulder and hugged her back. When they broke apart, he turned to her son. "Then you must be Nathaniel."

Mother and son both beamed at him. "It's so good to see you," Elaine said. She had the curvy, plump look of someone who loved sweets, worked around them every day and was happy about it.

Micah smiled at her before addressing her son. "I'm surprised you remember me."

"I'll never forget what you did," the boy said solemnly.

Elaine's brown eyes were suddenly over bright. She placed one arm protectively around Nathaniel's shoulders while the fingers of her other hand touched the pin Micah had given her years ago. "We never got a chance to thank you after what happened with…" Her voice trailed off, and she sniffled quietly. Micah reached out and clasped her hand in both of his. After a moment, she pulled herself together.

"Obviously, you are here for something sweet. Nathaniel, get me two of the caramel and toffee bars. And don't you dare," she added as Micah reached for his wallet, smiling. His love of salted caramel and toffee chocolate was apparently very memorable. "You will insult me if you even think about paying for this," she continued before her eyes fell on the case behind him and suddenly gleamed. "What kind of truffles were you looking for?"

"Bittersweet dark chocolate," the dark-haired woman said when he hesitated.

"That's different," Elaine said to herself, but then she broke into a mischievous grin. "I love a challenge. So what's the filling?"

"Raspberry cream?" Micah said, half asking.

"Fascinating. Consider it done." Elaine turned to her son. "Nathaniel, go turn on the water for my smallest double boiler. Rebecca, hurry down to the market. See if they have any fresh raspberries and get some cream."

"Wait! What?" The dark-haired woman Rebecca asked. "I bought cream three days ago, and it's not the season for raspberries."

"Then we'll make do with some of the frozen ones from last season. Don't worry," Elaine added for Micah's benefit, "you won't be able to tell the difference." Looking back at Rebecca with a preoccupied air, she said, "Hurry!"

"But we have cream!" Rebecca said. "I'm not going to make a trip across town for cream we don't need when we're about to have our morning rush." "

Elaine stared her down. "Three-day old cream is great for cakes, tarts, and breakfast pastries. But for this order, I will have nothing but fresh."

"I'm sure they'll be fine without," Micah tried to cut in, but Elaine forestalled him.

"I'll humor you enough to let you pay for these truffles because I can tell they're for someone special, but I will not hand you anything less than the best I can offer. Now, here are your chocolates with caramel and toffee. Come back in a few hours, and I'll have your truffles." She then forcibly escorted him and her bewildered assistant to the door.

"Special," Micah mused as he opened one of the chocolate bars. "Caroline was definitely that." She'd been special to him for a long time. They'd been casual lovers a few times over the years, but then necessity would take them separate ways. When they came back together, the spark of romance had gone, but the friendship remained.

He took a pensive bite of chocolate and was totally distracted. Elaine had put a hint of a savory herb in the caramel. It was unique and fantastic—but what was it? He took another bite but still couldn't tell what she'd used.

Micah was over the bridge and six shops away, enjoying the final bite of deliciousness before he realized he still had no idea where the cobbler was. Crumpling up the wrapper, he spotted an older gentleman enjoying the sunlight in a wooden rocking chair on his porch. There was an empty rocker next to him. "Seat taken?" Micah asked.

The gentleman nodded his head in a gesture of welcome, and Micah sank onto the warm wood gratefully. Then, stretching his long legs out and fighting back a wince of pain, he saw his companion look questioningly at his ruined boot. "My friend's kid just discovered scissors," he lied easily.

The older man laughed. "You'll want to go back the way you came then. Cobbler is four alleys down on the left."

Micah nodded his regard but settled deeper into the chair. It rocked smoothly and comfortably. Taking a minute to survey his surroundings, he noticed several demons hanging out across the street, staring at the house. Small demons could survive without attaching to a human, but they rarely tried to or congregated in groups like that.

"Nice, isn't it?" his companion asked. Micah switched his focus and gave a soft grunt of agreement. "My son makes these himself. He gives my wife and me a new rocker every couple of years. Somehow finds the time in between working and raising four little girls."

As if on cue, the tinkling sound of breaking glass reached them.

The man sighed. "That sounded like my last vase. The wife loves flowers, but now she's got nowhere to display them."

"Know the home goods store on the other side of the canyon?" Micah asked.

"Can't say I do, but I don't get over there much since it got so cold. Honey!" he turned and called through the open door. "Come out here a second."

A harassed looking woman with flyaway, grey hair charged onto the porch, shepherding three girls under the age of ten. They giggled and tried to stay out of reach as she attempted to comb their hair. "What is it, Markus?" she asked.

"Have you been across the bridges recently?" Markus asked while he rocked and made a feeble swipe at one of the girls.

"Can't say I have." his wife responded, deftly catching one of the girls and producing a comb and hair tie. "It's been enough looking after these three while their mother recovers."

"May I ask?" Micah inquired politely. He was surprised neither Markus nor his wife had a demon on them. With the attention their house was getting, he was sure something big was attracting them.

"Oh, I suppose," Markus's wife said after a pause. "It's already all over town anyway." She paused again to catch a second little girl as the first danced away with her hair tamed into twin braids. "She had her fourth a few weeks ago and hasn't quite seemed right since. It was a difficult birth, and the child is very colicky. She cries all the time, for no reason at all, and won't calm down until someone else takes her from her mother. It's been a very troubling time for our daughter-in-law."

Micah tapped his fingers on his leg and considered a moment. While the older couple was engaged with their granddaughters, he snuck a glimpse at his compass. The red needle was pointing directly into the house behind them. That meant there was something closer than the gaggle of demons across the street and powerful enough to cut through the interference.

Curiously, the silver needle was moving. He looked in that direction and saw the woman from the chocolate shop Rebecca hurrying past, clutching a carton of cream. He filed that information away for later and turned his attention to the matter at hand. "If I may," he said, interrupting the monologue of the last little girl

30

about her favorite doll as her grandmother finished her hair. "I have some experience with delicate matters like these. I'd like to talk to your daughter-in-law."

"You can help mommy?" the oldest girl, who wasn't more than ten, asked excitedly before Markus or his wife could answer. Children always seemed to know subconsciously when an exorcism was needed and took immediately to someone who could do it. Micah had seen it too many times to think it was a coincidence.

"He can help mommy?" the middle one echoed from under her grandmother's arm.

"Mama?" said the youngest, a toddler of about three. She reached a tiny hand out and grasped Micah's pant leg. He patted her head gently.

"I'd like to try," Micah said kindly, "with your grandparent's permission, of course." He looked up at them while the girls vied with each other to plead his case.

They stared at him for several long moments. Then Markus narrowed his eyes. Something seemed to click in his mind, and he said, "It couldn't hurt." He smiled at Micah. "You just want to talk to her?"

Micah nodded. "I have no intention of distressing her in any way, and of course, this will go no further than your front door."

Markus' wife was still uncomfortable, but she finally gave in to quiet down the older girls who were now skipping around the porch chanting,

"Help Mommy. Help Mommy," while the youngest toddled in excited circles.

She gathered them all together and herded them into the house calling, "Angelica" as they filed through the front door. "There is a gentleman here who'd like to talk to you."

"Privately, if at all possible," Micah added in a murmur. "You have my word I will not harm her in any way." She looked unhappy at that but nodded after looking at her granddaughters' pleading faces.

The bedroom she led him to was dark and stuffy inside with all the curtains drawn. A woman, deep circles under her eyes, looked up at them from her position on the floor by a crib. She had reached in and grasped her baby's hand, cradling her tiny fingers gently but was shaking with silent sobs.

It was clear to Micah what had happened. He stepped into the room and closed the door with a muted but decisive thud. Certain demons preyed upon the exhaustion of new mothers. They snuck in during the stress of childbirth and sought to remove all the mother's affection for her child. He hated them the worst among all demons. He could see it too. The slimy, sickly, yellowed creature was grinning at him from its perch. One of its claws wrapped around the mother's neck while the other waved mockingly at him. Micah refrained from scowling. It didn't know he could see it yet.

"You love her very much. I can see that," Micah said gently.

"I'm trying to," Angelica responded sadly. "I want to...so much." Her voice broke, and she bowed her head, too exhausted and stressed to wonder why a strange man just entered her room.

"But something feels like it's pulling you away?" he asked in a soft, calm voice.

"Yes," she whispered. "I keep having horrendous dreams of hurting her." Tears began running down her face. "I'm scared to hold her, to touch her, and to tell anyone."

"Thank you for telling me," Micah said seriously. "Now answer me clearly. Do you want to feel this way?"

"No," she said with a quiet sob. The demon wasn't smiling now.

"Do you want to pour the love in your heart out to your children?"

"Yes."

"To the rest of your family?"

"Yes!" Her voice rose now. The demon looked shaken. It bared its fangs and tried to dig its claws in deeper.

"Will you love your daughter to the best of your ability?" Micah asked as he knelt by her on the floor.

"I will." The force of the exclamation, even though it was said quietly, rocked the demon back. It scrambled not to lose its perch, but Micah's hand shot out and grabbed it by the throat. Angelica didn't notice as she focused her full attention inside the crib.

"Don't allow anything or anyone to tell you differently," Micah said, ripping the demon off her back.

The change was immediate. Angelica gave a decisive nod, then stood and reached into the crib. Gently, she lifted her little girl into her arms and held her close. The baby cooed and snuggled in, wrapping one tiny hand in her mother's shirt.

The demon was fighting to get out of Micah's grip. It snarled and flailed and tried to get its teeth into his hand. He held it firm, and when Angelica turned away to walk out of the room, snapped its neck. The demon fell limp, and its body fell to dust before it hit the floor. Micah took a moment to open the curtains and bring light back into the room.

"It's good to see you smiling," Markus's wife was saying when he joined them in the living room.

Angelica smiled. "I know I'll be all right now."

The three older girls looked at Micah, and he gestured them over. Then, sitting on the floor so he could be closer to their eye level, he pulled out the second chocolate bar Elaine had given him. Their faces lit up with pleasure. "Do you want to help your mother?" he asked them as he opened the candy.

"Of course, we do," replied the oldest one. "Even Sarah." She gestured to the toddler, who was clutching her other hand.

"Good. I'll share a secret with you," Micah said as he broke the chocolate into pieces. "The best way to help her is never to let her forget that she loves you all and your baby sister."

The older girls nodded solemnly and took their treats. They rushed over to their mother and grandparents, asking to play with the baby. Micah stood and strode toward the door.

He was halfway across the porch when Markus called out to him, "Wait!" Micah turned and paused. "You need to come with me," the old man said.

"Why?"

"There is someone else who wants to see you."

"I'm afraid I have other commitments—" Micah tried to say, but he was interrupted.

"No. It's my son's best friend Joshua and his wife. Her name is Miranda. They made me promise if I ever came across you that I would bring you their way."

"Why?"

"It's Miranda. Eight years ago, a group of men accosted her when she had to work late and were dragging her down an alley in the middle of the night. She hasn't spoken of what they planned to do to this day, but they never got the chance. You intervened, broke up the gang, and sent her home unscathed."

Micah couldn't recall the exact incident without seeing the woman. Sadly, this happened far too often for him to keep all the details straight based on just a name. "How do you know it was me?" he asked.

"You're memorable," came the reply. "Miranda couldn't see much given the poor lighting, but she said you were tall and lean, had piercing blue eyes and scars all over your arms."

"That could be any number of men," Micah protested.

"You intervened," Markus emphasized. "That's how I know it was you. You could have passed us by when you heard about Angelica just as you could have passed by that alley, but you didn't. You stopped and helped. For Miranda, you prevented what could have been the worst—or last—night of her life. Now tell me honestly, was it you?" He fixed Micah with such a stare that he couldn't lie.

"I think so."

"I knew it! Now follow me; they live just up the road here." Markus set off with a purposeful stride, and Micah followed him pensively.

A few minutes later, they reached their destination, a quaint single-story house painted white. Markus entered without knocking and called out their presence. Joshua, a burly red-faced man with dark hair and beard, looked up from the couch and closed the book he was reading. "Markus, good to see you. Escaping all the ladies at home?" They shared a laugh as Micah stood politely by the door.

"Where's Miranda?" Markus asked.

"She's just putting together some tea. Fancy joining us?" Joshua glanced at Micah to include him in the invitation.

"Always. You have any of those little iced biscuits?" Markus asked.

Joshua laughed again. "We keep a stack handy just for you. I'm sure you and…" he trailed off.

"Micah," Markus supplied.

"I'm sure you and Micah will demolish the lot."

They walked through the house into the inviting kitchen. Joshua walked up to his wife and pecked her on the cheek.

"Guests again?" she asked as she turned. "I heard voices." When she saw Micah, she gasped, and all the color drained out of her face as she raised shaking hands to cover her mouth. Joshua's brows furrowed, and he held on to her protectively. "It's you," she finally managed to squeak.

Micah gave her an awkward smile. "Been hearing that a lot recently." Seeing her brought all the details of that night to the front of his mind.

"Thank you," she said with profound gratitude. "I've waited years and hoped I could say those words to you." Her eyes welled up with tears.

"You mean this is the guy that…?" Joshua asked.

Miranda nodded, making no effort to stem the tears trickling down her face. "I'd never forget him."

Joshua let go of her and walked to Micah with his hand outstretched. "If we can ever help you—anything—you name it."

Micah shook the offered hand. "Just pay it forward. Stop and help someone else when they need it."

"We have, and we will," Miranda said sincerely, unshed tears gleaming in her eyes. "But for now, let us feed you lunch." She wiped her face and began bustling around the kitchen, waving off all help, as the men retreated to the living room to enjoy their tea.

It was well into the afternoon when Micah left. The company had been pleasant, and he felt relieved that the demons hadn't infiltrated the entire town. Looking at the small package they'd forced on him, he smiled. Caroline would love the tea and biscuits. He spent so much of his time alone or in hostile environments; it was nice to have a friend to share things with.

The cobbler's window featured some fine mid-calf boots in black and brown leather. Micah paused to admire them and mentally selected the style he wanted. They were dark brown and plain except for a small decorative seam near the top. He thought he could ask Caroline to expand on that with a protection charm. She'd do a better job than he and probably accept payment in raspberry truffles.

He trained his face into neutrality when he walked in. The cobbler had a fat, ugly demon, a garish shade of pink draped about his head. It had small yellow and gold streaks around its mouth and eyes. *It's some kind of hatred demon,* Micah thought as he waited for the cobbler to finish with another customer. He analyzed it further while it was looking away. *The coloring reminds me of jealousy or envy, but those demons usually have three arms. However, the claws and the shape of the arms look like self-hatred, but it is oozing too much. Ah, yes, it's self-loathing.* He reached this conclusion just as the cobbler turned to him.

"Good afternoon, sir. How may I help you?" The man was an excellent actor. He smiled and listened to Micah's request before taking his measurements.

"Your shop seems in good hands," Micah commented. He would have praised the man anyway, he was very free with deserved compliments, but he covertly watched the demon. At hearing the kind words, it leered at him and sunk its claws deeper into the cobbler's neck.

"Very kind of you to say," the man said before holding out a receipt. "The sum for your new boots."

Micah paid half upfront then took his leave with the promise his boots would be ready in a few days. The cobbler promised to send a message to Caroline's home goods store.

Two people stopped and started whispering as he left the store and started back toward the chocolate shop. Ignoring them and their demons, Micah rechecked his compass. The red arrow was spinning lazily in a full circle while the silver one wavered in the direction he was heading.

"Sit!" Elaine commanded forcefully the moment he closed the door of the chocolate shop behind him.

Micah jumped, and his hands twitched toward his belt where his daggers usually sat. Calming himself, he obeyed and laughed as she brought him a gift-wrapped box, a steaming mug of spiced hot chocolate, and one of his favorite candy bars. "You are too good to me," he said as he blew on the hot chocolate. While taking a small sip, he had to ask, "What is in this?"

Elaine smiled before calling for her son. Nathaniel emerged, looking sheepish, from the curtain where he'd been eavesdropping.

"He's been flavoring all the hot chocolate for months now," Elaine said proudly.

"It's excellent," Micah remarked after another sip.

Fidgeting and blushing in embarrassment, Nathaniel explained that he steeped cinnamon, cloves, and just a hint of black pepper in the hot chocolate.

Caroline was finishing up some three-egg omelets when Micah limped up her stairs. She called for him to wash up and take a seat.

He smiled broadly when she brought the plates of egg, sausages, and breakfast pastries to the table and remarked, "Breakfast for dinner, your favorite."

She happily rolled her eyes. Micah never turned down breakfast, no matter what time of day it was.

As they ate, Micah explained about the people he'd met.

"Elaine is a sweetheart, isn't she?" Caroline said as she pushed away her empty plate. "I just wish she did truffles on commission."

"Speaking of," Micah said with a mischievous smile, and he placed the wrapped gift box from the chocolate store on the table.

Caroline grinned in anticipation and sent the wrapping paper flying. Inside were nine beautifully shaped dark chocolate truffles. Three had small, candied mint leaves on them, three had a decorative sprinkling of pink sugar, and three had grated lime zest. "What are these filled with?" she asked excitedly.

"Try one and find out."

Caroline selected the middle truffle from the box, one of the pink sugared ones, and bit into it. She closed her eyes as the bittersweet chocolate began to melt on her tongue mixed with the tart raspberry filling and just a faint hint of strawberry sweetness from the sugar. She popped the rest of the truffle in her mouth and sighed with pleasure.

She opened her eyes to see Micah smirking at her across the table as he bit into his chocolate treat. "How did you get her to make these?" she asked eagerly, selecting one of the lime ones to try.

"She volunteered."

Caroline paused with the truffle halfway to her mouth. "It's been her policy for years not to make truffles on order, or so I've been told. She makes what she makes, and it's, 'Take it or leave it.'"

"Yeah, well…" Micah hedged. He got that kind of half awkward, uncomfortable look he always got when talking about people he'd saved.

"What happened?" Caroline asked, setting the truffles aside. "It was the last time you were here, right?"

He frowned and thought a long moment before nodding, obviously deciding how much to tell her. "You know Elaine was married, right?"

"Of course. They started the shop together. I've heard around town that her son may look like her but has his father's genius with cocoa."

"Well," Micah paused and tapped his fingers on the table as he gathered his thoughts, "Elaine's husband fell under a demon's sway. It was a hideous thing, and I've rarely met one of that caliber. I'll spare you the details, but it had convinced him to plan out a dreadfully detailed and gruesome murder-suicide." He paused again and looked off to the side as he rubbed a hand over his face. "My compass led me to them, but I was late. He'd already started through with his plan."

His shoulders slumped, and he seemed to curl into himself. "The only thing that saved them was how elaborate it was. Nathaniel was only a child. He shouldn't have seen his father like that. Anyway, I fought him back and prevented the murders. It wasn't easy," he added as he straightened and traced a specific fine scar across the back of his right hand. "However, the demon had such a hold on him that I couldn't stop the suicide."

Caroline let the silence stretch after he finished the story. There wasn't much to say anyway. They'd witnessed similar scenes and stories enough that the platitudes had run out. She got up, put on a pot of chamomile and mint tea, and pulled out some petit fours from the bakery down the street. Neither of them ate the small decadent cakes but sat in companionable silence with their tea.

"You know," Caroline said later as she prepared to go to sleep, "your hair looks atrocious."

Micah sighed and reached up to tame it. His left arm didn't make it all the way, and he grimaced.

"Here," Caroline said and gestured him toward her bedroom.

He brightened immediately. "Head scratches?"

She laughed and settled down on her bed. Micah sat on the floor in front of her, leaned back against her legs, and closed his eyes. She started by undoing the remnants of braiding left in his hair and gently combing out all the tangles; then she began to play. She lifted locks of hair and let them fall back down over his neck, ran her fingernails over his scalp, and massaged the uninjured parts of his neck. He relaxed against her as her touch soothed away the tension and pain. Eventually, his breathing deepened, and his head started to tilt to one side. With the ease of long practice, Caroline quickly braided his hair and gently laid her hands on his shoulders.

He turned his head slightly and nuzzled her wrist before she slid out from behind him. Draping his good arm around her, she helped him to his feet and nestled him in the bed before he woke up.

Three

The intimate mood had burnt itself out by the following morning. Micah agreed to help Caroline in the shop, although he quickly regretted this act of chivalry. She happily assigned him the job of dusting all the top shelves while she puttered around at waist level arranging tableware. As he dusted, Micah subtly rearranged some of the vases and knickknacks. Several were just close enough in color to be clashing, and others weren't even close to matching. He did the same with decorative pillows and napkins when he thought Caroline wasn't looking. Neither of them said a word about it.

They were in a back corner having a serious, if somewhat ridiculous, discussion on the merits of teapots with external strainers when they heard the front door open. "Micah!" someone shouted genially. "I hoped you'd be here, and I didn't drag my old bones across the bridge for nothing!"

"Markus!" Micah called back. "I'll be right there." He hurried Caroline to the front and introduced her to Markus and his wife, whose name, he finally learned, was Maria. "Looking for some new vases after all?" he asked after the introductions were completed.

"Indeed," Maria said wistfully, looking at a dinette set in polished walnut wood. Markus cleared his throat loudly, and she continued, "I'd like a matching set, please. Angelica used to love the smell of fresh flowers in her room."

"Of course," Caroline said. "My most beautiful vases are located back here." She led them down one of the aisles while Micah made a beeline for the stairs.

Once there, he hesitated and returned to the group. "Where are your herbs?" he asked Caroline under his breath.

She looked at him curiously, "In the usual place."

"Top cupboards left of the icebox, thanks," Micah interrupted her. He turned abruptly and headed back to the stairs. He thought he heard the door to the shop open as he began climbing.

The charm he had in mind was simple and beautiful, but it packed a punch. He rummaged through the cupboards and quickly found the sage and baby's breath flowers, but he could not find lavender. Usually, he counted himself lucky if he went weeks without seeing the purple flowers. He hated the smell, but this wasn't for him.

"Micah, what are you doing?" Caroline asked. She'd come to see what he was up to after agreeing to give Markus and Maria some time alone to peruse the vases.

"I need lavender. Do you have any?"

"Of course, I do," she said, nonplussed. Micah never used lavender. "It's above the icebox. I set it aside so you wouldn't have to smell it." The words were hardly out of her mouth before Micah was reaching to get it with his good arm. She changed tack when she spotted the plants on the table. "That's the couple from yesterday, isn't it?"

"That's right," Micah said as he separated and laid out four baby's breath flowers.

"Don't use four," she said critically. "Never use more than three baby's breath. You get diminishing returns."

"There are four children in the house," Micah said, defending his choice.

"Then use three for maximum effect and cut the lavender to four different heights. Place them around the baby's breath at cardinal points to account for the four children," Caroline said as she came around to stand over his left shoulder and stared hard at the plants he'd laid out.

"That will throw off the symmetry," he objected.

"Not if you counterbalance it with different heights in the sage and two tall stalks of lemongrass at the back for extra purity."

"You don't put lemongrass with lavender."

"Not normally no, but in this case, it will add to the aesthetics and rebalance the bouquet."

"I really don't think," Micah tried, but Caroline shoulder checked him out of his chair and onto the floor. With a flourish, she took his seat and began arranging the plants.

"Hand me my thread," she said once everything was to her liking. "I'll tie an infinity knot to keep the herbs fresh."

"Use pink thread," Micah said as he located the large package of thread. Each bundle was carefully labeled with type, thickness, and color.

"No. Infinity knots concerning love always use red."

"Maybe I'll hand you the pink thread anyway," Micah teased.

Caroline scowled at him. "Hand me both, and I would know the difference." He did, and she laid the pink and red threads on either side of the bouquet. "Why pink anyway?"

"All four children are daughters," Micah said with a superior smirk.

"Fine, pink."

"And cross it four times."

"I will not. That is a useless waste of time, and usually, the thread gets tangled anyway and negates the effects." Caroline resisted Micah's efforts to take the charmed bundle of plants from her and neatly tied the pink thread into a complex knot. "Now it's done."

They took the charm for Angelica and walked back downstairs, breaking off the conversation about thread colors for different infinity knots when they saw Maria and Markus still in discussion about vases.

"Have we any front runners?" Caroline asked.

"Well," Maria hedged, "we love these silver ones, but I'm afraid the girls will break them."

Caroline smiled and picked up one of the vases. It was a beautiful creation of gentle curves and clean lines. "These are stronger than they look."

"But will they survive four little girls?"

"I think they will," Caroline responded with a grin. "These are made of metal."

"Really?" Maria looked delighted. "We'd love them."

"I'll ring you up. If you'll follow me?" They headed for the register in the back.

As they were wrapping up the vases, Micah stepped forward and presented the charm he and Caroline had made. Maria and Markus might not understand its power, but that didn't matter. "For Angelica," he said. "Please take it."

"This smells divine," Maria said as she held the little bundle up to her nose. "Thank you."

"That was a good thing to do," Caroline said a minute later as the door closed behind Maria and Markus.

"Seems a little odd," Rebecca said, appearing behind them. Micah flinched, and his hands moved to the daggers on his belt, but Caroline didn't react.

"Why would you just give away a powerful charm like that?"

"Because there was a need," Caroline answered. Her voice was mild, but she bristled slightly.

Rebecca scowled at her but spoke to Micah. "I didn't know you knew how to make charms."

He looked back and forth between the two women but didn't answer. Clearly, something had happened between them, and he did not want to be part of it.

"I see," Rebecca said haughtily. "You're like her. You think I'm useless because I taught myself."

"I think nothing of the sort," Micah said diplomatically. "I don't know anything about you and have formed no judgments."

"Don't bother," Caroline said nastily. She stood with her hands on her hips and was practically spitting the words. "She doesn't know much and wouldn't learn even if we offered."

"I know enough to keep myself alive," Rebecca snapped. Micah took a prudent step back as the two women squared off.

"You haven't faced anything life-threatening," Caroline snarled. "Anything beyond a simple hatred demon would clip your pride and shove it down your throat right before cutting it."

"Caroline!" Micah said, shocked out of his neutrality by her vehemence.

"She needs to hear this," Caroline said viciously before turning back to Rebecca. "You haven't seen what is out there. You haven't fought them in the middle of the night trying to stop something horrendous. You haven't dealt with the infection, the wounds, and the scarring. You haven't watched them rip apart your friends or stitched your family members back together." She was nearing hysterics now. Her eyes were full of tears, her face was bright red, and her hands were shaking.

Rebecca looked like she'd been slapped, but then she went on the offensive. "Oh, I've seen plenty, you pretentious bitch. I've seen what they do, but they never face me directly. I'm too powerful."

"You are dumber than I thought," Caroline cut in. "The *only* reason they haven't killed you is that they know there are bigger fish to fry. They won't waste time on a pathetic weakling like you while powerful exorcists are around."

"Like you?" Rebecca shot back skeptically.

"Like him!" Caroline shouted and pointed her finger at Micah. "Look, I mean, really look at him. Do you see the number of scars on his hands? The fresh wound on his neck? The way he stands with his back to a corner? The fact that he reaches for weapons before anything else? *He* is who they are after. They don't care about you and barely care about me. Don't talk about your power in front of him."

"Don't bring me into this, please," Micah said, his hands held up before him as Rebecca's eyes swept up and down his frame.

"He doesn't look that special," she said dismissively.

Caroline uttered a wordless shriek of rage. She snatched Micah's compass chain, ripped it out of his pocket, and shook it in the other woman's face. "How do you think he got this?"

"Why should I care about a pocket watch?"

"You ignorant bitch!" Caroline ranted. "This is a demonic compass granted to him by the International Witches Council. Only seventeen have been given out in the last fifty years! Most witches have to reach a T.P.A. of nineteen or more before they even dream of seeing one."

"What rubbish is a T.P.A?" Rebecca said, clearly ignoring the evidence presented about Micah.

Caroline sneered at her. "Tiered Practicum Average. Do you even have one?"

"Never tried, but I don't need one—"

"Yes, you do!" Caroline interrupted. "You need one to be able to interact intelligently with any other witch! It's a statement of your skill level and power."

"I'm plenty powerful without one."

"You are not listening to me." The compass rattled in Caroline's shaking hands and gave her an idea. "Micah, use your compass!"

"What?" he said, bewildered.

"Stand between us and see which one the silver needle points to. That will show her. It'll point toward the most powerful one around," she added scathingly to Rebecca.

"Then won't it just point at him if he's so powerful?" Rebecca sneered.

"It won't point to the holder," Caroline snarled.

"This is not what the compass is supposed to be used for," Micah said, really regretting his involvement in this argument.

"I don't care!" Caroline shrieked.

Micah hesitated. He desperately did not want to be in the middle of this fight, but Caroline pushed him between her and Rebecca. He sighed, ignored the jostling to his healing injuries, and opened the compass. The silver needle spun around once and pointed toward the front of the store, away from both women. His eyes followed that direction, puzzled at the answer.

Rebecca snorted. "Seems like your compass doesn't work."

"Of course, it works," Micah snapped. He hurried toward the front but stopped in his tracks as he saw the fourth person in the shop.

A tall, broad-shouldered black man with warm golden eyes wearing the traditional sky-blue robes of a monk stood before them. They had not noticed his entrance, but he seemed unconcerned by the argument and exuded a sense of calm and serenity. Caroline forgot her anger when she saw him and rushed up next to Micah. Both put their hands together and bowed slightly before they took the time to examine the newcomer.

He smiled at them and nodded while propping the walking stick he carried against his shoulder. His other hand rested on a satchel slung across his chest. His pale blue robes hid his physique and were covered in red and gold protection symbols.

"Madam," he said, acknowledging Caroline in a deep, slow voice. "Do not dismiss intelligence and experience different from your own."

Caroline grimaced and flushed in embarrassment for losing her temper until her eyes found a deeply special crest stitched into the left shoulder of his robes, and they went wide. "Thank you for your wisdom," she said politely.

"Miss," he said, turning to Rebecca. "If you continue to let your pride push away potential allies, you will find yourself alone in the darkness."

She scowled at him and sputtered, but he ignored her and addressed Micah. "My friend…do not carry your burdens alone. They will twist your soul."

Micah looked thoughtful as he digested this advice and bowed again.

"What is going on, you two?" Rebecca said, having found her voice and clearly annoyed that she had been dismissed. "Who is this?"

"Look at his shoulder," Caroline said exasperatedly.

"That swirl of stitching doesn't mean anything to me!" Rebecca shot back, her temper rising again.

"Gegan," Micah said, interrupting the argument before they could get going again. "That's his name."

"That's a title," Rebecca scoffed. "That's not a name."

Caroline threw up her hands in anger and turned to the man. "I am so sorry, Gegan. Please don't take offense."

"It is fine, madam," he responded calmly. "We teach those who do not know, not condemn them."

Caroline flushed deeper but kept her mouth shut. Finally, Micah tried to explain to Rebecca. "Gegan is a term used in this monastic order. Often it describes a person who has received extensive training and is placed in front of their name. However, in special cases, the name is dropped."

"Why would they do that?" Rebecca asked, distracted from her anger.

"Because it doesn't matter anymore," Gegan said.

"He's right," Micah said. "His training and skills are so evolved, so...I don't even know the word that his order dropped his old name."

"It matters not," Gegan said as Rebecca tried to ask another question. "It is my name and how I wish to be addressed. The rest is history."

"Why are you here?" Caroline asked.

At the same moment, Rebecca asked Micah, "How did you know what to call him?"

Micah looked apologetically at Gegan (who nodded his head) before answering. "There is a mark on the shoulder of his robes. It signifies his name and title."

Gegan raised his hand and indicated the elaborate crest on his left shoulder as he turned to Caroline. "My order received intelligence that a large demon has roosted nearby. I came here to see if you had any knowledge about it or any supplies you would part with."

"Anything I've got is yours," Caroline said promptly. "My skills and my services as well. What do you need?"

"Really?" Rebecca muttered. "Kiss up a little more, why don't you?"

"Are you fucking kidding me?" Caroline shouted, completely losing her temper again. "When a freaking Gegan asks for your help, you give it! No questions asked. No payment, no favors. Nothing!"

"Madam, no need for that," Gegan said. "Lack of education should be calmly corrected, not cursed."

"I do not need to be corrected!" Rebecca snapped back.

Micah had enough. With another apologetic look at Gegan, he wrapped the fingers of his left hand around Rebecca's upper arm and dragged her from the shop. She threw him off once he had marched her two doors down and turned to face him with a look of rage undiminished by his gasp of pain as he grabbed his injured shoulder.

"Just don't," he said, interrupting her rant before it could begin. "I am going to give you a piece of advice, and you are going to listen to it. Like it or not, Gegan was right. Your pride is holding you back. Caroline has a T. P. A. of seventeen. The highest you can get is twenty-three. She could teach you a vast array of techniques and skills, but you don't want to hear it. There is so much in this world that you don't know, and you are driving the people who would help away. Continue to do that, and no one will be there when you need them most." His piece said, Micah turned on his heel and walked back to Caroline's shop.

"There you are," Caroline said, plainly grateful he'd returned alone. She was sitting with Gegan in her small living room with her stocks of herbs spread out on the coffee table and overflowing onto the floor. His satchel and walking stick were resting next to the couch.

Micah smiled at her as she carefully moved the lavender to the far corner.

"Thank you both for your assistance," Gegan said. "I have traveled a great deal over the last several weeks and am grateful for the chance to rest. I'll be on my way soon to face the demon."

"It's a leopard one," Micah said.

Gegan gave him a calculating look before nodding his head slightly and sinking deep into thought. "That is very unusual," he finally said. "Have you seen it then?"

"I fought it," Micah admitted and gave the details when Gegan pressed.

"I am impressed," Gegan said after Micah finished. "How did you prevent its pursuit?"

"I shot it in the stomach with my last enchanted crossbow bolt."

"Interesting," Gegan said. "I will integrate this into my strategy. Thank you."

"Can I interrupt?" Caroline asked. She'd made tea while Micah was telling his story and brought it out with some biscuits and cakes.

"This smells divine," Gegan said as he picked up his cup. His huge, scarred hands enveloped the china and looked one twitch away from crushing it. After taking a sip, he selected a ginger biscuit and sat back contentedly.

"Is the leopard demon the only thing that brought you here?" Caroline asked delicately.

"Yes," Gegan responded promptly. "My order found a record of it in one of their rituals several days ago and dispatched me. I was in the area already on unrelated business. Hence my need for resupply."

"Of course, anything you need," Caroline said quickly. "But could I ask you for help?" Gegan inclined his head for her to continue. "My friend is a seer, and she foresaw something terrible happening here in Canyon Town. But, unfortunately, her vision was too murky to make out any details, and the Council won't help me. Could you help us?"

Gegan took another sip of tea and twirled a biscuit between his fingers for a moment as he thought. "I can help you, and I will. However, to find the information you seek will require external assistance."

"How so?" she asked.

"The rituals of my order are very complex. Even the simplest of them require four participants. Are there any witches or sorcerers in the area you trust?"

Caroline grimaced. "No, but there is one I don't...Rebecca."

"The young miss from earlier?" Gegan asked. Both Caroline and Micah nodded. "Do not fear. She is hungry for knowledge and will overcome her pride to get it. We need merely wait for her to do so. In the meantime, there is much we should prepare."

They spent the afternoon shifting all the furniture in the living area and cramming it along the walls to create ample space. Caroline excitedly reclaimed a bracelet that had fallen beneath her loveseat, as well as two silver pins and a skeletal-looking bundle of herbs.

"Why were those there?" Micah asked.

"I was looking at them and sitting on the couch," Caroline said primly.

Micah just chuckled, but it quickly turned to a grimace as the heavy lifting irritated his injuries. He was healing fast, though, and the work was worth it. Gegan then sat down with Caroline and examined all her herbs and accouterments. He pronounced himself nearly satisfied. "This area is so abundant with sage; we should use some fresh-picked." He gracefully rose to his feet and reached for his satchel. "I shall go walking this evening and return with it in the morning."

"Wait, you don't mean to sleep outside?" Micah asked.

"I often do," Gegan replied. "I find it peaceful."

"I wouldn't recommend it," Micah said. He didn't want to correct the man but felt he didn't fully understand the situation.

"Why?" Gegan asked.

"There are many, many more demons here than you would expect. And they'll know you're here by now. So I don't want them to gang up on you in the middle of the night."

"Your advice is sound. Thank you."

Caroline said, "I was worried about the same thing. But you can stay here. I'll lay you out some blankets, and you can stretch out on the floor."

"Thank you," Gegan said. "I hope it is no inconvenience?"

Both Caroline and Micah categorically stated that it wasn't, and they spent some time digging out spare blankets and pillows to give Gegan a comfortable place to rest.

"I will go now to gather some sage and return soon," Gegan said as he headed for the door.

Later, as they retired for the night to Caroline's bedroom and the only other place with space to sleep, Micah said quietly, "I'll take the floor."

"You will not," Caroline said back forcefully. "We'll just share. It'll be fine."

Micah was too tired from shifting furniture on a not-very-healed-yet ankle and shoulder to argue. So, instead, he slid under the blanket, stripped off his shirt, and was asleep within seconds.

Caroline studied him for a minute as his breathing evened out. Soon, he shifted position and tossed the blanket down to his waist. His shoulder looked healthy and well on its way to being fully healed, but the scars would be worse than usual. She sighed as he rolled onto his right side, facing away from the center of the bed, and then frowned. It was still there. A small circular mark, almost like a red brand on Micah's right lower back, just below his floating ribs. It wasn't a birthmark. She'd seen him before he had it, but he never spoke about it. Any question she'd asked over the years had been shut down cold.

Four

Consciousness came to Micah slowly and peacefully the following morning. A warm bed and restful sleep left him wanting to snuggle deeper into the covers, but his stomach growled. He mentally laughed at himself and rose slowly so as not to wake Caroline. He stepped into the crowded kitchen space, hoping to find something to eat. Careful maneuvering through the furniture got him close enough to the stove to start the kettle, but none of the cupboards were accessible for breakfast.

"Screw it," he said out loud, turning off the heat. He pulled on his boots and waistcoat and grabbed his weapons belt before striding toward the door. Gegan was awake but deep in meditation. He sat cross-legged with his fingers laced and resting gently in his lap. His eyes were closed, and his face was relaxed though his mouth moved slightly as if he were talking to someone.

"Good morning, Micah," Gegan said just as Micah laid his hand on the doorknob. He turned rapidly to see the man sitting still on the floor, eyes closed.

"Good morning," Micah said back. "Sleep well?"

"Very. Thank you," Gegan replied before finally opening his eyes. "This space is extremely well defended." He rose fluidly to his feet and stretched. His fingertips nearly brushed the light fixture hanging from the ceiling.

"How did you know that was me?" Micah asked curiously.

"You do not smell of lavender," Gegan said simply. "Nearly all witches do as they enjoy its amplifying effects."

"Yes, they've told me about those effects many times," Micah said, grinning. "I've just always hated the smell."

"Why?"

"Well, when I was young, a friend was practicing, and she put way too much lavender into a charm for me. It overpowered everything and made me feel sick. Ever since then, I feel nauseous when I smell it."

"I'll keep the lavender to a minimum then," he said, one corner of his mouth ticking up. "Where are you off to?"

"A friend owns a chocolate shop, and I figured I'd go there for breakfast since the kitchen here is out of commission. Interested?"

"No, chocolate is not a weakness of mine," Gegan said with a true smile. "But thank you. I'll stay here and prepare more for the ritual. When Rebecca overcomes her pride, I'd like us to be ready."

"So you think she will?"

"I believe her hunger for recognition will eventually force her pride into submission."

"Interesting thought...do you mind if I activate a small charm before I head out?"

"Of course not. I find all such things stimulating. What will you be doing?"

Micah pulled a metal bottle from his pocket. It looked like a small lady's perfume bottle but was made entirely of copper. He sat down on the floor, and Gegan joined him with a curious look. Micah opened the bottle and lay his belt across his lap. Then, he dripped one drop of clear liquid onto a symbol on each of his dagger's sheaths.

"Is that purified water?" Gegan asked.

"Yup," Micah said, offering the bottle.

"May I?" Gegan asked as he reached for the blades instead.

"Of course," Micah replied.

"I've not seen a pattern like this before," he said, tracing the imprints in the hardened leather grips. "What does it do?"

"Well, it's a charm to make the daggers less noticeable. They're not invisible, obviously, but with this, people don't tend to notice them. I make similar charms into buttons and pins."

"Fascinating. How did you purify the water? I've used it before but never known how to make it."

"It's not technically difficult," Micah said. "It's just somewhat annoying and time-consuming. First, you must pull the water directly from a spring and bring it to a boil in a copper kettle with chunks of clay and sandstone. Then you have to condense the steam from the kettle onto another copper surface, and that is what becomes your purified water."

"Why copper?"

Micah laughed. "Honestly? I've no idea. Caroline told me to do it this way, so this is the way I've done it. She has an apparatus in the kitchen- you can just see it there- and has probably forgotten more than I will ever know on the subject."

Gegan chuckled and returned his attention to the daggers. "And how did you get this impressive pattern into the leather?"

"With great difficulty," Micah said as he laughed. "I made a tiny brand and imprinted each detail of the leather myself. It took two days."

Gegan stared at him. "This is extremely well done. What's your T. P. A.?"

"Last time I had it checked, I think it was a twelve, but that was years ago. I never seem to have the time to update it. What's yours?"

"I don't have one. We use different scales within the order, but I was curious about you. It is extremely uncommon for someone to have a demonic compass."

Micah gave him a self-conscious smile and absently played with the compass chain but didn't answer.

"Will you tell me how you got it?" Gegan pressed.

"That story," Micah said as his stomach rumbled, "is too long to tell on an empty stomach."

"Welcome!" Nathaniel said enthusiastically as Micah entered the shop. "Mom is in the back talking to Rebecca. Should I go get her?"

"What are they talking about? If it's serious, I'm in no hurry." He'd happily spend a few minutes waiting in the peaceful atmosphere.

"I'm not entirely sure," Nathaniel admitted. "Rebecca wanted to ask Mom's advice. It was something about learning something new, but she's worried her teacher won't be good, and it'll be a waste of time."

"I'll see myself to the back, instead," Micah said as several people entered the shop.

The curtain shielding the kitchen was closed, but it sat at the end of a small hallway. Micah pulled his copper bottle out of his pocket and took a deep breath. He put a small drop on each cufflink and on his collar, where symbols matched those on his daggers. Provided he stood very still and made no noise, he should pass unnoticed by the other customers.

He twitched the curtain slightly, giving himself a few inches to see through into the kitchen. Rebecca was separating eggs into two large bowls. She had rolled up her sleeves and was wearing a white apron with her bracelet peeking out of the pocket. Her hair was tied up in a messy knot on the top of her head.

Elaine was carefully pouring tempered cholate into small truffle molds. "Just say it," she commanded.

"It's hard to explain," Rebecca said, a slight whine in her voice. "I've been interested in this…topic for a long time. I taught myself, got a pretty good skill set, but so-called traditionally trained people have burned me."

"What subject?" Elaine asked curiously.

"I'd rather not get specific…," Rebecca hedged.

"It's fine; keep going."

"Well, I learned yesterday that there are some other people in town that have similar skills. I want one of them to teach me, but I'm kind of afraid to ask."

"Once burned, twice learned?"

"Yeah, plus the other woman is…"

"Other woman? Is this some kind of—"

"NO! It is nothing like that," Rebecca said as she flushed a dull red. "She is gorgeous for an older lady, but there is no romance or anything like that involved."

Elaine snickered and said, "So that is your taste then? Gorgeous, off-limits, older ladies."

Rebecca glared at her, and Elaine relented. "I'm sorry," she said. "Please continue with your non-romantic, serious subject."

Rebecca continued to glare as she washed her hands and began whisking the egg whites.

"Come on. I can't give you advice until I know what's going on," Elaine wheedled.

"All right, I would have to ask him to train me. I guess you could call it an apprenticeship. And I would still be able to keep all my hours here," Rebecca added rapidly. "But I'd have to deal with the crazy bitch on a daily basis."

"Is learning from this guy that important to you?"

"Yes," Rebecca said without hesitation. "I've been stuck for a while now. I can't access any new information, and I want to get better."

"Ask him then."

"The thing is, he's friends with the bitch. She hates me, feels threatened by me, and will probably try to make me miserable."

"Tell her to piss off then," Elaine said as she straightened up from her molds. "If it's important to you, don't let her stand in your way."

"You're right," Rebecca said, brightening up.

"Go on then, go find your man."

"He's not my man."

Elaine gave her a patronizing look. "Go find your man and ask him to teach you. We'll be fine here."

Rebecca smiled at her and started taking off her apron.

Micah hurriedly backed away from the curtain and sat down at a vacant corner table. Rebecca ran out a minute later but didn't notice him.

Nathaniel wandered over with some nutmeg-spiced hot chocolate and a croissant. Micah ate in contemplative silence as he thought about how to gently tell Rebecca that he wouldn't take her as an apprentice. He'd never had one, never wanted one, and no one cared since his T. P. A. was technically a twelve.

He'd never admit it, but that was one of the reasons he had not sent in his paperwork for an updated one. For anyone over a fifteen, it was expected to train an apprentice or two. It was one of the reasons exorcism and witchery knowledge didn't die out.

He was surprised to see Rebecca standing outside Caroline's shop when he made his way back half an hour later (the hot chocolate had been too good to stop at one cup). She'd changed into a sleek green dress over tights that flattered her figure, and her black hair hung down her back in a shining curtain.

"You're blocking the door," he said jokingly as he halted behind her.

She spun around and stumbled. Micah grabbed her elbow to steady her but let go quickly.

"Thanks," she mumbled as he held the door open for her. She walked in with her head held high and headed directly for the voices coming from the back.

Caroline and Gegan were debating twisted versus braided thread for charms.

"You have some of the strangest conversations," Micah said with a smile.

"I save all the ridiculous ones for you, love," Caroline teased, but her expression immediately changed to a scowl when Rebecca cleared her throat.

"I have something to say," she said.

"I don't care," Caroline snapped.

"Gegan, would you teach me?" Rebecca blurted out.

"No," he answered serenely

Five

"What the fuck?" Rebecca said, incensed.

"I will not teach you," Gegan said calmly.

"Why not?"

"I am not a teacher."

Everyone stared at him. Rebecca's blue eyes seemed to frost over as they filled with tears, and a red flush worked its way up her neck. None of them knew if they were tears of sadness or rage or if a heart attack or fistfight was in their immediate future. "Why not?" she spat the words again as her fingers curled into fists. "Afraid of my skill like the others? Afraid I'll be better than you?"

Caroline gaped in horror and tried to intervene, but all that came out of her mouth was a weak stuttering sound.

"Teaching you to be more does not make me less," Gegan said. "Improving your skill set and ability to survive does not negatively impact my value. I am simply not equipped for this task. However, there is someone here who is."

Rebecca dashed tears from her eyes and glared at him before swinging her gaze to Micah, who raised his hands in front of him. "I'm not a teacher either."

"But you could?" she asked.

"He is not who I meant," Gegan answered instead. "She is."

Caroline grimaced. She couldn't argue. Technically, she was the most qualified to teach, and worse, it was expected of her. She didn't have a current apprentice, and it was bad form to refuse someone.

"I'd rather not," Rebecca said stiffly.

Gegan sighed. "I'd hoped to avoid saying this directly." He rose to his full height and towered over Rebecca. "You stand at a fork in the road. You cannot turn around, you cannot avoid this choice, and you will *not* walk away. There is no wilderness for you to hide in. You will learn from Caroline, or you will die."

"What!?" Rebecca stammered, completely taken aback.

"You are not strong enough to withstand a demonic onslaught," he continued in his calm, quiet manner. "They can see you and will come for you eventually. As you are now, you will not win. So, you have your choice—learn or die."

Rebecca stared at him as the silence stretched on. Micah finally broke it by saying gently, "He's right."

"He is," Caroline commented sadly. "The demons get us all eventually. So it's a matter of choosing your exit or having someone else find your body."

Rebecca ran her fingertips over her belt distractedly as Gegan's warning echoed in her mind. Micah noticed a faint shimmer coming from the belt. Then it was gone.

Some of the fight drained out of Rebecca as she looked around at them all. "You've seen both then?"

"We have," Caroline said, speaking for herself and Micah. "Neither is pretty. We just make sure to pass on our knowledge before we go so others can take up the fight."

At that moment, Rebecca stopped to look at the people before her for the first time. She saw the light glint off tears in Caroline's eyes, saw the streaks of grey in her magnificent red hair, and noticed the scars peeking out from her clothing.

Micah met her gaze unflinching, but she sensed he wasn't seeing her. His blue eyes had a thousand-yard stare full of regrets. A movement drew her eyes to his hands, which were nervously tapping on the daggers at his waist. They were crisscrossed in scars. Some were thin from knives or daggers; others were punctures from teeth, and many were long rough-edged tracks from infection-ridden claws.

Gegan was watching as her eyes swept over him, so she did not linger.

"I'll learn," she said quietly.

"Excellent," Gegan said. "We begin now."

"Wh-what?" she stammered.

"We begin now," he repeated. "There is a ritual we wish to do that requires four people. You have just been nominated for the fourth spot. Come."

"I didn't know this kind of thing could take that many people," Rebecca said as she trailed behind Gegan up the stairs.

"Some of the things the monks do take up to twelve," Caroline told her. "But we outsiders rarely see that."

"Why do you know about it then?"

Caroline grimaced slightly at the accusatory tone in Rebecca's question. "I know because I bothered to ask someone about it, and I listened to their answer."

"Who?"

"A friend of a friend," Caroline said evasively.

"So, what are we doing then?" Rebecca asked, changing the subject.

"Well, something strange is going on here, and Gegan is going to help us find out what."

Rebecca frowned and scratched her head. "I've never heard of this kind of scrying, and I thought I knew them all."

Gegan gave a low rumble of laughter. "This is not scrying. This is interpreting symbols for information."

"Oh…" Rebecca's voice faded as she looked at the transformed living room. The floor was covered in symbols drawn in red, orange, and yellow chalk, all surrounding concentric circles in white. Three small candles stood 120 degrees apart from each other around the outer edge of the largest circle. A massive skein of red and yellow yarn lay in the middle. Three incense burners were sending smoke fragrant with sage and lavender into the air.

"First, we cleanse ourselves as a gesture of respect to Gegan and his order and prepare ourselves for the ritual," Caroline instructed. They went into the kitchen to wash their hands and then rinsed them again with water steeped with fresh rosemary.

They returned to the living room, and Gegan directed them to choose a candle and stand in the appropriate space. "There are a few minor touches to be completed. Ask away while I attend to them, but once we start, it is imperative to remain still and silent."

"Why yellow and red yarn?" Rebecca asked as she tried to take the candle in the corner.

"Nope," Micah said and beat her to it.

"Hey!"

"Let him stand there," Gegan said. "The airflow in the room will keep that corner mostly smoke-free, and he requested that."

"Lavender makes me sick," Micah explained.

"But everything has lavender in it," Rebecca said back.

"Now you see the problem," he added playfully as he took his position with his back to the corner.

Caroline was already standing in the spot by the door, so Rebecca took the remaining one by the window. Gegan took his place in the center of the circles.

"To answer your question," Gegan said once they were all situated around him, "my personality corresponds to these colors. My order discovered this and using them amplifies my abilities." He stepped across to Rebecca and shifted her slightly to the right. Satisfied, he turned his attention to Caroline. "Hold the candle at waist height. I'll be wrapping the yarn around it as I go, so please provide some tension for me when we get to that part." He turned to see Rebecca had moved again to see what he was doing. Calmly, he repositioned her, then said, "Micah, shift back another inch or two. Perfect.

"Now for the demanding part. Each of you is acting as a pillar to hold up the framework of this ritual. It will only work if you remain rooted in the present. You must suspend any thoughts, bonds, and wishes you hold in your minds while I work. You exist in the present, and nothing exists outside of this space."

Caroline took several deep breaths with her eyes closed. Her shoulders relaxed, and the lines around her eyes softened. She nodded to Gegan.

Rebecca tried to cast all thoughts from her mind. It was difficult, but she found herself copying Caroline's deep, slow breaths, and that helped.

Micah adopted a loose, ready stance wherein no energy or movement was wasted. He kept his eyes open, but the room began going in and out of focus as he turned his attention inwards. Thoughts and memories bubbled up in his mind, but he gently acknowledged them and set them aside as he would books upon a shelf. He would read them, but not right now.

Satisfied, Gegan took a deep breath and shrugged his right arm out of his monk's robes, revealing a fitted, dark, long-sleeved shirt underneath. There were patches of ornate lace sewn onto the fabric. He tucked the empty sleeve of his robes into his belt and pulled the collar on his left side close to keep it from slipping. His right arm seemed to shimmer slightly as he moved.

"Why'd you do that?" Rebecca asked, coming out of her trance.

"To keep my robes from interfering with the smoke," Gegan said. "Now the time for questions is over." From within a pocket, he drew a spherical amulet. He took three calming breaths and muttered a few words. Soon smoke began to waft from the amulet.

"Hold this down," he instructed Rebecca as he motioned her to lift her foot slightly. He placed the end of the yarn under her foot and began to chant as he moved clockwise around the symbols on the floor.

Rebecca was so fascinated by what he was doing that she forgot to act like a pillar. She shifted her weight, and the yarn came free. Gegan immediately stopped what he was doing and walked over to her. "Stay still, please," he said as he replaced the yarn.

She tried, but she just couldn't seem to stand still and recover her peace of mind. She was humming with excitement at being part of this ritual. The third time Gegan had to start over, his patience ran thin.

"Rebecca," he said sternly as he wiped the sweat from his forehead. "If you move again, I will seal your shoe to this floor until the entire building crumbles into the canyon."

"It's my favorite pair," she said plaintively.

"Then don't move again. It is exhausting to keep starting over."

"I think I can stiffen her up with some temporary paralysis," Caroline offered. The repeated distractions had broken her focus too.

"Don't! Please, I can do this," Rebecca pleaded with them.

"Just stay still. That is all you need do," Gegan said. He took a few deep breaths to restore his energy while he waited for her and Caroline to regain their composure.

Again, he placed the yarn beneath her foot and began his chanting. He walked sedately around the circles on the floor, swinging the smoking amulet and winding a web about himself. The web moved higher as he went, starting at the base and rising past waist level, finally reaching the end of the skein. Gegan swung the amulet high and shouted the final verse. As the smoke billowed around him, a blast of glacial air howled through the circle and made all of them gasp. Then it was over.

The smoke cleared instantly and left Gegan drenched in sweat and shivering in the middle of the circles. He blew out a breath that hung like vapor before him and said, "That's not supposed to happen."

Micah shuddered as a slithering sensation ran up his spine that wasn't all due to the freezing air around them. He started shaking but hid it by looking uneasily at Caroline, whose eyes were full of fright.

Gegan swayed and said, "Something exceedingly forceful interfered." Small shards of ice broke off his arms and chest. "I need to sit down." He overbalanced, but Micah caught him before he crashed to the ground.

Caroline came over to help while Rebecca, wisely, blew out their abandoned candles. She glanced around the glittering, frosted room again, then joined the others.

"What was that?" both women asked.

"I've never felt anything like it," Rebecca added as she rubbed her arms. The warmth began to seep back into the room, but all of them were shaking badly, and their fingertips were turning blue.

No one answered right away.

"It was the winds of hell," Micah finally said.

Gegan gave him a very sharp look. "How do you know that?"

"Now is not the time," Micah said, evading the question. Then, he rubbed his hands together to warm them and drive away a flash of memory.

"Yes—it bloody well is the time!" Rebecca countered. "What just happened?"

"We just felt a draft from the winds of hell," Gegan answered as he struggled to rise. "I need to go inspect the portal."

"I'll go with you," Micah said immediately.

"Where is the portal?" Rebecca asked.

"It's all the way down...at the bottom of the canyon," Caroline told her before adding to the men, "I'm not going."

"I'd like to go," Rebecca said nervously.

Gegan looked at her thoughtfully for a moment. "Yes, you may. But, first, we need to gather supplies and prepare ourselves."

"Can I ask you guys questions while we hike?"

"As long as you don't get offended if we don't want to answer," Micah told her.

They left early the following morning after spending the afternoon and most of the evening returning Caroline's living room to normal. Nearly all of the work fell to Micah because Gegan took several hours to recover from the ritual, and neither Caroline nor Rebecca was strong enough to heft the furniture.

Experiencing a sense of despair that made him feel vulnerable, Micah checked and double-checked his protective charms and weapons, stealing glances at his compass whenever no one was watching. He did not speak except to respond when someone asked him a question.

The two-day hike down the canyon played havoc on their shins and lower backs as they fought to retain control of the descent. Micah's injured ankle began throbbing after lunch on the first day, but he bore it in silence. His injuries were well on the path to being healed, and he silently thanked Caroline for her healing skills. Micah's attention drifted in and out as he was distracted by unwelcome memories. Rebecca filled the daylight hours with questions ranging from specifics on scrying to demon lore to the history of Gegan's order.

The canyon got colder and colder as they went, but nothing like the icy blast they experienced in Caroline's living room. When they stopped for a rest, Rebecca made a fire to help warm their spirits. The flickering light brought out shades of umber, cinnamon, and rust in the striated canyon walls. Their moods lifted at the warmth and beauty, but their bodies felt as if nothing would ever warm them again.

They reached the bottom of the canyon late morning on the second day. The walls had sloped inwards until there were barely thirty feet between them. Shadows lingered as they wound their way through the curving, dried-up riverbed until an eerie purplish light lit their surroundings.

Gegan called them to a halt, mainly for Rebecca's sake. "The portal is just around the next bend. It will," he paused to gather his thoughts before speaking directly to Rebecca, "try to play tricks on your mind. Just don't let it."

She looked nervous but nodded.

The portal glimmered at shoulder height. It was the size of a billiards ball and glowed purple, not a deep, rich plum color or the pale purple of dawn. Rather, it was the purple of a deep, bone-painful bruise. Lines of silver and black stretched across it like veins. Periodically, almost like a heartbeat, it would pulse, and the silver and black would stand out starkly as if a surge of blood flowed through them. At every pulse, a blast of ice-cold air shimmered out from the portal condensing mists and vapor from the air before drifting lazily up between the narrow gap in the walls.

Micah looked at it and grimaced before turning his attention to his backpack. Gegan sat cross-legged and began intoning in a low rumble. Rebecca stared at the portal and kept staring at it.

"It's pretty," she said as a blast of cold air raised the hair off her neck.

"No," Micah said harshly, "it's not."

She flinched and looked at him before returning her gaze to the portal.

"Rebecca," Gegan said, rising to his feet, "please go back around the corner."

"Why?" she asked immediately.

"It's luring you. Go out of sight."

"But I—" She stopped abruptly as Micah firmly grasped her arm, spun her around, and escorted her back around the bend. She glared at him as he released her.

"Make camp," he ordered as he turned around. The portal looked more sickening the second time, and it pulsed as if to mock him.

"That was the right call," Gegan said as they began to work. "Her mind isn't strong enough yet to withstand this." Micah nodded tersely and pulled a coil of thick black and silver rope from his borrowed bag while Gegan began scratching symbols in the dust with the end of his walking stick. They worked together over the next hour to put together the elements that would force the portal to close.

But the portal did not close. By the time Gegan and Micah gave up—after repeated attempts—they were both sweating with exertion, despite the cold. The portal continued to pulse as if laughing at them, and a vivid red glow suffused them for a moment before fading.

"Damn it all," Micah gasped, becoming nauseated. "Why didn't it close?"

"I've heard of this happening once before, but it was nearly seventy years ago," Gegan said in between deep breaths. Finally, his heart rate and respiration began to slow down. "My order has the data. I need to contact them, but I don't have my tools," he explained.

"We need to get back then," Micah said and hesitated, as he could see that Gegan was suffering. "It's going to be a long night."

"Unfortunately, yes."

They walked back to Rebecca, who had built a small fire and laid out some of their remaining supplies for lunch.

"I want you to pack it up—we need to leave," Micah said as he grabbed a blanket and started to fold it.

"But you told me to set up camp," she said, irritated.

"Rebecca," Gegan cut in to put a stop to the argument. "We don't have time to debate. We are walking out of here *now* with or without you and these items."

She shut her mouth and helped.

"What happened?" she asked a short time later as they began the long hike uphill out of the darkness.

"The portal refused to close," Gegan told her wearily.

"And something may have come out while we were there," Micah said, remembering the red flash of light. Rebecca shivered and looked over her shoulder. "Odds are it won't attack us as long as we keep moving and stay together," he added to reassure her.

It was nearly midnight when they finally stopped. Rebecca was swaying slightly on her feet while Micah walked with his head bowed, and Gegan began falling behind.

They slipped into an exhausted sleep only to wake with the first fringes of dawn. Gegan rolled the kinks out of his massive shoulders while Micah stretched and circled his ankle several times. It was hurting more now, and he winced in pain as he put weight on it. Luckily, it quickly loosened up. Without a word, they were off.

The morning passed in an exhausted haze for all three of them. Trudging ever upwards, they took turns leading and following each other along the steep path. While in the lead, Rebecca sensed something, looked to the right, and stumbled in shock. "Stop!"

A magnificent gray wolf stood observing them. Gegan and Micah were astonished and just stared at it. Slowly he approached Rebecca and sniffed her. She was trembling, but she showed her hand to the wolf. He licked it and then turned to the others. After studying them, he appeared to be satisfied. Then he glanced at Rebecca and headed in the direction they needed to go, repeatedly checking to be sure they were following.

They felt energy emanating from the wolf that made the long and treacherous climb easier. When they stopped to rest, he vanished the way he had appeared. Only Rebecca was able to see him walk into the folds of space. No one said anything as they rested. Rebecca smiled inside, honored by the wolf's visit, and she wondered if she would see him again.

They resumed their journey, and Micah started to feel as if something ominous was watching them, but he never saw anything. At length, the evening shadows painted the rocks around them vibrant hues of red and gold, and the top of the canyon came into sight. The three of them stumbled onto level ground and had to pause for several minutes before they could summon the strength to walk the last quarter mile to Caroline's shop.

"What happened to you?" Caroline asked as they trooped in and slumped on her display furniture.

"The portal didn't close," Micah said dully. Then he stretched out one of his calves and groaned in pain. "As soon as Gegan recovers, he will contact his order and see if they know what is going on. Would you contact the Council as well?"

"Micah, darling, there is no need for that," a soft feminine voice crooned.

Everyone jumped at the unfamiliar voice, except Micah, who closed his eyes and clenched his hands into fists so tight his knuckles turned white. *Not now,* he thought. *Please—not now.*

"What is *that*?" Caroline shrieked.

Micah opened his eyes and was not surprised at what he saw. A small demon, roughly the size and shape of a bat, fluttered just outside the window. It was ruby red with bulbous, milky white eyes and had lengthy claws extending from its feet. Its open mouth showed needle-like fangs glistening with saliva as it eyed them all.

"Now that you are looking at me…" said the soft, female voice from the bat's mouth.

The bat abruptly flipped over and dove through the window. It hit the floor with a muted *crunch* and lay face up. The air above it began to flicker before a life-size image of a demon materialized.

The four of them were transfixed, almost paralyzed.

She looked like a humanoid wasp. Faceted, large, black eyes stood out on her pale face above high cheekbones and ruby red lips. Two magenta antennae sprouted from her forehead, but they swept back over the top of her head and merged with her mane of luscious black hair. Her shoulders and chest looked normal though banded in black, magenta, and yellow, and she trimmed down to an impossibly thin waist, like that of an insect. Below, she looked like she was wearing a belled skirt in black and magenta stripes. Her arms were thin with double-jointed elbows and ended in four-fingered hands.

"Micah, darling," she cooed, smiling to reveal pointed teeth, "you have not aged well."

"I wish I could say the same," Micah replied angrily, standing up. It was as if all of his pain and fatigue were forgotten as dread and adrenaline flooded his system.

She laughed, a horrible buzzing sound, and looked more closely at him. "Such a welcome! I'd almost think you weren't happy to see me." Micah raised his eyebrows, but she continued. "Don't think you stayed beneath my notice. The awful, purified water that you kept near my mark and the protection charms you stitched into every shirt for twenty years were not enough." Her grin turned predatory. "You carry around a piece of me, and I've always known where you are."

Micah stared at her, not noticing his hands were shaking at his sides.

"What in hell are you?" asked one of the witches. But he couldn't tell which one due to the ringing in his ears.

No, no, no! he thought. This can't be happening.

"Darling, you should answer the lady's question," the demon taunted.

"This is the Mistress of hell," Micah said between clenched teeth.

"WHAT?!" someone yelled.

The Mistress glared the others into submission before speaking again. "Darling, it's time you paid a debt to me. I've waited years to see your face again, disappointing as it is with all that grey hair, but now you will help me."

"Yes, my Mistress," Micah ground out.

"You see, pet, it's a simple request," the Mistress purred. "Another demon, calls himself the Baron, has overthrown me and set hell into chaos. It is most inconvenient."

"Inconvenient?" Caroline said indignantly. "That's what you call it?"

"Quiet, little witch!" the Mistress hissed. "My image may not have the power to affect you out there in your realm, but I can affect him." She snapped her fingers, and Micah let out a howl of pain. His legs gave way, and he fell heavily to the ground clutching his right side and twitching. After several very long seconds, the pain passed, but he remained on the floor, pale and shaking. "No more interruptions," the Mistress snapped at her audience.

"As I was saying, Micah dear, I am currently deposed from my rightful rule. You will rectify this. The Baron is as insane as I have ever seen. He wants the destruction of both realms. This is why *you* will set me back in power. I don't care what goes on with you mortals. Keep out of my hell, and we can all continue in peace." She waved one of her hands in a dismissive gesture.

"Who is the Baron?" Micah ground out, unclenching his teeth. His jaw cracked.

The Mistress looked at him coyly. "The Baron is a demon of renown, of high intelligence, and ruthless drive. He adores the quiet and the still. He has been my adversary through much of my reign. Always, he is biting, baiting, pestering, but never causing actual harm—until recently," she paused and hissed in agitation. "Now his followers increase. His legions grow. Many a time, I let him be, for I do not appreciate change." Her tone soured on the last word, and a muscle in her face twitched. "He will cause imbalance, chaos, upset, and you must stop it." Her gaze sharpened, and she smiled at Micah as he unsteadily pushed himself to a sitting position. "Once already, you foiled his plans. You are my instrument, and thus I wield you." She studied Micah fondly.

"My lady," Gegan said into the silence in a servile manner with his head bowed low, "may I ask how he intends this destruction?"

She regarded him imperiously. "Monk, I'll answer only because you asked so politely. He has stopped the machinery. Last one of my servants saw, it had frosted over completely, and the ice was heading farther out."

"What does that even mean?" Rebecca snarled.

"Clearly, you are incapable of following directions." The Mistress snapped her fingers again, and the air resounded with Micah's screams.

Rebecca was terrified and stared at Micah helplessly while he writhed.

After he quieted, curled into the fetal position with tears streaming into the sweat on his face, the Mistress continued. "Normally, I would not care if your world turned into a desolate plain of ice; however, it would destroy hell first. But, of course, I can't have that, which brings us back around to the issue at hand. Micah dear, you will fix this problem for me." She started to turn away but paused. "I suppose you will need the help of these pathetic little beings, so I release you from your silence." Her image faded, and the bat demon turned to dust as Micah gave one final scream of agony and passed out.

Six

Confusion reigned in Micah's mind. He did not know where he was or how long had passed. His right lower back felt like it was on fire. All his muscles were sore, his head was fuzzy, and his joints simply hurt. He tried to roll over but let out a whimper as his entire body rejected the idea of movement.

"I heard something," he heard Caroline say, and a moment later, she entered the room, which he belatedly realized was her bedroom. Gegan and Rebecca followed. All three looked very worried.

"How long was I out?" Micah rasped. His throat felt dry and scratchy.

"All night," Caroline said as she slipped a straw into a glass of water. She sat on the bed, ran a soothing hand across his hair, and held the glass out for him.

"Shit," Micah said after taking several long drinks. He wanted to move again but knew better.

They all stared at each other for a few moments before Caroline lost her composure. "Can we talk about how the fuck the Mistress of hell knows your freaking name?" she ranted but restrained herself from touching him roughly. "How come you've never mentioned that?"

"I couldn't," Micah said. "Not that I ever wanted to," he added, but then stopped and looked surprised. "I've thought that many times but never been able to say it before... Anyway, she put a ward of silence on me. I couldn't talk about what happened. I hoped never to see her again."

"What happened?" Gegan asked.

Micah licked his lips and hesitated, clinging to the small amount of peace Caroline's touch gave him. "Could I get a painkiller, at least?" he asked. "This topic hurts enough without all the physical torment she put me through."

"I've got one," Rebecca said.

"You do?" Caroline asked, surprised.

"I brought it back with me when I went home to water my plants and change my clothes," Rebecca said, slightly embarrassed.

"What's in it?" Caroline asked with interest as she got up from the bed.

Micah closed his eyes and let his mind drift in and out of focus. Their voices washed over him like a calming balm as they discussed ingredients. Caroline thought she could improve on the potency of what Rebecca had, so they retired to the kitchen to sort it out. Gegan stayed by Micah's side. He sat down on the floor by the bed and placed one hand on Micah's shoulder. Slowly, he began chanting in a soothing rumble, and Micah felt some of the tension drain out of his body. "That's better," he said drowsily.

Gegan continued until Caroline and Rebecca returned with the upgraded painkiller, but Micah was already asleep again.

He awoke a short time later, and while still hurting, was able to sit up. It took him four tries, but he made it.

Looking over at the bedside table, he saw a small glass filled with green liquid. A small note rested against it saying, "Drink me!" He chuckled and reached for it. The liquid was thick and cold, but he felt better immediately after forcing it down. "Hello?" he called out hoarsely.

Gegan walked in and smiled down at him. "You look much better, my friend. The ladies are arguing in whispers over what to feed you, so I came to escort you to the table."

"And no excuses," Caroline called from the kitchen.

Micah laughed and let Gegan help him up.

A stack of flatbread covered in melted cheese and a pyramid of his favorite chocolate bars lay on the table.

"No onions!" Caroline snapped as she and Rebecca crowded around her small stovetop.

"Onions are great for nutrition and healing," Rebecca said, brandishing a red onion.

"He's allergic to them. He'll get so much healing from them when his throat swells shut," Caroline said sarcastically.

"I stand corrected," Rebecca said, quickly putting down the onion.

A few minutes later, as Micah was cautiously eating his second piece of bread—swallowing was difficult—they brought over the main course. Ideally, they would have all sat at the table together, but it had been pushed into the corner, and there wasn't enough space. Gegan chose to sit cross-legged on the floor and ate contentedly on his lap while Caroline and Rebecca stood at the counter. Micah was left alone at the table with the food.

"Story time," Caroline trilled.

"Can we attend to the matter of the portal first?" Micah asked.

"It's been done," Caroline told him. "I've sent a message to the Council, no reply just yet, and Gegan has been in touch with his order."

"As we speak," Gegan said, "they are gathering all the information we possess about portals. I expect to hear back within a few days."

"Enough procrastinating," Caroline said. "You are out of excuses so talk."

"Fine," Micah snapped. "Let's get the whole damned story out then." He paused for a moment breathing hard before continuing. "First, I want you all to know that I don't want to talk about this. I don't want to relive what happened. I don't want

96

to even think about it, and I have done my best not to remember for twenty years. So, you will give me some patience here!" His friends all looked a bit shocked at the outburst but nodded. "Okay, it started with Devon."

"Devon?" Caroline said, surprised. "That girl who was top of her class but kicked out of her assistant tour?"

"Her what?" Rebecca asked.

"Yes," Micah said simultaneously.

"Yes, please explain further," Gegan asked a moment later.

Caroline scratched her head in thought then spoke, clearly trying not to be condescending. "In traditional witches training, we attend boarding schools. There are small ones in every major city. The witch or exorcist is sent off when he or she…" She paused and said, "I have to start over. Just to keep things streamlined, I will refer to all the students as she and witch. Men can be witches too, and there are exorcists, but they are so rare, they are usually just called witches. It'll take too long to keep indicating them all. Agreed?"

"Agreed," Rebecca and Gegan echoed. Micah didn't answer as his mouth was full.

"Good. So, witches are sent off to school when they are twelve or thirteen. They spend the next two years studying at the school closest to where they live. The schools operate in six-month increments: five months of studying and then home for a month. After that, witches attend a different school every semester. This way, they can form friendships and bonds with many other witches and learn from various teachers. We called them 'dames.'

"Anyway, after graduating at nineteen or so, most witches would stay on and work as assistants to the dames for a couple of years. That's what I meant when I said the assistant tour. This time would let them hone their skills, get practice for taking on apprentices, and research magic that interested them. It's so important to form this community. Without it, the demons would have isolated us and wiped us out decades ago."

"Correct," Micah said. He nervously tapped his fingers on the table before pushing his plate away.

"Take your time and start at the beginning," Gegan advised. "It'll make the telling easier."

Micah sighed. "I suppose I might as well. When I arrived at the witch's school, I was immediately part of the outcast group. The 'misfits' we called ourselves. We were the ones that stayed at the school during the month recesses. We didn't have homes to go back to."

"Didn't you come late, anyway?" Caroline asked.

"I was fifteen when I was enrolled," Micah answered.

"Why were you late?" Rebecca asked.

"Ladies!" Gegan scolded. "You are showing a remarkable lack of empathy here. Stop interrupting the man."

"I was seven when I saw my first demon," Micah said, resigned to the fact that all the details would be coming out. "After that, I saw them regularly, but my parents couldn't. They thought I had an active imagination or a series of imaginary friends. When they didn't go away after a couple of years, they sent me to physicians of every type. So much hassle would've been saved if they'd just brought in a witch, but they didn't believe in that. Finally, when I was fourteen, I ran away. I'd had enough of everyone telling me I was just seeing things. I knew the demons were real.

"I spent a few months sleeping in the gutter, scrounging food from the trash, and picking up odd jobs here and there. One bar—I'll never forget it—'The Wasted Scoundrel,' hired me to do dishes twice a week. I usually got some leftover food at the end of the night, so it was a pretty good deal for me. There was an older man who frequented the bar. He always sat on the same stool in the corner and drank brandy. All the regulars left him alone to drink in peace. Whenever some jackass would try to take his spot, the bartenders would turn them out.

"Well, a demon took a liking to me shortly after I started working there. I know it was some flavor of despair, but I can't remember exactly what kind. It was waiting for me to mentally crack so it could have a go. None of the other demons tried to whisper to me, but this one would hang out at the bar watching me. One night, someone dropped a tray of glassware, and it shattered all over the floor.

I volunteered to help clean it up, and the demon followed me around. We went near the man in the corner, and quick as I've ever seen, he snagged the demon and broke its neck. The demon fell to dust, and he was back to his brandy like nothing happened.

"There, finally, was proof that someone else could see them—and better—kill them. So, I watched for the old man to leave and stopped him. I asked him how he killed that thing. He looked surprised and asked how I knew what he'd done. I told him I could see them too.

"He looked me up and down and asked me why I wasn't in school. I told him I didn't have a school to go to. This clearly troubled him. He told me he was too old to take on an apprentice, but there was another way. I told him I would take anything, so he wrote down an address for me on a napkin. Then he said, 'If you can find this place, you might have a shot.'

"It took me six months to find it. I'd never seen a map in my life, so I had to walk the city streets every day looking. I went up and down them all: avenues, broad tree-lined streets, twisting alleyways, crossroads, corners. Then I found it. He'd given me the address of the witching school in my city. Not that I knew what it was at the time. I knocked on the front door without a clue about what I was going to find.

"Dame Helen answered. I'll never forget the look of shock and awe on her face. I'd waltzed in past protection charms and notification alarms like they weren't even there."

"I remember that day," Caroline said eagerly. "Everyone was talking about how some nobody had walked right in. The dames were in an uproar."

Micah smiled briefly before continuing his story. "They asked me all kinds of questions about who I was and how I'd found them. Then they stuck me in class with the thirteen-year-olds.

"If I'd had a home to go to, I don't think I would have caught up. The months when the school was out, we misfits worked our asses off. Sometimes an assistant would stay with us, but we usually ignored them.

"Getting back on track, Devon was two years older than me, right?" he said, looking at Caroline.

She nodded. "I think so. She split the difference between us."

Micah nodded. "She was an outcast, like us, but she didn't mind. She didn't want any friends."

"Didn't need them," Caroline explained for Gegan and Rebecca. "Devon was a genius. I taught her a lot during my assistant tour. You'd barely teach her the basics of a spell, and she was off experimenting, improving, heightening, and more. She was powerful, smart, and creative. Devon never spoke about where she'd come from or any family, but she always went somewhere on school breaks. She graduated top of her class with nearly perfect marks. The dames raved about her talent."

"But she was kicked out during her assistant tour," Micah cut in.

"That she was," Caroline said sadly. She wasn't sure how this led to the Mistress of hell, but she was confident they would get there.

"Devon had pulled several students in to help her with a new spell, and it backfired," Micah picked the story back up. "Three were injured pretty badly. They all survived, but one lost several fingers, and another had to wear a knee brace for months. Devon showed no hint of remorse at hurting the others and was immediately off devising something new. The dames decided she wasn't a good influence and sent her packing. No one heard from her for a couple of years.

"Meanwhile, I graduated. None of the misfits stayed for an assistant tour. We felt there was no reason to since all our friends were leaving, and we would no longer have access to our favorite instructors. I went back to my home city and tried to find my parents, but they'd moved, and no one knew where they went. So, I got a day job, picked up contracts from the Witches Council for extra cash, and proceeded to live my life."

"That was around the time we got to be friends, wasn't it?" Caroline asked.

Micah nodded. "You'd just moved there, and I helped get you settled in and familiar with the city. Another contract came through then. The Council was detecting something strange. It was demonic, but it wasn't a portal, nor was it a demon. They couldn't understand it, so they asked me for help. There were several other powerful witches in the area, but the Council knew me from the work I'd done for them and offered me good money.

"A few days of scrying, location charms, and power readings got me a rough location. After that, I got to spend my evenings hiking around the worst side of town until I found the exact spot. The discordant energies were coming from an abandoned warehouse on the edge of town. When I got there, I saw that the place had been protected from intruders. There were charms and tokens on every door and window to stop people from entering. The entire building had unbroken lines going around it at levels of three and five feet to warn of intruders. I only got in through a glitch. One corner of the building stood near a fence for the next property over. I climbed the fence and was able to jump over to a window above the warning line and climb to the roof. There I found a skylight."

Here he paused a moment in remembrance. "It was a sight to see. Every square inch of the floor below was covered in lines, diagrams, and symbols. They stretched six feet up the walls and over the windows and doors save one spot about two feet wide that was blank. I have never seen anything like it, but it was wrong." He shuddered as he tried to explain. "The principles were sound, but there was such a sense of wrongness about the whole thing. The air was practically pulsing with energy. I broke into a sweat and felt waves of nausea cascade over me.

"Devon walked up then. At first, I was so glad to see her. I was in way over my depth and really needed a friend, but then she walked through the protection charms and entered the building as if she owned it. Probably did. Without hesitation, she went over to the empty spot on the wall and began drawing arcane symbols on it, preparing it for whatever she had in mind.

"I'll never know for sure what she was planning, but I couldn't leave. I wavered at the edge of panic. I wanted to scare her, to delay whatever it was until I could get help, but I didn't know how. I must've made a noise, or she saw me through the skylight because she motioned quick as lightning and brought down that part of the roof. I fell with the rubble right in the middle of her ritual.

"She looked at me, and I felt terrified for the first time. Up close, I could see the changes in her. Her dark hair was stringy, dirty, and matted. She'd pulled it up into a messy knot at the top of her head. Her skin was grey and covered in dirt. She was dressed in filthy clothing covered in rips and tears. Her eyes stood out starkly in her face, red, shiny, and mad! That's what made my spine turn to ice. Her hands shook, and her fingernails were bitten down to the quick. 'I know you,' she said to me. I didn't reply, and after studying me, she smiled. 'I'd wondered if I needed some blood to make this work. Now they've delivered me the answer. Haven't you, my friends?'

"Sixteen massive demons stood there. They were the largest I had yet seen, ranging from eight to nine and a half feet tall. Coarse fur covered their dull grey bodies, and their hands sported four clawed fingers. Three twisting horns rose above their cruelly intelligent eyes and grinning mouths full of snaggled, misshapen teeth. All of them were taller than me, stronger than me, and far more vicious than I could ever be. Yet, they stood behind Devon, like colonels behind their general. She saw my look of surprise and laughed. 'I've taught them well, and they've returned the favor.'"

"How come you didn't see them before?" Rebecca interrupted.

Micah shrugged. "I'll never know. I can only guess that she shielded them with an inconspicuous charm so that any witch would miss them. After soundly laughing in my face for several minutes, they cleared out the rubble. Yes, I know demons aren't supposed to be able to interact with the physical world, but they did," he added to forestall any questions and kept going (over Caroline's gasp of alarm). "Even though the ritual wasn't quite complete, they started it. I don't know if it worked or if it went terribly wrong, but a portal opened. Devon was shepherded through it first, then they dragged me along for the ride.

"It was freezing cold. Hell is a..." He got up and started staggering around the room as he struggled to put it into words. His friends watched him agitatedly run his hands through his hair and bite his nails. "Hell is a city," he finally began after nearly a minute of pacing and muttering to himself. "Or I guess a slum, but it plays with your mind.

You start walking up a street toward a building only to find you are a hundred feet to one side of it once you get there. You climb staircases thinking you will arrive on one rooftop, but you are actually on the one next to it. You climb down a ladder thinking you are at the bottom, but there was always more. Slums, sewers, tunnels, mines, hell just kept going down." He shuddered. "It got colder and colder the lower you went.

"Everything about the place is slightly off. No corners meet at right angles; nothing is vertical or horizontal. It just messes with you. And the wind," he shuddered and unconsciously rubbed his arms, "there is a marrow-freezing wind howling around the place all the time. There is no sunshine. The sky looks like it is constantly murky and overcast, but they do have weather. Hailstorms, hurricanes, and blizzards are a regular occurrence."

His face stilled and his shoulders drooped as he continued. "Devon was shrieking when the demons dragged me through. It was the stuff of nightmares, so I'll spare you the details. She, um, didn't survive more than a few moments as they ripped her apart. They were so happy about it, too, jumping and prancing and waving their grisly trophies about in the wind. I fought free of the ones holding me while they were distracted by the spectacle and dove for the portal, but it wouldn't let me through. It was like looking through a pane of distorted glass. I could see through it, kind of, but it was beyond my reach.

"I set my back against it. I remember it felt warm and prepared to meet my fate. I…" All the tension leaked out of his frame, and he looked like he might collapse as he looked down at his hands and sighed. "They…" He took a deep breath, rubbed his face, and started again. "My wounds burned with frostbite instantly, and my blood froze to my skin wherever they struck me. One of them pinned my left arm to the portal and tore the dagger from my numbed fingers. Patches of skin came off, glued to the blade by my frozen blood.

"I felt peace then as two more grabbed me. They dislocated my shoulder and broke my right arm, so it fell limp at my side. I looked down at my right-hand dagger, frozen fast in a death grip, and was content. I had fought until I could fight no more. Then *she* arrived." A wave of goosebumps spread over Micah's arms, and he shivered.

"The Mistress had felt the portal open and was curious. She laughingly called it 'a disturbance.' The demons immediately stopped pinning me down and bowed before her. I can only assume she spoke to them. The keening wind drowned out most sounds. She was pleased with whatever they said, and then she turned to me.

"'A shiny new mortal!' she cackled. 'I haven't had one in ages.' The demons had let me go, but I couldn't support my weight. I slid down the portal to my knees and stared up at them all. 'And it knows its place!' she added delightfully. 'I think I'll keep it.' And so, she did."

Micah looked away in shame, his voice bitter as he returned to his seat. "I became a pet. All day long, the Mistress would parade me through the streets. 'Mortals only last a few days, so I need to show you off while I can,' she said. Demons would flock to the roadside to laugh and hiss at me. I lost the feeling in my fingers and feet that first day. My injuries didn't get infected, but they were frozen open. I stopped even noticing my dislocated shoulder and broken bones after a while. There is no food in hell, and I was allowed very little water. I slept huddled in the middle of an icy floor because the walls of my cell were always covered in frost.

"I only got out because I was lucky. The Mistress is attacked on a regular basis as other demons try to take her position. While we were making the rounds one afternoon, another demon jumped at her from the crowd." He glanced up with a look of pain and despair. "I don't even know what it looked like; I was so far gone mentally. I can't tell you why or how, but I intercepted it. It bowled me over, and we ended up in a heap at the Mistress's feet. She beheaded the other demon, and it fell to dust, covering me. 'That was quite a feat,' she told me. 'And it merits a reward.' I begged her to let me go. 'Go on then. You're free,' she said and turned away.

"'Wait!' I yelled after her. 'I want to go home.'

"'That wasn't part of the deal,' she said mockingly to me.

"'Then let's make another deal,' I said in desperation.

"She snapped her fingers, and a small piece of paper appeared. 'Sign here,' she said. The contract was short. By signing it, I would owe her one favor to be called in at her discretion. Contracts in hell are always three lines or less. I had no choice, so I signed it with a shivering, shaking scrawl. She sealed it with a kiss, then lashed out with her hand and sliced my chest from here to here." He gestured to his left side. "Flicking her hair forward, she pressed one strand into the wound and cut it off. Then she summoned a portal right behind me and shoved me through it. I landed flat on my back in a pile of trash in an alleyway. I managed to call for help, but then I passed out."

"I think," Micah said abruptly after finishing his story, "that I would like to go lie down."

"Of course," Gegan said as both Rebecca and Caroline opened their mouths to protest.

Micah waved off any offer of help and struggled to his feet. As he turned away, Caroline gasped. There was a small hole in his shirt directly over the odd mark on his lower back. The protection charm was gone. He felt the area, and his shoulders slumped.

"I'll repair it for you," Caroline said quickly.

"Just do it tomorrow," Micah said wearily and headed into the bedroom.

The door was barely closed before Gegan turned and scowled at Caroline and Rebecca.

"What is wrong with you two?" Rebecca looked angry, and Caroline was surprised at the outburst, but Gegan wasn't finished. "You couldn't just let him tell the story? You had to keep interrupting and bleeding out any kind of rhythm. You made that so much harder on him than it needed to be. It's embarrassing to think his friends would lack so much compassion for him."

"It's not that!" Caroline snapped back. "You weren't there. You haven't wondered for twenty years what happened to your best friend." She found herself, chest heaving, on her feet. "I was there," she continued quietly. "I was part of the team that healed him. It was bad.

"When he sent off that distress note, anyone sensitive to charms within five miles felt it and tried to get to him. The first person who did was a young witch. She couldn't carry him, so she sent another distress signal. Two signals from the same spot within ten minutes are cause for alarm. Every single witch in the city dropped what they were doing and headed for that alleyway. Four more arrived within five minutes. They carried him to the closest magical site, which was a school, two miles away.

"I arrived shortly after they brought him in. He was laid out on a dining table, bleeding on the tablecloth with the chairs thrown against the wall. One with such force, it hung halfway embedded in the plaster. The original witch who found him was talking to the dames. An exorcist was contacting the Witches Council; two more witches were assessing his injuries. The fourth responder (another witch) and one of the dames murmured over a tray of healing potions.

"I went to help them. We threw together this concoction that was either going to force him back to us or kill him. Luckily, it woke him up. His hands were black with frostbite, and he nearly lost three fingers and six toes. He teetered on the edge of severe hypothermia for an hour. We couldn't get him warm, and when we tried, he screamed in pain as the blood returned to his limbs. It damaged his voice to where he could barely speak for weeks. Then his wounds began to thaw, and the infection set in with a vengeance. He went from practically frozen to a raging fever in thirty minutes. It was terrifying, and he was awake for all of it.

"He couldn't even rest. As soon as he was barely coherent and the infection was contained, he was called before the Witches Council. What went on behind those closed doors, no one knows. Two dames half carried—half dragged him into a private room to communicate with the Council and then were banished. That's part of what made it so hard. He went in there to explain his actions and was carried out unconscious. No one said a word about it, and we were told to give him anything and everything he needed to heal. The rumors were that he fought another exorcist or some crazy demon. No one could think of another way to get that much damage in so short a time. I guess time moves differently in hell.

"He walked with a limp for six weeks until we finally healed all the damage to his feet and had to go through physical therapy for six months to get full use of his hands. If you look closely, you can still see where the pieces of skin were ripped off."

Micah heard Gegan start to speak as he closed the bedroom door behind him, but not a single word penetrated his brain. He wanted to lie down, but the thought of being on his back made him feel too vulnerable. Instead, he sat down on the floor, leaned against the bed, and stretched one of his legs out before him. Resting his arm on his other leg and tipping his head back onto Caroline's quilt, he thought about that meeting with the Witches Council.

The memory of waking up, surrounded by witches trying to heal him, was fuzzy. He thought Caroline was there but couldn't say for sure who it was that poured a steaming potion down his throat. It ripped him from his peaceful, warm fugue and sent him crashing into a world of stinging, biting, burning pain.

Then he was being carried, his useless feet dragging on the floor and settled gently into a soft chair. The Witches Council could send their images and voices across vast distances, and they were suddenly before him. All of them.

"Don't stand," the one dressed in green with grey hair said. "Just tell us what happened."

He tried to explain. Devon, the ritual, and when he got to the demons lifting rubble, some of the witches frowned at him in disbelief. He doggedly carried on in a whisper and described hell. They all looked very skeptical but stayed silent until he mentioned the Mistress.

"The Mistress?" one of the younger ones asked. "You really saw the Mistress and came back to talk about it?"

"Are you sure it was the Mistress?" the same witch in green asked. "No one has ever come back from seeing her. We don't even have a record of what she looks like."

"Maybe he's confused," a different witch said. "He's been through quite the ordeal."

There was a general murmur of assent. One or two mentioned a possible head injury, and several others pondered the possibilities.

"Micah, Micah darling. I can't have you spilling all my secrets," said a familiar voice that made all the hair on his neck stand on end. The Mistress appeared before them. Much like the witches on the Council, she wasn't physically present, but they could all see and hear her. She looked around at them and smiled. Micah cringed. "As I was saying, dear pet, this simply will not do."

"How are you accessing our spell, demon?" a black-haired witch asked, eyes wide.

"Silly, girl. I don't need your paltry methods," replied the Mistress scornfully.

"Excuse me?" the witch spluttered.

"You annoy me," the Mistress proclaimed, snapping her double-jointed fingers. The witch's image vanished with a small *pop* and a puff of amber smoke.

The rest of the Council were now paying full attention. The Mistress haughtily looked them over before ignoring them. "Micah, talking to others was not part of our deal. I'll be adding that to your contract." She held up the piece of paper Micah had signed, and another line of text appeared on it. Reaching out, she flicked her nails across his lower right back through a gap in the back of the chair. Instantly, Micah felt a stab of pain. "That should suffice." The Mistress vanished. He blacked out shortly afterward.

That was the last time he'd seen the Mistress and had spoken about what happened. The few times he tried, his mouth would not utter the words. The Council had heard enough to get a general idea, though, and with the added benefit of the Mistress's visit to give proof to his story. They awarded him his compass and let the matter go.

He'd gone back to his healing team, and one of them commented on the small brand on his lower back. He knew it was a curse of silence from the Mistress but could only watch as they tried and failed to heal it.

Seven

Micah took several days to recover from the ordeal with the Mistress. The aches and pains faded by the following evening, thanks to his friends' skills. However, he was damaged mentally. He ate in silence, went on long walks through Canyon Town, and disappeared for hours at a time. Caroline and Rebecca wanted to try and snap him out of it, but Gegan was adamant that they leave him be.

"He learned to deal with this trauma in silence," he told the two witches. "This is his healing process. You will not interfere."

To distract themselves, Caroline and Rebecca began lessons. Immediately, they started arguing. Rebecca didn't see the point in learning potions and protective charms: she wanted to skip straight to attacks and aggressive, offensive skills.

"No," Caroline said firmly as she added water to her countertop apparatus. "That is not where we start."

"I don't want to learn that." Rebecca looked scornfully at the unoffending pieces of metal. "I want to be able to kill any demon that I come across."

"You can't!" said Caroline in exasperation. "This is a fundamental flaw in your thinking. No one, save maybe Gegan, can kill any demon they encounter. And sometimes you need to be able to run and hide until you can get help."

Rebecca looked deeply offended by this reasoning. "I will not run and hide."

"If you want to live, you will," Caroline countered. "Everyone runs and hides."

"That's probably because they took lessons from you and don't know how to fight!" Rebecca snapped angrily.

"Micah ran from that leopard demon outside of town two weeks ago," Caroline shot back. "It's the only reason he's here to tell the tale, and he is miles farther than you in talent and experience. Purification potions are an essential item in a witch's array of materials and tools. Otherwise, most of us would be dead by now."

Losing steam, Rebecca grumbled and dropped the argument. Gegan tactfully stepped in and asked Caroline how she made the potions.

"It's a two-phase process," Caroline explained. "First, I have to purify the water. I begin by lighting the candle," she gestured to the small candle holder overflowing in melted wax that sat beneath the covered bowl of the apparatus. "It's specially made with white wax suffused with rosemary, lavender, and honey. It heats small batches of water that are further purified by these."

She lifted the heavily embroidered cloth off the bowl and tilted it to show chunks of rock and batches of herbs inside. "Clay, charcoal, and limestone to pull out impurities, and bundles of rosemary, sage, lemongrass, lavender, and peppermint to increase potency. I run each batch of liquid through a sixty-minute heat and pour it out into these small bottles."

In the upper cupboard, she showed them the rows of bottles, labeled, and lined up neat as soldiers. "They age for a week, and then I run them through the process again. Each week they become more potent."

"How long until they are ready for use?" Gegan asked interestedly. His eyes lingered on a small rack in the corner of the middle shelf holding four empty conical-shaped bottles. Rebecca had stopped listening.

"They can be used at any time," Caroline said. "The longer they age, the better they are. Although, after about six months, it's not worth it to keep running them through the heating process. For highest purity and effectiveness, they need to age a further six weeks in this." She gestured to the copper bowl sitting alone on the top shelf of the cupboard. "After that, I put the potions in these flame-sealed bottles." She indicated the conical bottles on the rack. "Then they'll keep permanently."

The two witches were quarreling about the merits of white sage versus wild sage when a messenger politely knocked to announce his presence. He stated that Micah's new boots were ready. So they decided to pick them up and present them to Micah as a surprise that evening.

The cobbler's shop was dimly lit when they entered.

"Something is here," Caroline said. The hair on her arms stood up, and she could almost feel the negativity in the room. Rebecca raised an eyebrow at her. "Just pay attention," she muttered as she rang the bell.

The cobbler came from the back, and they could immediately see the demon of self-loathing perched on his shoulder. It looked bloated and happy as it cradled his head and whispered in his ear. Its second tail swung back and forth contentedly as the first secured the demon around the man's neck.

Caroline explained their errand and placed the balance for the boots on the counter. The cobbler stared at her a moment with dead eyes then returned to the back.

"We have to act now," Caroline said urgently as soon as he was out of sight.

"Why?" Rebecca asked.

"That thing is about to kill him. When the second tail forms, it means the victim is close to committing suicide."

"What do we do?" Rebecca asked immediately. "I'm not good at taking out demons that are attached to people."

Caroline refrained from mentioning that this was how almost all demon exorcisms took place. "Compliment him but not his appearance. He needs to feel that he is valuable as a person. That will loosen the demon's grip. I'll do the rest."

Rebecca nodded. When the cobbler came back, she said, "Everything in here looks so high quality. You must be a master at your craft."

"I don't think so," the man muttered as he started boxing up Micah's boots.

"I disagree," Rebecca said forcefully. He looked up, and the demon hissed at her. She continued to elaborate on his skills, all of which was true, while Caroline sidled up beside him. The demon was focused entirely on Rebecca and didn't notice her until she grabbed its second tail and whipped it over her shoulder. The demon lost its grip and sailed over Caroline's head as Rebecca continued to compliment the beautiful decorative stitching on a stunning pair of lady's boots.

"What extraordinary talent it must take to get everything so even and consistent!" The demon snarled and attempted to claw at Caroline while the cobbler finally smiled. He strode around the counter, nodding to her as he passed, and engaged Rebecca in conversation. Caroline swung the demon in front of her and grimaced as its claws found her side on the way. Thankful that she was wearing a dark-colored blouse and the blood wouldn't show, she quickly broke its neck and let its body fall to dust.

She and Rebecca thanked the cobbler and hurried toward the home goods store, so Caroline could purify the injury before the infection took hold.

"How did you know to compliment him?" Rebecca asked as they walked onto the bridge. Her gaze drifted down to the bottom of the canyon as they crossed.

"Any demon like that is weakened when the victim's self-confidence increases," Caroline answered tensely. The wound on her side was starting to burn, and she had to keep her arm tight to her side so the tears in her clothing wouldn't show. "With self-loathing particularly, you have to focus on the person and not their looks."

"But how did you know that?" Rebecca asked again.

Caroline frowned at her, her face turning red from the pain. "Everyone knows that. Demon identification and weakness is essential for any witch or exorcist. Knowledge is one of the only ways we can fight back."

Rebecca trailed behind Caroline for the rest of the walk, deep in thought. When they arrived at the store, Caroline immediately went to her kitchen and pulled the bottle out from under the spout of her potion apparatus. She checked the label and splashed her side where the demon scratched her. Immediately her face paled to its normal color, and her shoulders relaxed.

"That's better," she mumbled and set about making a pot of tea.

"How bad did it get you?" Rebecca asked.

Caroline pursed her lips but didn't answer, so Rebecca asked again.

"Fine," Caroline said, "I'll show you." She lifted the hem of her shirt and revealed two three-inch-long gashes along her ribs.

Rebecca noticed a few other scars peeking out around her torso. "How long until that heals?" she asked.

"Three or four days, I'd wager," Caroline said as she inspected the injury. "I used my best medicines on Micah and haven't had a chance to replenish my supplies yet."

"Why not?"

"Because that particular purification potion needs to be aged for six weeks in a special copper and silver basin after six months of going through the normal aging process. This stuff," she indicated the bottle and chose not to be annoyed at having to repeat the lesson from earlier, "has been going about three weeks. I'll need to keep applying it, but I'll be fine."

"Will you teach me to make it?" Rebecca asked hesitantly.

"Of course."

Micah sat in the far corner of the chocolate shop again. A sense of calm and the beginning tinges of peace began to settle across his shoulders. He set his materials on the table and thanked Nathaniel for the nutmeg and clove hot chocolate.

Instead of nodding shyly and carrying on with serving the other customers, Nathaniel lingered. The lunch rush had passed, and the chocolate shop was empty but for themselves and a couple deep in conversation. Elaine was busy puttering around the kitchen.

"What are you doing?" Nathaniel asked.

"Making Dorset buttons," Micah said. His voice cracked, and he cleared his throat. "Want to see?"

"Sure."

Nathaniel sat down, and Micah showed him the delicate wire rings he was knotting thread around. After completing the outer loop, he made a spiderweb through the center of the ring and wove the thread around to create a starburst pattern.

"This looks like the pin my mom wears," Nathaniel said as he picked up a spare ring. He struggled, trying to hold it and the thread, and at the same time, make a figure-four knot.

Micah smiled. "It should. I gave her that pin."

Nathaniel dropped the ring. It bounced between his fingers and rolled away. "She never told me that, but she wears it every day. Why did you do that?"

Nodding to show he heard the question, Micah considered his options. The pin was a marker for other witches to show Elaine had survived but might be vulnerable. It contained a hint of protection in the weave. Demons wouldn't realize it was there, but it would make Elaine appear to be *not* the easiest prey. He had given out many pins over his life. They were soothing to make, and he hoped they brought some peace. Finally, he looked Nathaniel in the eye, finished a button with a flourish, and said, "I thought it could help her."

"Thanks," Nathaniel said with emotion. "She pins it to her lamp every night and wears it every day." He paused and looked down at his hands, the seriousness of the talk making him uncomfortable. His brow wrinkled. "Are your cufflinks Dorset buttons too?"

Micah was surprised he'd noticed. Putting purified water on the cufflinks whenever he was in public helped the demons overlook him, and most people did too. "Yes, they are." With a practiced flick, he removed one cuff link and held it out. Nathaniel examined the intricate, brightly colored design and quickly handed it back.

"These look great," Micah said that evening. His chat with Nathaniel, accompanied by Elaine's bright smile when she saw them together, had finally conquered the feelings risen by seeing the Mistress. He was ready to put the experience behind him, and a new project was exactly what he needed. He pulled off his old, torn boots and tried on the new ones. They fit him perfectly. He sighed and said, "I was getting tired of my mismatched ones."

"Are you going to charm them now?" Caroline asked. Rebecca looked up interestedly.

"Naturally," Micah said, but then his face fell. "Damn, I don't have my equipment anymore. Remember the nest of hate demons that I was dealing with before I came here? Well, they ambushed me when I was on the move, and I dropped my bag in a fighting retreat. By the time I could get back there, someone had stolen it." He looked plaintively at Caroline and Gegan. "Do you have anything I could use?"

Caroline grimaced. "I don't usually work with leather. I doubt I'll have anything suitable."

"My order has the equipment," Gegan said, "but unfortunately, I travel light and did not bring anything with me."

Micah nodded to them both and started pacing around the room, thinking hard. The boots *clacking* against the floorboards as he moved.

"What exactly do you need?" Rebecca asked.

"Usually, I use a large steel needle with the end flattened," Micah explained. "A sailing needle or something of the like. I heat it and inscribe my protective charm into the leather. It passes for simple tooling if you don't look too close." He sighed and proceeded to take his new boots off. "I'll have to wear the old ones until I can get these charmed."

"It matters that much?" Rebecca asked.

Her companions stared at her—dumbstruck! Caroline opened her mouth to say something, but no words came out. Instead, she gaped like a fish for several seconds before shaking her head.

Micah finally broke the awkward silence. "Yes, Rebecca, it matters." He held up his old intact boot. "Do you see the patterns and intricate detailing here?" he asked. She nodded. "I put all of that on myself. Each cut is part of a protective charm. If I hadn't done that, the leopard demon would have sliced my foot clean off when it got me. Instead, the charms worked, and I only got cut."

He gestured to the pink scars crossing his other ankle. "If you truly want to be a part of this lifestyle, you need to understand this. Everything we do and everything we wear is steeped in protection charms." He grabbed her hand and ran it down the stitching Caroline had put into his shirt sleeve when she repaired it. "That is another series of defensive symbols."

Caroline nodded. She held up her hands and noted for Rebecca to look at her cuffs. There was nothing unique about them until she muttered something. Then they shimmered slightly and were awash in threads of various colors but subtle enough to escape casual notice.

"Another one?" Rebecca asked. When she received an affirmative answer, she asked tentatively, "How did I miss that?"

"It's an extra thing we usually do," Caroline explained. "See this band of white thread around the outside of the charm? It entices the eye to look elsewhere and helps the charms pass unnoticed."

"Gegan?" Rebecca asked.

He pulled the left side of his monk's robes open and showed her one of the most intricate pieces of lace she had ever seen sewed onto his undershirt over his heart.

Caroline and Micah shared a surprised look then got up for closer inspection.

"This is stunning!" Caroline said. "Where did you get it?"

Gegan smiled at her and ran a finger over the lace. "I made it."

Several seconds of stunned silence followed this statement. "You tat?" Caroline finally said weakly. "Of course, you do."

"Naturally," Gegan said without a trace of self-consciousness. "I find making lace very relaxing. Would you like to see my latest project?"

"Let's see it," Micah said.

Gegan strode over to his bag and began rummaging through it.

"Is tatted lace that different from normal lace?" Rebecca asked in an undertone.

"Tatting is a nearly lost art of making lace by hand," Caroline told her. "It gives a wide variety of specialization."

"Here you are," Gegan said as he returned. He was holding a strip of lace, an inch wide and four inches long. Tiny metal beads were sewn into it at regular intervals. "This is going to go around my wrist when I've completed it. My old one fell apart during my last intense fight."

"This is gorgeous," Caroline reached out for it but stopped. The energy emanating from it was palpable at a few inches, and she didn't want to alter it accidentally. She had also been taught that one does not grab at another witch's charmed objects, especially if they are still in creation. "Can you teach me?"

"It will likely require more time than I will have here, but I'll be glad to get you started," Gegan responded. As he gently folded the lace back up, Micah noticed the small tool attached to it.

"That is perfect!" he exclaimed.

"What?" Rebecca asked, startled by the outburst.

"That tool, the one you use for tatting."

"A shuttle?" Gegan interjected.

"Yes," Micah continued, "I can use one to charm my boots. Look at it. It fits in the hand easily enough, it's metal, and the one end is slightly sharpened."

"That's far too small," Caroline argued back. "You'll burn your hand trying to hold it." Her eyes went wide, and she practically flew into her bedroom without another word.

Micah stared at Rebecca and Gegan until Caroline was dashing back. "You can use this!" She crowed triumphantly as she thrust a metal crochet hook into his hand.

"That's far too large," he said, trying not to laugh, "but you have the right idea. Do you have any smaller ones?"

"Are you insane?" Caroline asked. "I would lose my freaking mind if I tried to crochet with anything smaller."

"What about knitting needles? Don't some people use those?" Gegan asked.

Caroline gave him a withering look. "I wouldn't be caught with knitting needles. Crocheting is the only way to get one unbroken line."

"I agree, tatting is the same," Gegan said. "But you can use knitting. Simply layer the effects."

"It's far too easy to screw that up," Caroline argued back. "And you have to invert the pattern every other line. It's a nightmare."

"Then use the purling technique. That way, you stay on the primary side."

"You still have to invert everything, and don't get me started on the effects of different tension."

Micah started to laugh. The argument, combined with the look of utter confusion on Rebecca's face as she unconsciously fussed with her bracelet, was too much for him. His whole body shook, and tears were running down his face by the time he calmed down enough to speak.

"This takes the lead for the most ridiculous conversation I think we've ever had," he said as he wiped his face.

Caroline snorted. "You're wrong. That crown belongs to the two-hour discussion we had on sheep versus alpaca wool for use in these kinds of things."

Gegan now mirrored Rebecca's confusion. "There is no difference," he said. "They have proven that the differences in the animals are far too removed from the process and final result to cause any effects."

"It doesn't matter," Caroline said, regretting that she'd brought the subject up.

"We know that," Micah chuckled, looking at Gegan and Rebecca. "Caroline still refuses to use alpaca wool, though."

"Don't you dare," Caroline said, her face turning red.

"Why?" Chorused Rebecca and Gegan.

"Well," Micah drew out the word to add suspense, "alpacas are far too like llamas for Caroline."

"Llamas?" Gegan asked, raising an eyebrow.

"She had a bad experience," Micah began, but Caroline threw a ball of yarn at him, and it bounced off his nose. He threw it back and hit her shoulder before continuing. "When she was a kid, her grandparents kept llamas." He deflected the yarn ball with his forearm as Caroline went for another hit, and it bounced away. "She was out playing in the field one day when a llama sat on her."

"You got...sat on...by a llama?" Rebecca asked. Her shoulders began to shake as she fought not to laugh.

"It was traumatic at the time!" Caroline shouted. "Thanks for that," she added sarcastically to Micah.

He shrugged. "They would have found out anyway." After a dramatic pause, he added in a stage whisper. "There is no escaping the llamas."

That was the end of Rebecca's self-control. She let out a peal of laughter and doubled over in her chair. Eventually resting her head on the table as she howled with mirth. Gegan kept control of himself, but only just. He kept his mouth covered with one hand and didn't speak, but everyone could hear the deep chuckles emanating from him.

"All of you can kiss my ass and sleep on the damn floor!" Caroline shouted as she stalked into her bedroom.

"It's easy for you all to fall into a rhythm, isn't it?" Rebecca asked the following morning.

Micah looked up from his chocolate bar and around Elaine's empty sweet shop. They technically weren't open for business yet, but they'd made an exception for him. "What do you mean by that?"

"I just feel like you, Caroline, and Gegan are so much farther than me," Rebecca said, a little embarrassed. "You know everything about demons. You can have arguments about charms and reminisce about old times."

130

Micah smiled. "I know it can seem intimidating to be around us sometimes, but Caroline and I have…a long history."

Rebecca sighed and nodded her head. She thought back to her elderly neighbor, the one who had taken her in and taught her everything she knew, the only person she'd had a long history with.

She was seven years old the first time she heard a whisper. It was a simple, small voice in her ear telling her to laugh at a friend who'd fallen. She ignored it and instead held out her hand to help. Two months later, she heard another one. This one tried to coax her into punching a boy who was laughing at her. Instead, she walked away. They came more frequently after that, small whispers, and ideas in the back of her mind. Occasionally she was tempted to listen, but she never did. She wanted to be a nice person. She wanted to have friends and laughs and not have to look over her shoulder to see what was talking to her.

She noticed her neighbor Bella start to take more of an interest in her. The old woman would wave at her from her rocking chair on the porch as she walked home or invite her in for a treat. Her parents supported this because Bella was a kind old woman and usually alone. She'd been living there when they moved in, before Rebecca's birth, and had never had a visitor.

Bella was of a medium height and build with short white hair and dark eyes. She always wore dresses with long sleeves and high collars or shawls. Her hands were covered in fine scars and shook slightly whenever she tried to grab things. Rebecca found Bella's voice soothing and intriguing as it was soft and high with a trace of an accent.

Soon the whispers were happening daily. Rebecca tried to ask her parents about it, but they didn't understand and brushed her off. They became more agitated around her and avoided her during the evenings. The more she reached out to them, the more they recoiled. She felt very alone but found solace with Bella. She cried many tears into the old woman's handkerchiefs while they rocked on the porch. Bella always had time for her and always supported her.

One day, Rebecca spilled a platter of food. She'd tried to carry two large plates at once to the dinner table and wound up spilling one all down herself. Her father shouted at her for several minutes, swearing profusely before turning and punching a hole in the wall.

Rebecca's mother immediately hauled her across the yard and deposited her on Bella's doorstep. "We're calling in that favor," she said when Bella had shuffled over and opened the door. She thrust Rebecca inside, nearly knocking her into Bella, and walked away.

"What's going on?" Rebecca asked.

Bella took her time in answering. "Your mother and father are going through some difficulties right now. You stay here tonight and let them sort themselves out." That night became the first of years. Rebecca's parents were gone the next day. They'd left in the night with all their important possessions. All that remained for Rebecca was a short note that Bella refused to let her read.

The stress of the abandonment caused her abilities to manifest, and she started seeing demons a week later. Rebecca thought she was going crazy until she realized that the things she saw and the whispers were from the same source. None of her classmates or teachers could see them and accused her of acting out to get attention. The news about her parents spread fast, and by week's end, everyone she knew was talking about her, behind their hands, in not-so-quiet whispers.

A crowd of demons followed her home that Friday. She sprinted as fast as she could and collapsed in Bella's kitchen, crying and gasping for breath.

"What's wrong, child?" Bella asked concernedly.

"They're following me," Rebecca wailed. "Why can't anyone else see them?"

Bella looked alarmed. "You can see them?"

"Everyone thinks I'm lying," Rebecca cried. "They all said I'm making things up because Mama and Papa left me."

"Oh, sweet girl," Bella murmured. She carefully sat down on the floor and held Rebecca close as she cried. Nearly an hour later, Rebecca's tears were spent, and she hiccupped as her breathing returned to normal. "Listen to me. I know you are not lying. You are not seeking attention," Bella said.

The validation sent a surge of relief through Rebecca. Her eyes began to water again.

"It's okay," Bella said, calming her as she stroked Rebecca's hair and held her hand. "Most people can't see those things."

"Why not?"

Bella hesitated. "Now is not the time for that. Just be assured that I see them too. There is no need to bring them up to anyone else, and I'll teach you how to deal with them."

"Okay."

That began Rebecca's training. Bella tried her best, but she was an old woman, and her memory was failing. She couldn't remember any charms to completion but turned instead to her library. Here Rebecca read and learned about location charms and how to kill demons not attached to humans. These two topics were Bella's specialty before she retired from active witch's work.

Soon the demons left her alone. She mastered multiple techniques to attack them at a distance, and they no longer followed her home from school or ganged up outside the windows of her class. She pretended not to see them and always ignored their whispers.

When Rebecca was fifteen, Bella had a bad fall. She hurt her knee, hit her head, and sprained her wrist badly. Rebecca dropped out of school and spent her time looking after her friend as she began to fade away.

Rebecca brought Bella's morning tea and sat watching her dear friend sip it slowly. Bella looked across the bedroom to the dresser and motioned to a square walnut box inlaid with mother of pearl. "Please bring me that box." As Rebecca placed the box in Bella's hands, she felt a quiver of anticipation. Bella took the lid off and revealed a bracelet. The stones sat shiny and black, strung together with silver and steel wrought fine as any wire. Spaced periodically around the smooth, asymmetrical stones were four black pearls surrounded by silver rings. "I can't wear it anymore, and it needs to be worn by a powerful witch. Please accept this from me, my child."

"I...Oh, it's stunning, Bella!" Rebecca picked it up and placed it on her right wrist. She felt as if it "accepted" her and seemed to have an energy of its own. The black opals shimmered with contained fire, and the tourmaline felt solid and safe. The only color in the bracelet came from a single star-shaped lapis lazuli.

Bella watched and then smiled. "It is meant for you. No questions now. I must rest."

Rebecca plumped up the pillows behind Bella's neck and head and retired to her room to study her precious gift.

"I need to tell you something," Bella said one evening. Her voice held more strength than usual, and Rebecca took notice. She laid aside the book she was reading as Bella continued, "The night your parents left—"

"Please don't," Rebecca interrupted. "I've cried enough over that."

"This is important," Bella told her. "I've said many times that you will be a powerful witch. You have no trouble discerning demon voices and ignoring them. You still don't realize how unique you are. Most people can't do that. They can't just 'not listen' to the demons. When you refused to let the demons influence you, they rebounded onto those closest to you."

"My parents?"

"Yes. Your parents had so many demons fighting for control and fighting to make them do horrible things. The fact that they left you proves how much they cared. They somehow knew they could not hold out against the demons much longer, and so they did the best thing for you. They got away from you before they did something far worse."

That short conversation stayed with Rebecca as she tended Bella through the last weeks of her life. She passed away peacefully in her sleep, and Rebecca mourned her alone as her casket was lowered into the ground. The simple headstone read, "Bella, Friend and Mother."

Quietly, Rebecca packed up the house and sold everything of value. The sum left her enough to travel, and she wandered for two years before settling in Canyon Town and meeting Elaine.

All the memories passed through her mind in the blink of an eye, and she brought herself back to the present and Micah. He was watching her patiently.

"Sorry," she murmured, "was thinking."

He smiled. "Don't worry about it. I could tell that whoever it was, they were important to you. It would be callous to demand all your time." He continued before Rebecca had a chance to respond. "Are you coming by the shop today?"

She nodded. "Now that it's come out that I can't identify different demons, Caroline wants me there every possible minute."

"Can you blame her?" Micah asked.

"Not really," Rebecca shrugged. "I just miss my nights off. Sometimes I enjoy solitude."

"Don't we all," Micah agreed. "I'll talk to Caroline for you. One evening off shouldn't hurt."

Eight

Something grated against Micah's senses as soon as he stepped from the chocolate shop. The air seemed to hum with a nasty promise as he quickly returned to Caroline's shop. Near the front window, he found her neurotically turning all the teacups in one of her display cabinets, so the handles faced the same way.

"You feel it too?" he asked.

"Yes," she said curtly as she took a step back to look at her work. "I don't know what it is, but I don't like it." Two teacups were not in line, so she moved them slightly before starting on the next shelf down.

"Where's Gegan?"

"He's upstairs. He said he wanted somewhere quiet to meditate."

The shop door banged open, and a soprano voice screeched, "Where is he?" Micah and Caroline both flinched as the voice continued.

"Come out, you useless son of a bitch! I know you've been lurking here, hiding away like a coward since you dared show your face back in this town."

The voice's owner came into view and proved to be a medium-height, athletic, blonde woman with blue eyes. She was red-faced under her tan and wearing fitted, comfortable clothing. Her boots and hands were covered in dust, and flakes of dirt drifted to the floor as she pointed a threatening finger at Micah. "There you are!" she shrieked. "How dare you come back here after what you did?"

Micah didn't answer. He was completely distracted by the demon hovering above her. It was unlike any he had ever seen. Mottled plum and bright pink with a pale-yellow underbelly, its serpentine body ended in a scorpion-like tail wrapped around the woman's neck. Two front feline paws rested on her head, claws extended, while its body was kept afloat by draconian wings. Its head was that of a lion in horrible caricature. One side of its mouth was dented, broken, and drooling. Its eyes were muddy and dark but glinted with malicious intelligence.

"You are the reason she's dead!" The woman placed her hands on her hips as she continued to berate him.

"I know that demon," Caroline said quietly when the blond woman paused for breath.

"Madam, please," Micah tried to placate the blonde.

"Don't you dare to speak to me!" she snapped. "You do not get to lie to me."

"I wouldn't," Micah tried again, but the woman slammed her fist on the side of Caroline's cabinet of teacups. They rattled in their saucers as she ranted on. "You swore you would keep her safe—she told me so. She knew they were after her, and you failed her. She's dead and gone, and it is your fault!"

To his eternal shame, Micah didn't know who the woman was yelling about. Caroline's shop faded out as a parade of faces appeared before him. Each one the face of a woman he had failed. Some had survived his failure, but none had remained whole. A great weight settled across his shoulders, and he found it hard to breathe. He had saved people from demons, from fire and water, from ex-loved ones, and from themselves, but he was only one man.

Caroline placed a hand on Micah's shoulder for support and though he hardly felt it, the action drew the ire of the blonde woman to Caroline for the first time. "Do you think he can keep you safe?" she yelled scornfully. "He will leave you to die broken and bleeding in an alleyway."

With difficulty, Micah returned his focus to the present and listened as Caroline spoke directly in his ear. "That demon, I've heard of it. It's responsible for more witch's deaths than any other on record."

"How do we kill it?"

"I don't know."

"Shut up, bitch!" the woman screamed at Caroline. "I see you talking to him like he's worth a damn."

"He is!" Caroline roared back, flaring up at once. "He is worth more than any other man I've known, and if you calmed down, you would see it too."

"You do not get to tell me to calm down," the blonde shrieked.

"Then get out of my shop!"

Micah noticed something interesting as the two women began hurling insults at each other. The demon's tail twitched, and a long gossamer tendril, almost like a strand of spider's silk, flicked out of the scorpion-like barb. It flew through the air and landed on Caroline. At once, her voice rose half an octave, and her insults became coarser. The demon flexed its paws.

The strand looked insubstantial, so Micah surreptitiously grabbed onto it and attempted to break it. The thin band of material bit into his fingers and they began to bleed. The demon noticed and smiled a terrifying lopsided smile. Micah tried again, but all he succeeded in doing was opening another small cut. He began to sweat. It had been years since he'd encountered a demon he knew nothing about. Without knowledge, he couldn't hope to defeat it because the demon was clearly that powerful.

He heard Gegan thundering down the stairs, but his friend didn't spare the three of them a glance. Instead, he rushed to the front door and

142

began rapidly inscribing symbols around it in white chalk. Micah cocked his head in confusion before his eyes traveled to the front window. The woman's screaming, coupled with Caroline's scathing retorts, had masked the sounds of a large group of people massed outside. He looked closer and saw that many of them had threads glinting in the sunlight linking them to the serpentine demon. These people were yelling the loudest. They acted the most animated, and some carried multiple other demons.

Having finished his charm around the door, Gegan turned silently and rushed back to Caroline and the blonde woman. While he approached the demon, he threw off his loose monk's robes and revealed tight black clothing adorned with lace underneath. Both women were now shrieking obscenities at each other as the demon smiled broader above them. Gegan whipped his hand between them, and the demon suddenly stopped smiling.

The thread connecting it to Caroline was severed. As the strand fell away, it left a long, thin cut along Gegan's arm, almost like a paper cut. As Gegan turned to face the demon, Micah saw the blade of a small reverse grip dagger extending from the man's clenched fist. The ornately decorated blade had a wicked curve and fine saw-toothing along the inner edge. Gegan's face was a study in fierce resolve and terrifying intent, made all the more surreal by his graceful movements.

"What are you doing?" The blonde shrieked as Gegan began moving toward her, slicing the air in intricate patterns. Additional gossamer strands flew from the demon's tail, slid around him, and bit into his arms and hands again and again as he did so. Blood ran down his arms, but it did not deter him. Energy rippled through his frame, and the cut strands began shriveling to dust. He fought faster, his arms blurring with effort and flinging droplets of blood everywhere.

The blonde woman tried to flee, but Micah grabbed her and held her fast. He thought fleetingly of the daggers at his waist but decided against them. Micah could feel a hundred strands from the demon feathering along his skin like spiderwebs, but they did not harm him. He was not their target. Gegan advanced another step, and the demon puffed out its chest.

"Don't kill me!" the blonde cried, writhing and sobbing beneath the looming wings. "I don't want to die!"

Micah knew it was useless to calm her down. She was entirely in the grip of the demon, terrified and hysterical. He tightened his hold as she fought to free herself.

Caroline came to her senses and dashed up the stairs.

Gegan exhaled roughly in pain as one of the cut strands left a delicate slice along his neck. His hands were covered in blood. The dagger remained firm in his grip due to a small metal ring set in the handle for his thumb. With every cut, small shocks ran up his arms.

Someone outside threw something at the front window and cracked the glass.

Jumping down the last four stairs, Caroline flicked something at the blonde woman. The droplets of liquid hit her face, and she suddenly gasped for breath. Her arms flew up to her throat, and she felt the demon's scaly tail. Paling, she looked up and caught sight of the demon's head above her. "What is that?!" she choked out as she clawed at the demon's tail and redoubled her efforts to escape.

Micah held on, thankful his injuries from the leopard demon had finally healed. He grabbed the demon's body, just below the wings, with one hand and wrenched its paws away from the woman's head. Thanks to Caroline, she could see it now, so it could physically hurt her. His other hand went to the scorpion-like sting. Something dribbled onto his hand that immediately burned and stung.

Caroline ran forward, snagging the threads around her, pulled the tail from his grip, and tried to unwind it from the woman's throat as she gasped and struggled. The demon laughed at their efforts; drool fell in slippery ropes from its broken mouth onto the woman's head.

Gegan fought another step closer through the web of tendrils the demon had spun around him. He was close to breaking its power, and it knew he was. It was ignoring Micah and Caroline and focusing solely on him. Setting his feet, Gegan took a deep breath as another surge of power rolled through him. All the strands around him withered away as his dagger cut through another group.

The demon was starting to weaken. Caroline managed to pull its tail away from the blonde's throat as she fought and screamed. It left a ring of light purple bruises. Micah let her go as the demon turned to snap at him, and the woman dove behind the cabinet of teacups. She sank down to the floor, sobbing as the fight continued.

Gegan was within reach of the demon's body now. It snarled at him and flicked its tail. The remaining uncut strands wrapped around Gegan's arms and held him fast. It tangled him further when it lunged, nearly breaking from Micah's grasp and freeing itself from Caroline. It jabbed its sting at Gegan, who could not dodge.

Instead, Gegan summoned another surge of power. He let out a roar as all the strands around him popped and fizzled. The demon's sting froze inches from his chest before its tail swung away limp and dripping fluid from large, angry-looking blisters. The demon began to panic as Gegan sliced through more of its threads—less than thirty remained now.

Risking a look outside, Caroline saw people arguing and several fistfights starting between the main mob of people and a few who stood between them and her shop. The demon twisted and turned, finally breaking free of Micah's grip as his hand spasmed. It fluttered up to the ceiling as several thumps sounded on the shop's front door. Taking advantage of the distraction, the demon started flapping toward the door.

"Not again," Gegan growled. He leaped up and grabbed the demon out of the air. It clawed at him with its front paws and scored him down his already lacerated forearms as he landed with a crash that shook the furniture. Gegan grunted in pain, but his massive hands didn't loosen their grip on the demon's body. He pulled the demon down, hand over hand until he grasped it around the neck. With a heave of his shoulders that rippled down his entire body, Gegan broke its neck as it twisted back on itself to bite him.

As the demon's body turned to dust, Gegan faced the front door. The fights were growing out of control, and several people were yelling. Blood dripped off his fingertips as he strode forward. Then, taking several deep breaths, he readied the last of his reserves of power.

"This ends now!" he roared as he slammed open the door. All the demons in the vicinity jerked and twitched as they felt his power roll over them. They immediately drew back slightly. Gegan looked a fearsome sight. Covered in blood and cuts, he seemed to shimmer as small metal plates and chains about his person flickered in and out of sight.

People in the back of the crowd, those with no demons on them, looked uneasily at each other and slipped away.

Caroline and Micah hauled the blonde woman to the front of the shop and shoved her out the door. "Forget this happened," Caroline said.

"Or if you can't, come back tomorrow, and we'll explain."

"But. I…" the woman stammered, overwhelmed, and confused.

"Tomorrow," Caroline hissed. "Today, I have to heal the man that saved your life."

"But. I…"

"Come back tomorrow!"

"We have hurt no one," Gegan shouted, oblivious to the conversation occurring behind him. "There is no need for further violence."

"He's right," Elaine called. She, Rebecca, Markus, Nathaniel, Joshua, Miranda, and several others stood their ground in front of the shop windows. The crowd didn't look convinced.

"Help me!" Caroline whispered as she grabbed Rebecca. "Follow my lead." The two of them ducked back inside, and Caroline began chanting. Rebecca quickly joined in as the verse repeated itself. The atmosphere began to calm, and more people slipped away from the crowd. However, Gegan continued to berate them for falling into a mob mentality and for trying to destroy private property.

The demons seemed cowed and confused, then all flinched in unison as Gegan sent out another wave of energy. They looked around for support from the demon Gegan had killed, and not finding it, they began to withdraw. The last few demons shook their fists and hissed at Gegan as they slunk away.

"What happened?" Elaine asked as she looked Gegan up and down with alarm.

"Someone broke in and attempted…." Caroline trailed off, not sure what cover story to use.

"I get the picture," Elaine said quickly, glancing at her son. "No details required." Then, she looked at Gegan with concern. "Will he be okay?"

"I think so," Caroline said as Gegan swayed slightly on his feet. Micah and Rebecca moved to support him and carefully led him inside. "I need to…." She gestured awkwardly after them.

"Go, go!" Elaine said. She and the others started dispersing.

Caroline hurried inside to find Gegan sitting at one of her staged dining room tables. He was slumped down in a chair with his head back and eyes closed, breathing hard. His dark skin looked unnaturally grey underneath the dripping sweat. Rebecca and Micah stood at his sides, pouring water over his arms. The blood and water fell into large porcelain vessels on the floor.

"What happened?" Rebecca asked. "We saw the mob go by the shop, and I noticed all the demons. I knew it had to do with you, so I convinced Elaine and our friends in the shop to come here."

"Your intervention was timely," Gegan said, his voice rough. "I doubt the door would have held long enough without you."

"What did you do to it?" Caroline asked as she grabbed some towels and began carefully drying off Gegan's arms. She felt thin bracelets connected by chains.

He grimaced. "It's a simple charm to prevent demons from entering through a door for a time. In my haste, I used too much power, and we may have to replace your door."

Caroline, Micah, and Rebecca all looked at each other before glancing at the door. The symbols Gegan had written in white chalk were now etched into the wood and smoldering slightly.

"That's an issue for the future us," Caroline decided. "Let's get you taken care of first."

Gegan nodded and rested a moment while they cleaned him up. Most of the cuts on his arms were minor. They crisscrossed and overlapped but weren't deep. His forearms resembled a jumbled spider's web. Caroline used her highest quality purification potions on hand to clean them and quickly supplemented them with two silver and white charms placed carefully in Gegan's neck and chest. His wrists, elbows, two small bands around his arms, and a strip along the top of his arm were curiously absent of injuries. Rebecca commented on that quietly, but Gegan heard her. He waved off Caroline as she began to bandage his arm.

"I might as well explain," he said as he sat up. He carefully raised one hand and touched his left shoulder, dropping his illusion charm. Small metal plates across his chest and shoulders appeared first. They connected to a series of fragile-looking necklaces wrapped around his throat. Narrow metal plates ran down his upper arms to his elbows, where they met thin bracelets both above and below the joint.

His forearms carried multiple bracelets, all joined by a wide plate covering the back of his radius and ulna. He wore flexible metal gloves that covered the back of his hands, leaving the palm mostly bare, and extended up to the first joint on his fingers. The armor was completed by a loose belt that wrapped several times around his hips and waist.

"What's all this?" Rebecca asked, nearly dumbstruck.

"My armor," Gegan explained. "I keep it hidden to avoid questions, vandals, and extra demon interest."

"As do we all," Micah said, fingering his cufflinks. "How does it work?"

"It strengthens my bones mostly," Gegan answered. "My training focused on hand-to-hand combat and short-range weapons. I don't even use my staff to fight. This armor prevents my bones from breaking. It also can store my strength. I usually have six 'charges' available to me. They let me greatly intensify my power or destroy any demon that gets on me. I had to use all of them in this fight."

"That's what you were doing when you freed yourself from the demon's threads?" Micah asked.

Gegan nodded. "I used one on the door, three during the fight, and the last two on dispelling the crowd." He took a deep breath and leaned back in the chair. "I've seen the aftermath of that demon." His voice dropped in pitch and intensified.

"It wasn't getting away again. Three years ago, it led a mob of people to a witch's house. No one knew how it convinced so many demons to follow it. They overwhelmed the witch and killed her. She managed to send out a distress call, but no one was close enough to respond. We knew that she put up a fight, though. There was evidence of a long, drawn-out battle on her property.

"Shortly afterward, it struck again. This time against one of my order." His face hardened. "The young man stood no chance and was hanged by a group of people screaming with glee. We learned then it could influence demons *and* people.

Another gegan injured it last year before it nearly killed him. The man held onto consciousness long enough to give us details. That's how I knew to cut the strands from its tail. It draws power from the people and demons it is connected to. Once it has a critical number of connections, there is no stopping it.

"I've personally seen its work one time before now. Six months ago, it brought an entire town to bear on an older witch. She was a retired dame who wanted to spend more time with her grandchildren. Luckily, the children were at their parents when the demon attacked. It led a mob, just like today, to the dame's home and influenced them to burn her out.

When I arrived, she had already passed on, but her home was still smoldering. I used all my power on a divining and scrying charm to find the demon responsible. It escaped me then." His mouth curved into a fierce smile full of flashing teeth. "But not today."

"Thank you, Gegan," Caroline said sincerely. "The dame you mentioned was a friend of mine."

Gegan bowed his head in acknowledgment. "I need to meditate," he said a moment later. "That is how I store energy for my charges."

"I am going to finish bandaging your arm," Caroline said, advancing on Gegan. He submitted to her, and when she had removed the used charms and completed his bandages to her satisfaction, she glanced at Micah.

"Go," Caroline and Micah said. Then, after Gegan calmly walked up the stairs, they turned to each other.

"Well…" Caroline said.

"Yeah," Micah agreed.

"Come on," Rebecca said. "Let's get this cleaned up." She hefted one of the filled basins from the floor and began walking toward the back. Micah attempted to lift the second one but dropped it, splashing water and blood across the floor as he grimaced in pain. Looking at his hands, he saw one palm was red and burned with a large shiny blister forming.

He held his hand out to Caroline for inspection, and she wrinkled her nose while gently folding his hand between her own. "My current highest quality potions barely made a dent in this demon's influence, and I won't have any more of that until tomorrow. I'll run them through the heating process as soon as I can, but—" she trailed off.

"Shit," Micah said as Rebecca returned, falling into the chair that Gegan had vacated. Caroline stood by him and placed her hands on his shoulders.

They explained the situation to her and began debating on what to do.

"Could you wrap it in honey, at least for now?" Rebecca asked.

Caroline cocked her head in confusion and looked at her. "Honey?"

"It's what Bella used to do," Rebecca said hesitantly. "If I ever got injured, she would wrap it in honey for an hour before bandaging it."

"That might do for a scrape or a minor demon scratch," Caroline said. "But this is way beyond that."

"So, add to it," Rebecca countered. "What could intensify the effects? We don't need this to heal him; we just need it to keep the infection at bay until tomorrow."

"Lavender is a big one," Caroline responded. "White bandages or thread would help."

"Could you loosely crochet the bandages? Would that make a difference?" Rebecca asked.

"Yes, it would," Caroline said, brightening up.

"Just do it fast," Micah cut in weakly as his hand seized up painfully

Nine

"Do we really have to charm every single thing?" Rebecca asked in exasperation the following morning.

"Yes, we *really* do," Caroline replied, her irritation evident. "How else do you think we stop the graveyard demons."

"The what?!"

Caroline closed her eyes and took a deep breath. "Graveyard demons. They are a specific group of small demons that congregate wherever blood has been shed—particularly witch blood. They slink inside through the cracks in the defenses and lay in wait. They love battlefields, the scenes of accidents, and even cemeteries because there are usually fresh corpses about.

The critical thing to remember is they destabilize protective charms. They undermine everything we do and open the way for bigger demons." She glanced briefly at the charms in the corners of the room before eyeing the freshly scrubbed floor for any visible blood. "Now, we do one final check."

Removing an ornate hair ornament and shaking out her bright red hair, Caroline took a deep breath to steady herself. She pricked her finger with a large pin drawn from the ornament. Then, she traced the blood over the scars on the inside of her middle finger. Closing her eyes, she muttered, "I will see." Rebecca scoffed, but Caroline ignored her.

The dull, muddy shades of the world were overshadowed by bright swarming streams of color as Caroline opened her eyes. She glanced at Gegan to assess the color of his aura, and he stiffened slightly. The vibrant, almost neon, turquoise hit her enhanced senses like a firework, and she jerked a little. Gegan raised an eyebrow, but she waved him off and looked further. Currents drifted lazily in the spiral of a waterspout rising from his feet to the top of his shaved head. Flares and bright lines appeared where the currents eddied over his arms and shoulders, marking where his armor plates lay.

She swept her gaze around the shop, looking for any trace of the same vivid, liquid blue as surrounded him. She spotted three small glimmers and quickly released the enhanced vision as her stomach rolled unpleasantly. "Here, here, and here," she gestured. "We need to go over these areas again."

"There is nothing there," Rebecca said mutinously. "We've been cleaning for two hours here, and I don't even know how long we cleaned last night."

"You don't screw around with spilled blood," Caroline said. There was no room in her tone for argument. "Clearly, you are not content with my telling you the time, so I will build you a clock, as my grandfather would say. So, in excruciating detail, here is why."

Micah half listened to the explanation. His hand, though soaked in lavender honey and wrapped in a bandage, itched and burned, and the purifying potions wouldn't be ready until the afternoon. Caroline had checked her apparatus as soon as she woke up, but unfortunately, one of her herb bundles had soured overnight. She'd made a replacement, but it had to soak for several hours before she could make any more potions.

Meanwhile, Micah had shouldered the big pieces of furniture away from the bloody floor. Now that she was actively dealing with the blood, he had been relegated to a supervisory position. Gegan had been unanimously voted exempt from clean-up duty. He sat stiffly across from Micah in an overstuffed chair, clothing ragged where Caroline had torn it to expose his wounds. He'd left his monk's robes upstairs soaking and wore his fitted black shirt, now sleeveless, over loose, drawstring pants.

His hands and arms were bound up in bandages that bulged on top of his now invisible armor and were only slightly reddened with seeping blood. Caroline had placed a large cup of tea, complete with a saucer, in front of him as Rebecca arrived. He smiled and said nothing as she turned away. His fingers were so heavily bandaged that he could not grasp the cup's handle.

Instead, he brought his hands together as if trying to hold water and gently scooped up the cup and saucer. Carefully, he brought them to his mouth and tilted the cup and saucer to drink. Micah started to reach for the saucer, but Gegan shook his head. He didn't want to bring attention to it and embarrass Caroline. Besides, the heat from the cup and saucer was soothing.

Instead, they discussed his armor.

"How does it work?" Micah asked.

"I meditate every day," Gegan answered. "This method concentrates some of the latent power produced by my other charms. I don't choose to fully explain it, but the armor holds this excess power, and I can call forth surges of it in great need. I trust you, so I will tell you this. I can carry six surges, six charges of power if you will. Each charge takes a full three hours of meditation, and the charges will start to bleed off if I don't meditate every day."

Micah nodded and processed the information. He knew Gegan had power equal to a powerful witch from his aura and a formidable demon hunter from his name, but the magnitude of his skill was still astounding. It never occurred to him that others might view him the same way.

"Um…excuse me…?"

They all looked up, surprised to see the blue-eyed blonde woman from yesterday. She stood over them nervously. The ring of bruises around her neck had darkened overnight but were barely visible over a high collared shirt. She was accompanied by two men, one emanating fury while the second gave off no emotional cues at all.

The first had the lean look of an athlete or someone who did physical labor. His light brown hair and facial features resembled the blonde woman's. He was unshaven and had piercing green eyes. The second was a tall, wiry, young man with dark hair streaked with premature grey and light blue eyes. He had a vicious-looking scar along his left collarbone and small nicks and cuts all over his hands. He stayed a pace behind the other two as they all approached.

"Hi," Micah said awkwardly. Gegan carefully lowered his cup and saucer.

"I'm back," the woman said to Caroline, who straightened up wincing, as her knee popped loudly.

"Yes, you are," Caroline agreed, rubbing her knee. "And you brought friends."

"This is my cousin, Kane," she gestured to the light-haired man next to her. He scowled at them all. "This is his best friend, Derek." The other man nodded.

Caroline introduced herself and Rebecca, then looked pointedly at the blonde woman.

"Sorry, I'm Trish," she mumbled.

"Enough of the niceties," Kane snapped. Trish flinched as he went on. "What the fuck did you do to her?" His eyes darted between Gegan and Micah. Neither of whom had risen.

"They did nothing to her!" Rebecca said, firing up at once.

"It sure as shit wasn't you," Kane sneered, his eyes roving over Rebecca's slim figure. "Those bruises didn't just magically appear, and she didn't have them before she came here yesterday."

"Where were you?" Gegan asked in a calm, low voice.

"None of your business!" Kane shouted, his face red.

Micah shivered slightly and glanced at Gegan, who was frowning. Kane's demon had shown itself. The red monstrosity was a demon of hate and anger. Its four insectoid legs ended in furry paws with six extended claws. Its underbelly was furred in pale orange with small streaks of fiery red and fuchsia. Hardened and smooth crimson wings (like those of a cockroach) covered its back. A prehensile tail, framed by two long antennae, waved lazily over its grinning feline face.

"Now it all makes sense," Caroline said. "You saw it, didn't you?"

Trish's eyes shone with fear as she nodded vigorously.

"Saw what?" Kane snapped.

"Can you do anything about it?" Trish asked the room at large. Kane looked furious at being ignored, but Derek put a hand on his shoulder. Both the man and the demon quieted.

Rolling his eyes, Micah finally stood. He was slightly taller than Derek and had several inches on Kane. Neither man backed down as he approached and circled them appraisingly. Then, he plucked the demon off Kane from behind by grabbing one of its antennae at the base with his uninjured hand. The demon lost its balance and swung crazily off to one side before losing its grip. Its legs cycled wildly through the air as it attempted to claw at him, but Micah flipped it underhand to the floor in front of Caroline as he came back around the two men.

The gesture was small, precise, and none of their guests noticed. Caroline quickly set one foot on it, braced herself, and ripped its antennae off. She gave an involuntary shiver of revulsion and dropped the twitching antennae as they fell to dust.

Kane looked around him in complete confusion. Suddenly losing the influence of a demon in mid-rant was disorienting mentally and physically.

"How did you do that?" Derek suddenly asked. He had a rough, baritone voice.

"Wait, is it gone now?" Trish asked timidly.

Micah nodded.

"That's it?"

He shrugged.

Trish looked nonplussed. "But yesterday…" She trailed off, glancing at Gegan.

"Now, will you tell me what is going on here?" Kane demanded as he wobbled slightly. Derek agreed. Everyone looked awkwardly at each other for several seconds as the silence stretched.

Gegan finally broke it by addressing Derek. "Why don't you tell us what you know first?"

"I don't know anything," Derek said, without meeting anyone's gaze.

"Just start talking, someone," Kane grumbled. "My head is starting to pound, but I'm not leaving until I find out who hurt Trish." The woman colored but encouraged Derek to start speaking.

He grimaced and rubbed a hand across the back of his neck. "At first, I thought I hit my head during one of my rock climbs, but I showed no other signs of head trauma. I would catch movement out of the corner of my eye, but when I looked, there was nothing there. Then I started seeing vague shapes or shadows. Lately, they've been getting clearer, and I've seen some colors. Like that thing on Kane...it was red, right?" He smiled apologetically and hesitantly.

"What thing?" Kane demanded.

Micah ignored him. "It was red," he said to Derek, who looked relieved at the validation.

"What was it?" he asked.

Everyone paused. It was usually a bad idea to tell people about demons. They ran for a stake and torches or blamed every misfortune of the last ten years on the failure of the witches. Many didn't believe in demons and thought of them as mere bogeymen meant to scare children.

Caroline and Rebecca were exchanging grimaces while Gegan studied Derek. Kane looked about ready to start shouting again but suddenly grabbed his stomach. Micah's eyes found Trish. She looked hopeful for answers, scared of the truth, vulnerable, and haunted as she clutched the high collar of her shirt around her bruised neck. He decided to tell them the truth.

"It was a demon."

Trish flinched as Kane scoffed, drawing attention to himself. "Everyone knows those aren't real," he said.

"They are very real," Caroline said quietly. Something in her voice made Kane swallow his next dismissive comment. She continued. "If you'd seen what happened yesterday, you wouldn't scoff and laugh. This man here," she gestured to Gegan, "nearly died saving your cousin from a demon that would have flattened lesser men.

"That demon has haunted our community for decades, killing and ravaging. No one could stop it." Her voice rose as she said, "He put a stop to it, at great personal risk, and none of us came out unscathed. Your cousin is lucky that she came here! Otherwise, she would be dead at the hands of the mob she led." She was shaking now. Rebecca put a comforting hand on her arm.

"Is it true?" Derek asked. "Did you save her life?"

Gegan nodded. He stood slowly, unthreateningly, and gestured to Micah, Rebecca, and Caroline with his bandaged hands. "Without the aid of these exceptional people, your town would likely be burning ash and blood-spattered streets. That demon exerted an influence over more individuals than I have seen any other do. Your neighbors were prepared for violence. Trish was at the center of it all and would not have survived. The demon would have made sure its host could not report to people like us."

"So, who are you people?" Derek asked.

"Witches and exorcists mainly," Micah said, sensing that Gegan had said his piece. "We're the ones who have been fighting back against the demons for years."

"We're leaving now," Kane announced, grabbing Trish by the elbow.

"Wait! What?" she stammered as he marched her toward the front door.

"I have heard enough of this nonsense," he said. "It's all insanity."

"You didn't see it!" Trish said as she threw him off. She was shaking, her whole body practically vibrating, as she jabbed a finger at him. "You didn't feel it curling around your neck and whispering horrific things in your ear. You didn't feel powerless to resist it and watch it make you say things, do things you regret. I will not pretend this never happened. I will not leave and put this out of my mind. I couldn't think, couldn't act, couldn't stop myself, and I will not walk away from the chance to find out why."

Kane looked shocked by her outburst, but Derek moved up and put his arms around her shoulders. Together they stood and watched Kane's reaction. He turned on his heel and left the store. The door rattled on its hinges as he slammed it behind him. Out in the street, a rage demon perked up and watched him go by.

Derek gently led Trish, who now had tears streaming down her face, back over to the group and sat her on a couch.

For the next hour, they listened. Caroline and Micah explained about the demons, the witches and exorcists who fought them, and their methods. Rebecca recounted her experiences, nervously fiddling with her belt as she explained how demons attempted to make her parents do something unthinkable and how she had been taken in by Bella. Gegan spoke about fighting demons, how he knew what to do with the demon yesterday, and briefly about his order.

Trish's tears ran dry somewhere in the explanation of portals to hell. She sat straighter, though she still held Derek's hand for support and took in every word. For his part, Derek watched and listened, calculating. Both of them missed the worried look between Micah and Gegan as Rebecca's eyes lit up at the mention of the portals.

Finally, out of words, silence fell.

"Why could I see them yesterday...the demons?" Trish asked. She hadn't moved much through the entire explanation but now leaned forward. "What did you do to me?"

"I'm sorry about that," Caroline said sincerely. "I exposed you to a small potion that would let you see them. It's temporary, and there are no side effects. I just...I needed to break the demon's hold over you, and that was the only idea I had at the time. I knew if you saw it, you would want it off you."

Trish nodded emphatically and took a deep breath. "What am I supposed to do now?"

"That depends on you," Micah said gently. He knelt next to the couch so they were at eye level. "What do you want?"

She looked at him, lost for an answer, for several seconds before Rebecca cut in. "How about some lunch? I think we're all hungry, and conversation is usually better with a full stomach."

Caroline and Micah went upstairs to begin prepping the food while Rebecca stepped out to buy some extra ingredients from the market. Gegan, Derek, and Trish were left to their own devices. Gegan, unconcerned, began flexing his fingers and testing the range of motion in his bandaged forearms. It was minimal.

"Did that...demon really hurt you so bad?" Derek asked.

Gegan stopped testing his arms and looked the younger man straight in the eye. "Why don't you ask what you really want to know?"

Derek flinched. Trish looked at him questioningly. "Why me?" he finally asked in a small voice.

"You are not alone," Gegan said first. "No one knows why some people can see demons while others can't. Many see them because a loved one falls under a demon's control and attempts violence. It's hard to accept that a caregiver would do such a thing, so a child's mind seeks another answer. They reach out, questing for the truth, and they find it."

"Is that what happened to you?" Derek asked hesitantly.

"In a way," Gegan said slowly as he flexed his fingers again. "My father was a violent man. He beat my mother. She stayed because she had nowhere to go, no friends, and no family to assist her. I discovered later that witches and monks made regular visits to our town, specifically to see my father. He didn't want to change, and the demons always came back."

Though Gegan's body remained relaxed and at ease, a note of deeply held anger entered his voice. "When I was ten, he disappeared for four days. When he returned, he was drunk and in such a rage as I have never seen again, and he went after my mother. I tried to intervene; he broke my arm." His fingers unconsciously traced a scar hidden beneath the bandages on one arm. "Seeing my bones jutting through my skin and my blood dripping to the floor was the last straw for my mother. Once my father passed out, and it was safe, we got away with nothing but the clothes in the dirty laundry basket.

"I don't know how she did it, but she got me to the clinic in town. Both of us were crying and bleeding when we staggered through the doors clutching each other. I will never forget the sight of all our clothes, everything we now owned, spilling onto the floor as mom dropped the basket to support me.

"The clinic's entire staff knew my mother on sight and immediately began helping us. When they learned she was taking me away from my father, they treated us without expecting payment. The head doctor paid my mother all the cash he and his staff could spare for her wedding ring, and that gave us enough money to leave. We spent two weeks wandering the roads before some monks found us. They took us with them and gave us sanctuary."

"Is that why you became a...what you are?" Trish asked not sure how to phrase her question.

"In part," Gegan answered, his voice completely calm again. "I don't want another child to witness that, nor another woman to be trapped. When the monks took us in, I saw my mother happy for the first time in my life. I was educated with other people my age, and she did chores for the monks and filled her spare time with flowers. She loves flowers," he added with a soft smile.

"When I came of age, I was given a choice to continue in my order or to leave with goodwill and pursue my own path. I chose to stay because I was happy, and most of my friends were staying. I was skilled at my work, and it gave my mother somewhere safe to be."

"Do you see her often?" Trish asked.

"No." Gegan seemed to shrink in on himself slightly as he continued. "The repeated head trauma she suffered has caused early-onset memory loss. The last time I visited, she thought I was my father. She cowered and screamed and cried. I can't see her in such distress, so I don't see her at all. Friends and caretakers tell me she spends her time in the flower gardens of her home and is content." Sensing their discomfort, Gegan changed the subject and addressed Derek. "It is odd, though, that this would materialize now. Did something happen when you first started seeing the demons?"

"I don't think so," Derek said after thinking hard. "It just kind of started one day."

"What do you want to do about it?" Gegan asked.

Derek gave him a wry smile. "I guess going back to the way things were is not an option?"

Gegan shook his head.

"Well," Derek said after a long moment of introspection, "I guess that means I need to learn more. If this is my life now, I'd like to live it as long as possible, and knowing what to do about these demons is the first step."

"That is very wise," Gegan replied. He turned to Trish. "And you? You have the answers you came here for. What will you do next?"

She was saved from answering by Rebecca, who meandered through the aisles to them, clutching two heavy bags of groceries. Derek jumped up to help her, and all four of them made their way upstairs.

"Why don't you talk about your personal history?" Trish asked Caroline and Micah, thinking of Gegan's story, as they stood eating sandwiches slathered with garlicky pesto in the living room. "It'd be nice to know where you came from."

"Especially if we'll be working together," Derek added. He hid a smirk knowing Trish was nervous. She always deflected conversation off herself when she was.

Micah and Caroline shared a brief glance before Caroline said, "That wouldn't make for a good dinner conversation."

"Come on," Rebecca said. "Caroline, you never talk about your childhood. It can't be worse than mine," she added with a forced smile.

Caroline cringed. "I still prefer not to."

Gegan kindly shifted the discussion away by telling an amusing story about a monk who had to be extricated from a pile of books in the middle of the library.

The conversation never drifted back around to the future for Trish and Derek. They left after praising the food and promising the think about what they wanted. Rebecca cornered Caroline before the door closed behind them. "Why don't you ever talk about your past?" she asked.

"Because I don't want to," Caroline said succinctly.

"Come on," Rebecca wheedled. "Afraid it won't measure up?"

Caroline's temper flared. Micah saw it in her eyes the second before she spoke and hurried Gegan and himself down the stairs into the store showroom. "You do not get to play the wilting flower," Caroline snapped, unaware of Micah's actions. "If you are going to join the witch's community, you need to realize that no one had it better than you, and most had it worse."

Rebecca flinched as if Caroline had taken a swing at her.

"I grew up knowing exactly what went bump in the night because I saw them," Caroline continued. "I don't remember a time when I didn't. I saw the demons lurking around our house, testing our defenses every night, and attacking us whenever we were alone. Mama taught us about plants and herbs before we could read, and Papa handstitched defensive charms into our clothes from infancy. Why do you think I've got such a high T.P.A.? My papa cast a charm on all his children to make us prodigies in defensive workings.

"I was twelve years old the first time I got these scars." She gestured to the middle finger on her right hand. "I see how energy weaves together when I make my charms. I know exactly why this flower will work better than that because I see how the energy twists and turns for both options. It's not worth it, though," she finished bitterly before abruptly turning away.

Rebecca glared at Caroline's back before storming out of the apartment. She snapped at Gegan when he wished her a pleasant afternoon and fumed all the way down the street.

As she crossed the main stone bridge toward her small home, she felt a chill breeze lift the hair from her neck. It seemed to cool her fury and she paused to enjoy the sensation. Resting against the railing, she let her gaze sift through all the colors and patterns of the canyon. The reds and golds shone in the sunlight, and motes of dust glittered as they swirled in the breeze.

A strange feeling came over her, and her mind drifted down to the canyon floor and the portal to hell. She'd dreamed about it again last night, and the images blended into her thoughts. She'd like to see it again, she decided and was back on solid ground before realizing she'd moved. Rebecca barely noticed the distance as she began descending into the canyon.

The path lay innocently before her feet, but a shadow darkened her vision. Rebecca closed her eyes and shook her head, trying to clear it away. When she looked again, the wolf was there. He was the same one from the hike up the canyon; she was sure of it. His yellow eyes looked at her with benevolent intelligence, and he spread his paws wide, blocking the path.

Rebecca took a step forward, and he bared his teeth. She felt no fear and knew his gesture to be a warning, not a threat. She stepped forward again. The wolf laid his ears flat to his skull and growled. The sound seemed to vibrate through Rebecca's mind without ever touching her ears.

He would not attack her if she forced past him, she realized, but she would never see him again. That fragile bond between them loomed large in her mind, and she could just sense what was on the line for her in this choice. She stepped back, and the wolf opened his mouth in a smile, his tongue lolling to one side.

The following day, Caroline was working with Micah to reorganize some of the staged furniture areas. Micah had commented politely that one area was unpleasant to look at due to the multiple shades of grey and green in the accents. In addition, another contained clashing purple and brown upholstered chairs. His hand had recovered from the demon's poison, thanks to two doses of warm purification potion, and he had no problem shifting the furniture.

While they discussed the benefits of setting the table for high tea versus for a formal dinner, Gegan entered the shop. His color looked better, and he seemed to be on the path to recovery after the fight. He brought with him a bulky package the postman had left at the door. Still bandaged and unable to grip things properly, he had it pinned between his forearms.

Caroline went into a transport of delight at seeing the box. She abandoned all work on the table setting, telling Micah to set it however he pleased, snagged the package, and all but flew up the stairs. Gegan looked somewhat questioningly after her, but Micah smiled and shook his head. "She'll be back in a couple hours."

Rebecca showed up shortly after lunch and began questioning both men about the portal to hell. "I dream about it," she explained. "I keep going back to it in my mind."

Micah scowled. "It's not good. Try not to focus on it so much."

"But why?" Rebecca shot back. "You guys are hoarding the information about it—I know you are."

"No," Micah said. "It's not that..." He trailed away and tried to think of a kind way to explain that portals to hell drew curious or weak-minded people. They caused obsession and eventually would lead the person to try and go through to hell. It was one of the unfair tricks of life when dealing with demons. Trying to explain that, however, would only encourage further obsessing over the portal.

He was saved having to answer by Caroline emerging from the staircase. "Hey all," she said, beaming.

Rebecca immediately looked suspicious, and Gegan raised his eyebrows in surprise at her joyous tone.

"What?" Caroline said, her smile faltering.

"Why are you so happy?" Rebecca asked.

"I got my letters from my brother today," Caroline said.

"How are they all?" Micah asked interestedly. He'd met her extended family several times over the years.

Gegan and Rebecca looked on with interest as Caroline began explaining. "Jay, my oldest brother, is thinking about retiring. He was in a bad way after a nest of rage demons got the jump on him. Luckily, his wife kept massive amounts of purification potions around and was able to save him. But his bad knee was really messed up, and he is struggling to come back from that. It's always worse when the weather turns cold."

"We all face that struggle as we get older," Micah said sagely. "How are his kids?"

"His oldest one is pregnant again. Looks like a girl this time. She and her husband are over the moon about it. They want to name her Pearl, after my father's mother. Additional good news, Jay's youngest just got married three months ago. I'll have to send something along for them. Mom said it was about time." Caroline laughed. "Oh, this might interest you," she pulled a piece of paper out and held it to Gegan. "Jay's wife included a new pattern she worked out for a protective scarf. Do you crochet?"

"I don't," Gegan said with a chuckle. "But many of my friends do. So I will gladly take a copy."

Caroline smiled at him before sobering and resuming her narrative. "Joseph, my next elder brother, isn't doing so well. He separated from his long-time partner and moved in with Mama. Apparently, his partner had been cheating on him for years.

He was suspicious because the lies started overlapping but didn't know for certain until one of his friends came forward. Joseph didn't go into much detail, but his ex-partner had propositioned his friend…multiple times." Everyone winced. "Joseph decided that moving in with Mama and helping her for a while was the healthiest thing to do.

"Speaking of," she continued, "Mama sends her regards. She has been struggling this year since her hands have been having trouble. They've been painful and swollen a lot. Joseph is helping her clean house and get ready to downsize."

"She's moving?" Micah said, shocked. "She always said she would die in that house and be buried next to your father in the graveyard."

"She's not going far," Caroline replied quickly. "She found a small cottage near the center of town." The side of her mouth quirked into a sad, little smile. "She would never leave Papa."

Micah sensed the drop in her mood and swiftly jumped in to redirect her thoughts. "How are your younger siblings? How is Carmen doing in her shop?"

"Oh, Carmen," Caroline said, perking back up. "Baby number three is on the way, due late next month if my math is correct, and they are keeping very hush-hush about the gender. It's driving Mama mad. Carmen spends most of her time just being a mother these days. She'll have three under five once the new little one arrives. Her husband handles everything in the shop. They make and sell equipment for our community," Caroline added to Rebecca and Gegan. Both murmured with interest.

"I need to write them," Micah said contemplatively. "I wonder if they could make me another portable apparatus to make purified water."

"What else do they keep in stock?" Gegan asked.

"Generic stuff on the shelves, mostly," Caroline answered. "Their true value is in custom jobs. Both Carmen and her husband are so creative. Tell them what you want, and they'll find a way. She's been that way ever since she was a little girl. Papa used to be so proud when the baby girl of the family came up with things he'd never thought of. And...she found a man who is just as passionate and creative, and it's been going great ever since.

"We can't forget David," Caroline said, preventing Gegan from asking another question but gesturing that she saw his intent. "He's married now."

"What?" Micah said. "I thought he was a confirmed life-long bachelor."

"Nope, he found a woman who turned his world upside down and knew she was a keeper. She's got one in the oven, due in the summer, and he took on an apprentice. Yeah," she continued as

Micah looked surprised. "Apparently, she convinced him to actually care about his T.P.A., so he took the paperwork seriously, now he has a sixteen, and a friend of a friend asked for help a few weeks later."

"Wow," Micah said. "Send them all my regards. Congratulations on the babies and everything else."

Caroline smiled at him. "I will."

"How come you never mentioned a family before now?" Rebecca said churlishly.

"Never came up," Caroline said and shrugged.

"I asked you about it directly yesterday!" Rebecca snapped. "You go on about how we can't complain when our lives are terrible, and you had a family waiting in the wings. You don't have to be alone like the rest of us—hypocrite!"

Caroline looked like she'd been slapped, but her composure snapped back into place with an almost audible *snick*. "I will not allow you to ruin this day for me," she spat and left the room gracefully.

"You are a fool," Gegan told Rebecca once Caroline had disappeared up the stairs. She turned to him, her face turning red, but he forestalled any refute. "You had the opportunity to share something positive with her. You had a chance to peer into the brighter side of her life." His voice became intense.

"You just witnessed proof that you need not be alone, yet you mocked it and threw it away."

Rebecca sputtered at him as he continued. "Your pride and arrogance and mockery will always drive people away. Keep up this attitude, and you will be alone in the end. I will say it again," he paused for emphasis and leaned forward, his bandages rustling. "Continue down this path, and no one will help you in your hour of need."

"Are we really going to do this again?" Micah asked in a resigned voice once Gegan turned on his heel and left.

"Do what?" Rebecca snapped.

"I'm going to explain why what you said was wildly inappropriate, and you are probably going to ignore me and carry on acting the bitch." Micah stared at her with a neutral expression until she huffed in anger and strode out of the shop.

Caroline returned downstairs once the door swung shut. "Thanks for that," she said.

Micah inclined his head. "Think we got through to her?"

"Only time will tell," Gegan replied, entering behind Caroline and unwinding one of his bandages. "To be honest, I'm surprised a demon hasn't found her."

"There is something about her that they don't like," Micah replied. "No idea what it might be, though."

Ten

Later that day, Micah dusted the shelves and debated going out for some spicy hot chocolate and extra raspberry truffles. Trish startled him as she burst into the shop, and the door complained loudly as it banged against the wall, rebounding into Derek's face. The young man prevented it from breaking his nose but stumbled on the entry and nearly fell flat. He flushed in embarrassment as Micah quirked an eyebrow at him but didn't say a word.

Trish, meanwhile, rounded the display furniture and flung herself into Micah's arms. He staggered at the force of the blow, realizing she was far sturdier than he'd thought, as she collapsed against him and burst into tears.

Knowing the futility of trying to talk to her, Micah settled them both onto a mildly uncomfortable antique couch and waited. He hummed quietly some old songs he didn't know the words to and let his arms rest gently around Trish's shaking shoulders. Derek stood awkwardly until Micah jerked his head at a chair nearby. He sank into it gratefully.

Gegan and Caroline joined them as Trish's sobs mellowed into hiccups. Finally, she coughed and sat up, releasing Micah. He politely moved to the other end of the couch but kept one hand resting on her arm for reassurance.

"What's this about?" Caroline asked with evident concern.

"Th-the demons," Trish said, her voice breaking. "They're following me. They k-keep waiting for the chance to attack me. I'm so scared, and I can't t-talk to Kane about it. He's been so angry with me." Her eyes welled up with tears again.

"We'll get you straightened out," Caroline said soothingly. "We won't abandon you."

Trish sagged in relief and wiped her eyes. "Y-you won't? Hic."

"We won't," Micah and Caroline confirmed.

"What will you do?" Trish asked.

"I'm not sure at this exact moment," Caroline admitted, pursing her lips. She looked at Micah, who was tapping his fingers on the arm of the couch. The tic told her he was deep in thought.

"You were suppressed by the large demon we battled," Gegan said. "You have not recovered, and the other demons sense the weakness."

"How do I recover?" Trish asked immediately, her eyes looking hopeful despite fresh tears.

"The quickest way is with a ritual," Gegan answered. "However, if you wish no such thing done upon you, time will heal you."

Caroline looked sideways at Gegan. "Really?" she asked. "What happens in this ritual? And why do you know about it when the Witch's Council does not."

"Within my order, many people have neither the skill nor the inclination to take up the direct fight against the demons," Gegan explained. "Their lives have been deeply affected, even nearly destroyed, by the demons, but they cannot fight back. So then, they devised this ritual. It helps those like themselves."

He drew an oval gingerly in the air with his bandaged hands. They were better today, and glimpses of his dark brown skin could be seen between the dressings. "Around each of us is an aura. Some call it the soul: others call it spirit. I've even heard it described as the possession of space outside the body. Demons burrow into this aura and suppress it. The larger the demon, the more the aura is suppressed."

"And that's what happened to me?" Trish asked.

"Yes," Gegan answered. "Your aura has been suppressed and weakened. However, there is a ritual to suffuse it with the aura of another and boost it until it can repair itself."

Silence greeted the statement. Micah and Caroline shared a confused look. Derek's expression said they'd lost him a while back, and Trish looked hopeful and scared. "I want to do it," she said with a bit of hesitation.

Gegan nodded. "I will need all of your help." Everyone agreed though Derek admitted he didn't know what he was doing.

"All I need," Gegan said to the young man, "is for you to stand still and hold a candle."

Derek brightened. "I can definitely do that."

"Whose aura will you use?" Caroline asked.

"There is only one person here who qualifies," Gegan answered, and his gaze swept to Micah.

Micah looked very uncomfortable with the attention as everyone stared at him. "Why me?" he asked.

Instead of answering, Gegan asked, "Have you noticed that demons don't try to whisper to you? They attack you outright or avoid you."

Micah nodded reluctantly. "It's always been that way, but most witches—"

Gegan cut him off by asking, "You've spent your adult life hunting them, killing them, and destroying the havoc they wreak, right?" Micah nodded again. "It's made you into an exorcist. I know we usually use the words exorcist and witch interchangeably," he added for Trish's and Derek's benefit, "but this is a case where they are not the same.

"Witch is the umbrella term and includes all exorcists, but few witches are exorcists. An exorcist has made himself a weapon against the demons." He turned back to Micah. "Your mind has hardened through long years of struggle and war. Your aura cannot be penetrated by lesser demons, and greater demons cannot get close enough to try unnoticed. Your senses are attuned to demons, and you are surrounded by protections large and small. The demons know who you are and are wary. That is why it must be you."

A dark flush rose up Micah's neck, and he looked supremely uncomfortable as everyone shifted uneasily. No one spoke, and the very air seemed to vibrate with the truth of Gegan's words. Caroline bent forward and placed a hand on Micah's shoulder. Some of the tension drained out of him, and he nodded.

Gegan rose at once. "Derek, Caroline, let us retire upstairs and commence preparations."

They left Micah and Trish alone on the antique couch. Trish sniffled and wiped the tears off her face and sniffled for a few minutes more before she asked, "Do you think this will work?"

"Of course," Micah replied.

"What's Gegan going to do?"

Micah shrugged. "No idea."

Trish stared at him. "Then how do you know it will work?"

"Because I trust Gegan," Micah replied. Seeing her anxiety, he looked for a change of topic. "How is your cousin?"

187

"Kane? I don't know. He's furious with me right now, but he's seemed so angry lately. Is it all due to that demon?"

"That's hard to say," Micah said honestly. "Anger and rage demons are some of the hardest to exorcise. I can tear them off and break them every time I see him, but it doesn't mean he'll recover."

"Why not?"

"Because a man is never truly angry unless he is, in some way, fundamentally right," Micah explained. "Kane's anger started out as something legitimate, but he has held on to it too long, and that is making him vulnerable. Yet, he'll have to heal from that initial event before he can start addressing the demons on his own."

Caroline came downstairs and motioned to them before Trish could say anything else.

Upstairs, the furniture had, once again, been pushed up against the walls. Caroline hadn't bothered to get any decorative items back out since the last time, so it was easy to clear a space. Derek sat on the loveseat; slowly, but calmly, braiding purple, dark grey, and white thread together. The long braid coiled at his feet while Gegan held the other end. The monk gestured for Trish to stand in the middle of the room. And he positioned Micah a foot behind her and slightly to her left. Once they were in place, he lifted Micah's right hand and placed it on Trish's left shoulder. Strangely enough, Micah looked the most anxious as the ritual began.

Gegan lit three candles with fumbling jerks, gave one to Derek as he finished the braid, one to

Caroline, and the two of them took up positions on either side of Trish and Micah. Gegan took up the third candle and the braid and began chanting. He carefully laid the braided thread in an oval around the five of them and seated himself in front of Trish.

The ritual took barely five minutes to complete. As Gegan's voice trailed off and he blew out his candle, Trish felt something. It was as if a powerful presence leaned against her back. A set of invisible arms reached around her shoulders and crossed at the wrist in front of her stomach. She felt their weight upon her body. The strong presence protected her, and she felt as though nothing could get to her. Tension and fear drained out of her body. She couldn't help it and let out a deep sigh.

At the same instant, Micah staggered. His face went pale, and his hands started to shake. He felt fatigued and weak. Caroline and Derek caught him under the arms as if they expected this to happen and half-carried him to the loveseat. Gegan rose and came over to him. "It'll pass," he murmured. "It'll pass."

Micah nodded, then put his head back and sagged into the too-small couch. Caroline and Derek turned him sideways and laid him down. His legs stuck awkwardly off the edge of the loveseat, but he didn't care.

Gegan turned to Trish. "How do you feel?" he asked.

"I'm…good?" She wasn't sure how she felt, really. "I'm less tense, and I don't feel afraid anymore, but I," she rubbed her shoulders and looked around, "I don't feel alone. I feel like someone is standing right behind me."

"That's what it should feel like," Gegan explained. "The demons will sense that too, and they'll leave you alone."

Trish nodded and looked at Micah. She opened her mouth to speak, but Caroline laid a hand on her arm and shook her head.

Micah wasn't sure how long he lay there, but he heard Caroline's ringing voice shout something about a funeral, and he thought Rebecca might've said something in reply. Images of the last funeral he'd attended rose from his memory. Caroline's voice sounded faint and far away as he remembered.

The service had been for Caroline's father. The old man had been retired from active exorcism work for over a decade. He'd raised his five children and doted upon his numerous grandchildren. But that was all that was said about him before the entire funeral came under siege.

The funeral was the only time in nearly fifteen years that Caroline's entire family had been together. They'd wanted to mourn and comfort each other, but the demons found them. Chaos reigned for about forty-five seconds until Micah and the other witches, brought in for security, regained control. In that time, Caroline's mother had been thrown to the ground with a concussion, one of her brothers had gashes running the length of his forearm, a niece nearly lost an eye, and her very pregnant sister-in-law started having labor pains.

"Why does everything happen at the same damned time? Every freaking time!" Caroline ranted as she stormed across the living room. She didn't notice Micah twitch in surprise and blink open his eyes as she marched out and down the stairs.

Shaking his head, Micah sat up and took stock of himself. Apart from the usual cold and stiffness in his fingers, he felt fine. But he did notice a twinge in his knee from the couch.

"Oh, shut up!" Caroline yelled at someone downstairs. "This has nothing to do with you."

Wisely, Micah decided to not get involved with that situation. However, noninvolvement and not knowing what was happening were two very different things. He padded over to the top of the stairs and sat in the doorway. He listened while stretching one leg out in front of him and rubbing his knee. From here, he could just make out the voices from down in the shop.

"You look very impressive," Rebecca said sarcastically.

"Let's see you try it," Caroline snarled back. "These are always temperamental."

"Worry not," Gegan said calmly. "My connection to my order is stable, and we are in no rush."

"There it goes," Caroline said before adding, "Madam, I apologize for the delay."

An unknown female voice answered back, "It's all right. I know that connecting us through a different long-range communication method is tough. Most would take over an hour to manage anything."

"Thank you," Caroline said smugly, and Micah could just picture her throwing a look at Rebecca. "What is the purpose of this meeting?"

"The portal," the voice answered back. "The information you sent us required much debate, but we have come to a conclusion, and please, call me Clarice."

Now Micah realized what was going on. Clarice, a representative of the Witches Council, was communicating long distance. Further, Gegan was in touch with his order, and Caroline had rigged up something to allow them to all talk to each other.

Meanwhile, Clarice paused. "Who are all these people? This conversation is sensitive."

"We'll just go then…," Trish said cautiously. She sounded extremely nervous.

There was another pause before Clarice asked, "And you?"

"I'm staying," Rebecca said obstinately. "It's the only way to learn something meaningful."

"Piss off," Caroline spat. "And get out."

"I will not!" Rebecca snapped back as Micah wondered what had set them off today. "You're supposed to teach me, and you are failing."

"This woman is learning under you?" Clarice asked.

"She was," Caroline said with venom. "Now, she is an unwelcome intrusion."

"Get off your high horse," Rebecca retorted.

"Ladies," Clarice started, but they ignored her.

"Enough!" Gegan said. His voice rang through the downstairs, and silence fell. "We are not here to listen to bickering witches. Set your squabble aside and pay attention."

"Thank you, good monk," Clarice said. "Now, Caroline, there is something you must do for us. Eighty years ago, records show that the machinery in hell froze over. A monk from Gegan's order, incidentally also a Gegan, went through to hell to stop the ice. We believe he succeeded, although he did not make it back. We need his echo."

Silence reigned for only a second before Caroline answered. "For Micah, anything, but I don't know how."

"When the demon Mistress interrupted our conversation last week, we sent word to all the seers. They meditated together, and one thing became crystal clear. You are to be the caster and Micah the anchor." Clarice explained. On the staircase, Micah got to his feet. "We have gathered all the documents, and they are on their way to you," she continued as Micah entered the room. She nodded to him but did not pause her explanation. "Gegan's order should also be preparing their contribution." She raised an eyebrow questioningly.

"We are," Gegan answered her. "The items are in good condition, and I will leave tomorrow to collect them."

Clarice nodded. "You should be receiving everything from our end late today or early tomorrow, depending on the couriers. I trust this will receive your utmost attention?"

Caroline nodded, and Clarice added. "As a token of our appreciation for your efforts and should you succeed, your T. P. A. will be raised to twenty-one." Her image flickered out.

Trish and Derek stepped back inside as Rebecca asked, "An echo?"

"I don't know how it all works," Caroline hedged but held up her hands as Rebecca opened her mouth to argue. "Stop, just stop arguing for two minutes and let me collect my thoughts." Rebecca glared but stayed silent.

"Okay," Caroline sighed a minute later. "Clarice was talking about bringing back an echo of the soul of the Gegan who went to hell eighty years ago. To my knowledge, it's been done successfully only three times in the last century."

"How many times has it been attempted?" Micah asked.

Caroline shrugged. "When I know, I'll make sure to tell you."

"What does the T. P. A. matter?" Rebecca asked next.

"Anyone above twenty receives a monthly installment from the Witch's Council," Caroline answered. "They expect you to spend your time in research and training and so pay for your living expenses."

"That's nice," Rebecca grumbled, but she caught sight of the look on Gegan's face and flinched.

Caroline ignored the grumbling tone. "You're right. It means, should I continue to educate you, that I can give you more time and attention."

"You make it sound like you won't," Rebecca said defensively.

"I'm currently on the fence," Caroline admitted. "Give me a reason why I should… You know what?" she continued, cutting across Rebecca, "don't tell me now. Go home, think hard on what you want to say, and come back tomorrow."

As Rebecca stomped across the shop and slammed the door behind her, Caroline sank down onto one of her display chairs and rubbed her hands across her face. Micah stepped up behind her and started rubbing her shoulders.

"Why do you hate her so much?" Trish asked.

Caroline looked up, startled. "I don't hate her."

"You've fooled us," Derek said.

Caroline gave Micah a look of thanks and returned to her feet. She began pacing around the display of dining room chairs as she spoke. "She won't learn. Her education has been extremely specialized. There are one or two fields where she is very advanced, but the rest is like teaching a child. "She's exceptional at scrying," Caroline said. Everyone looked at her with skeptical looks. "She is," Caroline defended. "And I can admit it when I see the skill and be envious if it is a skill I do not possess."

"You're not good at scrying then?" Trish asked, fumbling over the words.

"I am horrible at it. Once, and only once, have I done something complicated with scrying. It was an emergency situation, and it worked." She chuckled. "I've often thought I used my entire lifetime's worth of skill on that one time. She is better at scrying than I'll ever be. Yes," she repeated as everyone continued to look surprised, "I can admit that, but she knows no color theory, no botany. She can't embroider or knit or crochet. She doesn't understand why I do what I do, and she refuses to learn. All she wants to do is attack, attack, attack."

"Why is that a bad thing?" Trish asked.

Caroline cocked her head as if something had just fallen into place in her mind. "That's it." She beamed at Trish. "You asked just the right question. That is my issue with her: she's selfish. In our community, we attack the demons to protect ourselves, and we defend against them to protect

196

others. I care more about keeping those around me safe, and she does not."

Casting around for a change of subject to break the silence after that pronouncement, Micah addressed Trish and Derek. "Why'd you both come back in?"

"Oh," Trish colored slightly as she stuttered. "I wanted to thank you." She fidgeted with her blonde hair. "For helping with what Gegan did earlier, and um, is there anything I can do for you?"

Micah smiled warmly at her. "You don't need to do anything."

Further conversation was halted by the sound of the door opening. Two men walked into the shop and made a beeline for Caroline. The first had a satchel slung across his chest, and a long tube wrapped in cloth hung down his back. The second had a large woven basket tied to his shoulders.

"Miss Caroline?" the first man asked. At Caroline's nod, he began rummaging around in his satchel. "The Council sent us. Please read and sign." He handed her a piece of paper and began helping his companion with the basket. The second man heaved a sigh of relief as the basket came free and stretched. Several popping noises accompanied the movement.

Setting the basket down with a heavy *thunk*, the first courier unhooked the tube from its straps and pulled away the cloth covering. "Will you confirm that documents arrived unopened?" he asked Caroline.

She approached him and took the tube. There were no signs of damage to the smooth wood, and the top was still sealed with wax and bore the Council's insignia. "I will."

"There is one more coming," the first courier said as he accepted back the signed paper from Caroline. "We were separated at a ferry crossing several days ago. He should be here soon."

Caroline nodded. "Do you need anything before you go?"

"No, thank you." Both couriers nodded to her and walked out.

"Well, I guess it's really happening now," Caroline said and broke the wax seal on the tube. She turned the tube sideways and gently shook it until a roll of papers slid out. She looked Micah in the eye and took a deep breath. "Here we go."

She quickly read through the first two pages and pronounced them a summary but refused to let Micah look at them when he asked.

The next four pages were the list of items and ingredients needed to call the echo. "This will take days," Caroline groaned. "And that's not even counting the time it'll take to infuse them all."

"All what?" Trish asked.

"All the plants," Caroline replied as she separated one of the pages and held it out. She went back to rummaging in the large box while everyone else read through the pages. No one noticed the glint of silver as she transferred something from the box to a pocket.

"Sage, Damiana, Lavender, Thyme, Orange peel, Cedarwood, and Black Pine," Trish read aloud. "All infused in highly concentrated juniper oil." She paused and looked up. "Do you have all this stuff at the ready?"

"Most everything but the juniper oil," Caroline sighed. "I keep some juniper at hand, but the volume needed is ridiculous."

"I know where the juniper groves in the area are," Trish offered.

"Really?" Caroline exclaimed. "Tell us!"

"How?" Micah asked.

"I'm a wilderness guide," Trish said, smiling brightly. "I lead backpacking and hiking trips around the desert. I'll take you."

Micah and Caroline both flinched at the offer. "I'm not sure that is a good idea," Caroline said gently.

"I want to help," Trish said firmly. "You guys saved my life from that demon, and you helped out Kane even though he was a jerk."

"Trish," Caroline said delicately, "doing this might make you a target."

Trish tensed but forced herself to relax, then exhaled. "Then teach me how to do something about that."

Caroline put down all the papers and turned to face Trish. The blonde woman's face was flushed with anxiety but still determined. "If you want to join our community," Caroline said slowly, "we would welcome you with open arms, but I'm not sure you understand the risks involved."

"Being tormented by that demon wasn't enough?" Trish countered.

"That's not it at all," Caroline said quickly. She sighed and tapped her fingers on her thighs, clearly searching for the words. Her gaze shifted to Micah who was rubbing one hand across his neck. The motion opened the collar of his buttoned-up shirt, and a scar peeked through the gap. An idea formed instantly in her mind, and she said, "Micah strip."

He jerked. "What?"

"Strip out of your shirt. I need to make a point."

"No."

"Micah," she ordered, green eyes blazing and hands curling into fists, "just do it."

He held her gaze for a solid five seconds before complying. His fingers shook slightly with anger as he jerked off his cufflinks. Reaching into his front waistcoat pocket, Micah withdrew the steel demonic compass. He placed it precisely on the table in front of him with a small *clink*. The chain rattled as he released his grip. His knuckles were white as he tossed his waistcoat on the table, untucked his shirt front, and undid all the buttons. Jaw clenched, he shrugged out of it and faced everyone with shoulders back, head held high, and hands rigid at his sides.

The scars were the first thing Trish noticed. They stuck out white and silvery against his pale skin except for some recently healed claw marks that still showed pink across one side of his chest. Caroline lightly ran one finger over his collarbone, tracing the scar that inspired this idea. He flinched away from her touch.

"Broken collarbone," Caroline told everyone. "From catching a young woman whose abusive partner threw her out a window." She pointed to a round shiny scar on his lower left abdomen. "From a man infested with rage demons. He shoved a lit torch into Micah while he was ripping the demons off." There were others, but she didn't dwell on the details. "Infected bite marks, puncture wounds, teeth, knives, and…turn around."

Micah spun without a sound with his shoulders hunched and head bowed. "Claws," Caroline finished. The claw wounds had been vicious. Three separate scars ran up his back. Two claws had arched sideways across his rib cage, while the third had gotten caught by his vertebrae and ran straight up the other side of his spine. Caroline made to lay a hand on his shoulder, but Micah shrugged her off.

"Made your point yet?" he snarled.

Trish flinched as she realized it was more than the scars that made him uncomfortable. The bumps of Micah's spine stuck out a little too much. The indentations between his ribs rippled as he turned back to face them, and she noticed his collarbones were too defined and his waist too thin. The muscles in his forearms stood out like cords as he pulled his shirt over his arms. He flipped up the back of the shirt and tucked it in before doing up any of the buttons. Trish noticed the daggers then. Both were sheathed and looped into his belt. One ran crossways across his low back while the other nestled by the bump of his left hip bone.

He didn't bother to finish tucking in his shirt or grabbing his waistcoat. Gripping the compass in one white-knuckled fist, he left the shop.

Eleven

"Hey, are you okay?"

Micah flinched and looked around. The sun had set without him realizing, and twilight shadows were lengthening. Nathanial was looking at him.

"Wh-what did you say?" Micah asked as he shook his head to clear it. He'd been wandering around in a haze since storming out on Caroline.

"Are you okay?" Nathaniel repeated.

For a second, Micah considered saying he was. He wanted to believe he was, but he had never been one for self-delusion. "No," he admitted instead. "Is your shop still open?"

"Technically, no," the young man answered. "But Mom will make an exception for you."

Elaine had just finished cleaning up when Nathaniel ushered Micah into the shop. "Welcome," she said sincerely. "What can I get you?"

"A quiet place to sit, again?" Micah asked half apologetically. He rubbed his left hand across his right forearm and noticed he'd forgotten his cufflinks. It had been a long time since he'd been without those cufflinks, and a bad feeling settled across his shoulders.

"Of course," Elaine answered, breaking into his thoughts.

The three of them sat at the long worktable in the back room of the shop. Nathaniel made sandwiches with turkey, homemade spicy spread, and pickled carrots. They didn't talk much while they ate. Nathaniel wolfed down three sandwiches as only a teenage boy can, while Elaine munched steadily and watched Micah pick at his food.

"Do you want to talk about it?" she finally asked.

Micah met her gaze for a moment before settling back into his chair. The movement caused the compass in his pocket to dig into his leg, so he took it out and set it on the table with a muted *click*. "Thank you for your hospitality," he said first. "I didn't feel like going back yet."

"Was it something to do with your friend that likes raspberry truffles?" Elaine asked.

Micah shrugged and played with the compass chain. "Among others," he answered after a moment.

"Stay here tonight then," Elaine said.

Micah raised his eyebrows and gave her a questioning look.

Her cheeks turned a delicate pink, and she cleared her throat. "The guest room is made up. Nathaniel, go work on your recipes in your room."

He started to whine, but Elaine shut it down with a glare and a finger jab to the stairs. Once his door closed, harder than was strictly necessary, she asked, "Tea?"

"I'm surprised you don't drink hot chocolate for your nightcap," Micah replied.

She laughed. "I spend so much time around sweet things and sugar that I crave savory and spicy by the end of the day."

"Tea sounds nice."

A sense of weight on his chest woke Micah from a deep sleep. In the dark, his first instinct was to raise his arms and protect his face. A blunt snout hit his forearms as heavy, thick coils fell across his body and started wrapping around his limbs, their weight making it hard to draw a breath.

The demon's eyes glowed faintly orange as its coils forced his arms apart, and it slithered closer to his face. Micah thrashed around and managed to free his arms from the sinuous ropes before the demon could pin them. Valiantly he grappled with the snakelike head, trying to prevent it from sinking two-inch fangs into him.

The forked, reptilian tongue flicked over his cheek as he lay pinned to the bed, barely breathing and running on pure adrenaline. He managed to get one hand over the demon's mouth and held tight with his fingers digging into the hard scaly flesh.

With its poisonous fangs now contained, Micah began pounding on the demon's body with his other fist. The sounds of the impacts were flat and monotone against the hard scales and muscles.

The demon's movement defied logic, and it looped another coil of flesh around his forearm. Rotating his shoulder, Micah delivered a punishing elbow blow to its body. The demon flexed, and Micah felt the delicate bones in his wrist grinding under the pressure. The pain swamped him, and he was temporarily robbed of the ability to fight back. The demon's head shifted under his slackening grip and nearly came free, jaws snapping near his face.

Gritting his teeth and fighting past the white spots in his vision, Micah twisted violently. He managed to get one leg bent beneath him and the fingers on the hand holding the demon's head found one of its eyes as it turned to bite him. He gripped harder with that hand and felt the jelly-like substance of the demon's eye oozing out between his fingers.

The demon spasmed in silent agony and rage but still held on. Using the distraction, his free leg, and all the strength in his core, Micah thrust himself up onto his side. The white spots vanished as he sucked in a deep breath of air, the suffocating weight of the demon now off him. He spun onto his hands and knees.

He managed to keep control of the demon's head—barely—and pushed it hard into the bed as the demon mastered itself again. Twisting himself around with the bedcovers catching on his feet, Micah brought his arms together and switched control of the demon's head to the arm still bound up in scaly coils. He pinned its head down with his forearm and leaned as much weight as possible onto it.

With his free hand, he began pummeling the demon. He rained punches down on the rough scales until he felt a small crack within the demon's body reverberate through his fist. He hit the same spot again and was rewarded with a bigger *crick-crack*. The demon's tail went limp around his ankle.

Breath coming in ragged gasps, Micah delivered blow after blow to the single weak spot in the demon's flesh until he felt it relax its grip completely. He freed himself from the heavy coils and used his feet and legs to push the demon off the bed. It flopped to the floor and began to stir weakly. Micah jumped off the bed and slammed his heel onto the demon's damaged head, once, twice. At the third strike, its skull shattered, and the demon turned to dust.

The light outside his door clicked on, and Elaine burst into the room. Micah stood there, hair and clothes in disarray, eyes wild, covered in sweat and panting. Elaine simply stared.

"I should go," Micah said and grabbed his compass off the bedside table. He bitterly regretted not having his cufflinks to shield his aura and felt sure that was why the demon came for him.

"Let me patch up your hands first," Elaine managed, catching him by the shoulder. Then, though clearly shaken, she pushed up the sleeves of her nightdress and led him down to the kitchen.

"I'm sorry," Micah said as she tended to him. The knuckles on his one hand were torn and starting to ooze blood from contact with the demon's rough scales, while the bruises on his other arm were already darkening to purple. Luckily, the demon never managed to sink in its fangs, and the injuries would not get infected. "At least it only came after *me*," he added under his breath.

"What was it?" Elaine asked as she gently dabbed off the blood.

"A demon."

She flinched. "Like what forced my husband to attack us?"

"A different kind, but yes."

"What kind was this one?" she asked as she wrapped his hand in a clean bandage.

"Despair." Micah forced his mouth into a sad smile that was half grimace. "It's the only one that can still sneak up on me."

Elaine finished doctoring him up but left her hands in his. "What comes next?" she asked.

"Next, we set something up to keep you and Nathaniel safe. Do you have any flowers or fresh herbs around?"

"Not really."

"Let me see your sewing kit then."

Elaine rummaged around in one of the drawers before handing Micah a small box filled with thread and needles. After selecting the spool with thread halfway between grey and blue, Micah pushed the box back at her and painfully rolled up his sleeves. "Choose your favorite color," he said. She selected a pale yellow and withdrew it from the box. "And what color for Nathaniel?"

"I guess, this one." She pointed to a vivid scarlet.

"Okay," taking the scarlet, the pale yellow and a dark, rich brown from the box, Micah measured out a few feet and cut the threads. "Do you have any silver jewelry you can part with for a while?" he asked as he measured out more.

"I'll go check."

She was back in a minute with a pair of small hoop earrings and a chain bracelet. "Will these work?"

"Does Nathaniel have pierced ears?"

"Yes, but he rarely wears earrings."

"They'll be fine." As he spoke, Micah skillfully tied six strands of thread: three blue-grey, one brown, one scarlet, and one yellow, together into a slip knot. He fed the short tail back through the loop and pulled it tight. "You'll need to do the next part."

"What exactly am I doing?"

Micah knotted another set of threads together and said, "Watch." Gingerly with his bandaged hand, he braided the brown, yellow and scarlet threads together. "Three turns only." Then he drew the grey threads together, looped them around the bottom of the braid, and tied a double knot. "Three turns, two knots again. Got it?"

Elaine nodded and began working. Micah started five more identical charms and laid them at her elbow. "What are these for?" she asked as she started on the third one.

"Front door, back door, and four corners of the building," Micah said distractedly while examining the bracelet.

"But what do they do?"

"They will keep the demons out until I can get my friend, who is much better at this than me, to set this right for you." He set down the bracelet and checked the earrings. "These are high quality."

"My husband gave them to me."

Silence fell while she plaited together the fourth and fifth little charms. Micah took the first three and headed into the front room. She was just finishing up the last when he returned. He took them, coiled two in the corners of the big kitchen, and tied the last around the doorknob.

He nodded appreciatively at her work, then returned to the table and sat down. "This is the hard part. Give me your foot."

Elaine cocked her head. "Why?"

"Because we need something to keep you personally safe whether you are inside or outside this building. I don't think they will come for you, and I'll be setting the situation to rights as soon as possible, but I'm not risking your safety after you gave me sanctuary."

She paused only long enough to tuck her nightdress around her legs and lifted her right foot. Micah placed it gently on his knee and looped the bracelet around her ankle. It didn't fit, but he seemed to expect that and measured off another length of blue-grey thread. "Something is going to attack me?" she asked in a small voice.

Micah clicked open his compass and set it on the table. The red arrow spun in a lazy circle while the silver one pointed directly toward Caroline's shop, but as soon as he withdrew his hand, the silver arrow spun back to point at him. "As long as the red arrow spins, you'll be fine."

"Why that color thread?" she asked next. The silence was too awkward for her. "You don't mind the questions?"

"Not at all and it's my favorite color," he answered as he attempted to thread a petite sewing needle. "I've used this color to represent myself in my charms for years."

"Oh," for some unknown reason, she blushed. "And this will protect me how?"

He absently tapped the fingers of his bruised hand on her calf while he thought of how to answer. "It's a promise," he said as he set the bracelet around her ankle and began working with the needle and thread. "By putting this on you, I'm announcing that you are mine, and retribution for any threat will be swift and violent."

Her blush deepened, and she coughed delicately. "Usually, men do that with a ring."

He chuckled. "This is temporary."

"Do you make these kinds of promises often?" she asked a minute later, unable to keep quiet as he carefully turned the bracelet.

"No." He looked up, fingers stilling around her ankle. "I'm not usually around people long enough to need to."

"But you were here just the one night."

"I know." He finished his work and gently lifted her foot off his knee. "I think that's part of the problem," he added pensively. "Everything has been happening so fast since I came to Canyon Town, but I'm still stuck here."

"What's happened?"

He glanced at her before turning his gaze to the earrings on the scarred worktable. "Demon fights, debts. Everything just keeps spiraling and becoming bigger and bigger. More and more people are getting involved." He selected one of the earrings and began working.

She watched him begin the delicate work. He fumbled the earring twice before asking her to hold it for him. "Doesn't it hurt?" she asked, nodding at the bruises.

"Yes, it does." He neatly tied off one knot and began again.

"Thank you for doing this for us."

"Anytime."

They were sitting and drinking coffee fifteen minutes later and discussing the merits of salt in chocolate and caramel when Rebecca and Caroline burst into the room. Elaine looked embarrassed to be found sitting in her nightdress with a man before the sun had risen, but Micah looked supremely unconcerned. He saluted them with his

212

coffee mug and stretched his feet onto one of the unoccupied chairs.

"You don't waste time, do you?" Caroline said, hands on hips.

Elaine blushed bright pink and coughed into her coffee cup.

"I'm surprised you weren't here sooner," Micah said back, taking another sip. With his rolled down sleeves, buttoned cuffs, and bandaged hand below the counter, the injuries from the fight were hard to distinguish. "Taking a breather from monitoring my movements?"

Both witches looked very uncomfortable for a moment. "How did you know?" Rebecca asked, fiddling with her bracelet.

He raised his eyebrow at her over his coffee cup. "Don't insult me."

"Then what happened?" she asked. "Half an hour ago, your signature exploded, and it cracked my mirror."

"Not important," he said with the hint of a smile. "You two find out where Trish lives? I need to speak to her." Nonplussed, they gave him directions. "Next order of business," he continued, "Caroline, I need you to purify the space. Cleanse it, so it is like I was never here."

"That will take all day."

"It will," he agreed.

"Why did you feel the need to claim this space?" Caroline asked him. "You never do that."

He cut his eyes to Elaine before answering. "My presence brought a demon here last night. I am not about to leave her with the cleanup."

"But you'll leave me with it?" Caroline challenged.

"Naturally." He set down his coffee cup to gesture at her. "You're better at this than I am."

"Your hand!" Caroline paled as she noticed the dark bruising. "Let me see it."

"Start purifying the space first," he countered.

She ground her teeth before snapping, "Fine. Come on, Rebecca."

"What? Why?" Rebecca asked.

"There is too much stuff to carry on my own," Caroline told her. "With you, we can make it one trip."

"Get Micah to help you," Rebecca said back. "I actually work here, and we might as well get started. We're all awake anyway."

"Can't," Caroline said sourly. She glared at Micah, but he just saluted her again with his coffee cup. "He has to stay here. He claimed this space, and it is his responsibility. The demons won't hesitate for long."

They trooped back out with Rebecca complaining that it was too cold to be traipsing back and forth across the bridges at this hour.

"Do you think the demons will come back again?" Elaine asked. Her hands trembled slightly as she set down her coffee cup with a *ch-chink*.

"Without Caroline, yes, they would," Micah told her. "The warnings I put up will give them pause because they know I am waiting and watching, but they are not a long-term solution. Demons attack me every chance they get. That's why it is so important to get my aura out of here."

"They know you that well?"

He attempted a casual shrug. "My presence invites challenge."

It wasn't long before Caroline and Rebecca returned. Both women were out of breath from hurrying, pink-faced from the cold, and laden down with small boxes.

"Elaine," Micah said, giving the woman a kind smile and completely ignoring the two witches, "thank you for the hospitality."

"Of course," Elaine replied.

He slid his feet into his boots without another word and left the shop.

He wasn't in any hurry to see Trish, and the town was peaceful in the pale green light that precedes the dawn. So, his first stop was Caroline's place. Bogging her down at Elaine's shop had some added benefits, it turned out.

The shop was dark, but he could see a light on upstairs, and when he entered, he heard Gegan's deep voice chanting from upstairs. The words were muffled, but the sound was somehow soothing.

Caroline had left the instructions and paraphernalia from the Council on the table near the door to the stairs. Micah lit a small lamp, noticed her satchel sitting there ready for an emergency, and began rifling through the papers. He didn't want to talk to Gegan and explain himself, and he especially didn't want to be caught lounging around in case Caroline forgot something and came back. He extracted the pages describing how to process the juniper oil from the pile and left the rest of the pages in disarray. Caroline would notice, right everything, and realize what he'd done.

Next, he checked the heavy box from the courier. It contained a dozen small jars, boxes, a portable water purifier, charcoal, a seamstress' kit, and a money pouch. He weighed the last before tucking it into a pocket, standing and hefting the strap of the box onto one shoulder as he looked around.

His waistcoat and cufflinks were lying where he had thrown them yesterday. He quickly put on the cufflinks and added a drop of purified water from his pocket flask for good measure. He didn't want to leave any extra difficulties for Caroline. He grabbed his waistcoat and stuffed it into the top of the box. He didn't own much else and figured Trish would have anything they needed for the actual hiking part of the task.

The sun was fully risen by the time he found her place. It was a decent-sized, one-story home with a well-tended front garden and a green, painted front door. He rapped firmly on the door, grimacing slightly at the discomfort of the contact on his bandaged hand, and waited a full minute before it opened.

Trish wore long pajama pants and an oversized shirt. Her hair was mussed and stuck out at odd angles from her pale face. She winced as Micah moved to extend his hand, and the sunlight caught her full in the face.

"It's cold," she told him, ignoring his hand, "and bright. Come inside." He followed her and was quickly directed to a chair at the kitchen table while she started coffee brewing.

"You still interested in helping me?" Micah asked.

"Yes," she yawned and stretched. "When? How?"

In answer, he held out the papers from the Council. "How long will it take to find enough juniper for this?"

"Coffee first," she said. "No reading without coffee."

Micah laughed as she poured hot coffee into a massive clay cup and took a sip. "Okay," she said. "Let me see them."

After perusing the papers and drinking half of the cup of coffee, Trish decreed it would take a week or ten days to collect everything.

"When can we leave?" Micah asked.

She raised an eyebrow and asked, "Don't you need to say goodbye to people? Tell them where you're going and all that."

"No. Do you?"

"I guess not. Thirty minutes then." She yawned again, got up, and started out of the kitchen while waving vaguely at him. "Sit. Eat. Whatever."

Micah merely settled deeper into the chair and closed his eyes.

Trish woke him half an hour later by plopping into the chair across from him with her coffee cup refilled. She'd changed into snug dark pants that looked comfortable and a purple long-sleeve shirt. Her hair was tied back in a tail, but one tendril escaped and framed the side of her face. "How much outdoor experience do you have?" she asked businesslike.

"A fair amount," Micah answered, sitting up and blinking.

"Where is your gear?"

He grimaced. "What you see is what you get."

She stared at him. "The clothes on your back and a box. This is all you're bringing?"

He shrugged. "At the current time, this constitutes nearly all my worldly possessions."

"What's missing then?" she asked.

"My small crossbow. I didn't bother with it because I have no bolts."

"Okay then," she said slowly while rubbing one hand across her eyes. "What's in the box?"

"Materials for processing and storing the plants we're hunting for."

"So, nothing useful for survival?"

"Nope."

"Right. I guess we need to go shopping before we leave then."

He shook his head. "Don't you have extras? I doubt the weather will change that much in a week."

"If you're sure, then we'll have to make do," she said. "You're itching to leave, aren't you?" She fell silent and stared into space with her eyes darting around as she made mental checklists.

"Food is the most pressing." She began tapping her nails on her cheek as she spoke. "I guess we'll bring some of Grandma's cookies. That'll take care of a lot of meals."

"Cookies?" Micah raised a skeptical eyebrow.

"Don't hate on Grandma's cookies," Trish said matter-of-factly as she walked to the icebox. "They've got oats, honey, carrots, dried fruits, nuts, mashed pumpkin, spices, and chocolate chips. They are a meal unto themselves."

"I stand corrected," Micah admitted.

"That's what I thought." Trish grinned. "No one hates on Grandma's cookies." She pulled out two bulging bags of large cookies and placed them on the table. "Next, of course …" she added a small pot, utensils, two bowls, two water flasks, and a bag of coffee.

She began flitting around, adding things to the pile, taking others away, and working through a mental process. Micah watched quietly until he noticed a little anxiety demon poke its head around the corner from the bedroom. It observed a moment before entering the kitchen. It looked agitated as it hopped back and forth, mirroring

Trish's steps around the kitchen. But, surprisingly, it didn't approach. Micah supposed whatever Gegan had done to strengthen Trish's aura was still active.

After an hour, Trish announced they were packed and ready. Her well-worn backpack was stuffed to the brim with sleeping bags, tarps, cooking and eating paraphernalia, other miscellany, and the cookies. Micah had a few extra pouches hanging from the outside of his large basket and a sleeping bag stuck on top.

"Your house is very nice," Micah said as they headed toward the edge of Canyon Town.

Trish adjusted one of the straps on her backpack. "Thanks. It belongs to Kane's girlfriend. She and her best friend needed a low-maintenance roommate. I'm gone half the time anyway, so they gave me the smallest bedroom and a deal on the rent." She turned into one of the last buildings and said, "Quick stop for final supplies. This baker is a good friend, and he'll give us a discount."

She greeted the baker, a red-faced, jolly-looking man in his thirties, and introduced him as Phillip.

"Are you going out far this trip?" Phillip asked as he sorted through some loaves of bread.

"A week or two," Trish said.

Phillip turned a suspicious look on Micah. "I'm surprised your cousin isn't going with you. It's rare for you to take a man out into the desert alone." He stared hard as if trying to memorize Micah's features.

"It wasn't supposed to be just me," Micah lied easily. "My life partner took ill last week, and we didn't want to cancel last minute."

"I'm sorry to hear that," Phillip said, mollified. "Will she be all right?"

"Yes, he will be," Micah said, emphasizing the pronoun.

Phillip coughed and said, "Of course, I hope you have a pleasant trip. Will you be needing anything else?"

"I'm sure this will be fine. Thank you," Micah replied and pulled out the money bag.

"Thank you for buying," Trish said as they left the shop. "And you are sure you don't want to purchase anything else?"

"It's not worth it right now," Micah said evasively. "But speaking of money, how much will I owe you for the trip?"

"You don't have to pay me," Trish said quickly and began walking.

"Trish, this trip has some personal risk for you. Additionally," he went on over her assurance that she would be fine, "I am taking you away from your regular income. I would be a poor friend if I didn't compensate you for your time."

"Fine," she mumbled. "We'll discuss it when we get back." More of her hair came loose from the tail, and she pushed it behind her ear. An idea struck her, and she asked, "Are you one of those people who have to talk all the time?"

"No. I have no problem with silence. Why?"

"Some people are always asking me questions and wanting to hear stories and anecdotes. So I was just wondering if you were one of them."

Micah tapped his fingers on the straps that held the box across his back as he put together his answer. "Anything you think would be helpful, say it. If you tire of the quiet, then speak. I'll do the same."

"I like working with you already," Trish said with a huge smile.

They didn't stop walking until mid-afternoon when Micah called a halt. The box was feeling heavier and heavier, and his shoulders burned for a break. Finally, dropping the box with a *thud*, he rolled his shoulders with several cracking sounds.

Trish yawned and looked around while accessing her mental area map.

"How long until we're done for today?" Micah's voice held no sign of complaint even though his shoulder cracked and popped again as he stretched.

"An hour, maybe?" Trish answered. "We've made impressive time, actually."

"You must have low standards," Micah teased.

She grinned. "I learned a long time ago that day one of any expedition needs to be short and easy. Otherwise, people just want to go home when they wake up stiff and sore."

"Well, we can't have that."

Twelve

Caroline rubbed her fingers over her face and took another deep breath. She'd been trying to follow Micah's instructions for the past hour, but her efforts had been thwarted. First, Rebecca had complained about her broken mirror the entire trip back to her shop, so she'd forgotten one of the white candles. Next, Elaine had insisted on feeding them an early breakfast. It was delicious, but now she was anxious to get to work. Unfortunately, Elaine's son just walked in and started asking questions of his own.

"Can I still open for business in an hour?" Elaine asked timidly once Nathanial was wearing the earrings and distracted with toast, bacon, and juice.

"Sure, yes, fine," Caroline snapped. "Just let me work."

Finally, she escaped the kitchen. Nathaniel was whipping up egg whites for meringues,

Rebecca stirred chocolate in a large double boiler to temper it, and Elaine used up every other available surface. So Caroline left and commandeered a table in the center of the main room. If she acted efficiently, she could still get everything done before the shop opened for business.

Forcing the irritation out of her mind, Caroline quickly lit three white candles in glass jars and began finely shredding sage leaves. Without disturbing the flames, she prodded the leaves into the pools of liquid wax forming on the surface of the candles. Next, she opened her kit of thread and selected the one that counteracted Micah's aura. Twirling it into small three loops, she passed them over each candle flame and down into the melted wax.

The first charm started working as she finished up making the third. The air seemed to pulse slightly.

"What was that?" Rebecca asked from the kitchen where she'd been working with Nathaniel on spooning out the meringues for the oven. They were always a lunchtime hit.

"Start of the process," Caroline called back. "I've got three charms scrubbing Micah's aura from the air. It'll take time, though."

"How much?" Rebecca started to call but cut her volume mid-question as Caroline brought one of the lit candles into the kitchen.

"A couple of hours at least. All day probably," she replied, setting the candle in the

226

corner of the counter. "I'll need to place one in the room he slept in and the other in some unintrusive spot. How much time did he spend here?"

"A fair amount," Elaine told her. "We saw him about every day, and there were several days where he sat in the corner from open to close. He was so quiet and still, I started to worry about him."

Caroline forced a smile. She had a nagging suspicion Micah had rested there in silence all that time after explaining about his debt to the Mistress of hell. Instead of mentioning the details, she said, "He is one person you rarely have to worry about. He always comes through."

"I don't know," Elaine said as she paused, stirring a bowl of melted chocolate. "Part of him seems broken somehow."

"That's not always a bad thing," Nathaniel said, entering the conversation.

"How so?" Caroline asked.

"Well," Nathaniel hedged but went on after an encouraging nod from his mother. "Life breaks everyone eventually. It's just that some people get stronger at the broken places."

"That's a fine piece of wisdom," Caroline said as she began winding the extra thread from her charms. "Where did you learn it?"

"My dad used to tell me that."

Elaine's eyes glistened, but she cleared her throat, looked at the candle to hide her teary eyes, and then asked, "Why did you use that yellow thread?"

"I'd call that orange," Rebecca countered.

Caroline shrugged. "It is the one best suited to canceling out Micah's influence."

"It's definitely yellow," Nathaniel said around a bite of toast. Now the meringues were in the oven, and he was having a second breakfast.

"It's one vote orange and one-point-five votes yellow," Rebecca said. Nathaniel attempted to glare at her, but the effect was lost as everyone else chuckled. "You need to break the tie, Caroline."

All eyes turned to her expectantly, but Caroline just smiled. "It'll remain a tie then."

"Oh, come on," Rebecca said. "Just answer."

"I can't," Caroline said simply. "I don't know what color it is."

"It's not like there is a wrong answer," Rebecca wheedled. "Just give us your opinion."

"I mean, I literally do not know," Caroline said. "I'm colorblind."

After several seconds of silence, Rebecca pursed her lips and said, "So many things make sense now, but how do you know anything about color theory?"

Caroline shrugged. "I wasn't born this way."

"So how—?" Elaine started to ask but thought better of it. She wanted to know but decided not to pry.

Caroline smiled at her and said, "I don't mind. Look." She held up her left hand with her fingers spread. Elaine noted the fine scars along one side of her middle finger. "These scars, when activated, allow me to see currents of energy, auras, and charms in, um, exceptional detail. The regular world is dull and grey to compensate."

"Welcome," Gegan said that evening as Caroline struggled through the door of her shop laden down with gear and chocolate. He held the door open and prevented one of the candles from falling to the floor when she stumbled over the threshold.

"Tired," Caroline muttered. "Supper. Savory food."

Gegan laughed and helped her unload everything onto a convenient dining table. "A moment, though," he said as she headed for the stairs. "A third courier dropped off more equipment this afternoon, and I believe Micah was here earlier."

"But not now?" Caroline asked as her gaze swept over the new equipment. "Where could he possibly be?"

"The items left by the first Council couriers have gone, and the paperwork on your desk was disturbed. I thought I would tell you before I left." His piece said, Gegan left the shop.

Caroline paled and turned to the little counter space she used for checking out customers. The papers were there but untidy. Some were turned sideways on the pile. Her hands shook, and not entirely from sugar overdose, as she put them to rights. The pages detailing the preparation of the juniper oil for the ritual were gone. Feeling the edges of distress fluttering around her temples, Caroline looked for the basket that accompanied the paperwork. It was gone. He was gone.

She crumpled to the floor and ran her hands up and down her arms, trying to ward off sudden chills. Even without her vision charm activated, everything seemed too bright. Tears blurred her vision as she whispered, "I'm not ready."

When sunset began turning the western sky shades of orange and red, she managed to find her feet. "I know you are out there," she called out to the silent, empty store. "I know you are out there, and I will not give in. You cannot get to me here." She checked each and every charm she had placed on the building since taking up residence. As she worked, she dragged her fingers through her hair to distract from the emotional hole opening inside her.

The charms were all fine, but she continued to pace the floors. First, she berated herself for becoming too used to Micah's presence. He always left, and it always made her vulnerable to the demons. Then, afraid to sleep because of nightmares of him never returning to her, she kept pacing.

The campsite was a very peaceful place. Micah breathed a sigh of relief seeing the small, cleared space at the base of a large boulder. It was quiet, it was calm, and most importantly, there were no people. While Trish started unloading cooking gear and laying out the camp, he strolled around poking at the surrounding sage brushes. After several minutes, he found twelve relatively straight sticks and brought them back to the camp.

In silence, he sat with his back to the boulder and began cutting the sticks to an even length of about eight inches. Next, he set about making the sticks as identical as possible. Then, he trimmed off small branches and leaves. He whittled down twists and curves and laid out six matching pairs in the dirt.

Trish sat back and watched him once she finished setting up. "Firewood is twenty minutes off that way," she said, gesturing to her right once he put down the final sage stick.

"Okay. I can finish this later," he said and rose to help her.

"What are you doing?" she asked as they walked toward a small group of pine trees.

"Making an awareness net."

"What does it do?"

"Warn me if a demon approaches."

She paled and looked around. "Do you think that will happen?"

Micah shrugged noncommittally. He didn't want to tell her that the answer was probably yes. Demons always approached him, but very few attempted anything more once he knew they were there. He usually woke before they got close, but the attack from the previous night left him unsure of himself.

He accompanied Trish the rest of the way to the pine trees in silence, and they gathered enough wood for the night and morning. Eventually, they settled down to eat toasted bread with melted cheese on top and sip warm tea around the campfire that Trish skillfully lit.

After he ate, Micah finished his project. Carving a small hole in the top of six sticks, one from each matching pair, he placed them in a small circle equidistant around the campfire. He carefully carved symbols on the second set of six and placed them several feet away from the campfire, so they formed a loose ring around their campsite.

Satisfied, Micah leaned back against the boulder and felt his eyes start to close. He was warm, well-fed, and pleasantly tired. His knives were close at hand, and he'd know if a demon came close enough to be a problem. He sighed and relaxed.

A small whimper had his eyes flying open and immediately searching for the threat. Trish wiped a hand across her face and hiccupped. "I'm sorry."

Micah set down the dagger he grabbed by reflex and resettled his back against the boulder. "What's wrong?"

More tears spilled down her cheeks as Trish took a shaky breath. "It's gone. The feeling I got after Gegan did that thing to help me. It just vanished." She ran her hands up and down her arms as if trying to ward off a chill. "I feel like … I don't …" She trailed off and took a deep breath. "I just feel very small—" Her voice broke on the last word.

"Come here." Micah sat up and held out a hand. Gratefully she took it and climbed into his arms. She took another deep breath and seemed to relax a little as she snuggled in with her back against him. He kept one arm loosely around her waist outside of the blanket and let the other rest on the ground beside them, fingers splayed over the hilt of his long knife. "What did it feel like?" he asked once she was comfortable.

Instead of speaking, she lifted his "free" arm over her shoulder and clasped his hands about her waist. Sighing, she nestled closer and said, "Like this."

Trish woke up lying curled on her side with her head pillowed on one arm. She stretched, rolled onto her back, and smelled coffee. Opening her eyes, she saw Micah sitting across the small campsite from her and fiddling with a piece of cordage.

"Morning," he said without looking up.

"Morning," she yawned back at him, pushing aside her sleeping bag. "Thanks for the coffee."

"I take no responsibility if it tastes awful," he said jokingly.

Trish sat up, poured some out into a travel mug, and took a sip. "I've had worse," she said. Looking around, she noticed she was sitting next to the boulder Micah had been using as a pillow. She colored slightly, realizing she must have fallen asleep in his arms. Hastily taking another sip, she studied Micah over the rim of her mug.

He frowned as he unknotted the pieces of cord and consulted a piece of paper by his side. He seemed entirely unaffected by last night's sleeping arrangements.

Trish shook her head to clear it and asked, "What are you working on?"

After checking it again, he held up the paper, and she saw lines of text surrounding a picture of a complex infinity knot.

"What does that do?"

"Any contaminants will be trapped within the loops and redirected."

Trish watched him a moment, hoping for more explanation, but he shifted position and bent his attention back to the cord. "Why is that important?" she finally asked.

"Before we can make any purified water, we have to place a charm on the containers," he explained. "If I can get it to work, this will keep everything free from external contaminants. It is vital to have this active before we start processing anything."

"How is it going so far?" Trish stretched again as she asked, then rose and walked over to her pack. She began rummaging around looking for one of the boxes of her grandma's recipe cookies.

"Not well," Micah grumped. "I can't get the tension right. I start out okay, but I lose it before I get to the last layer." He sighed and set it aside to

234

accept one of the cookies. "These are delicious," he said after a bite or two.

Trish grinned. "Told you not to hate on Grandma's cookies." She poured a little water into her hands and bent forward to wash her face but huffed in annoyance as her hair slipped out from behind her ears. She pushed it back before trying again and succeeding in splashing the water across her face. The cold water woke her up better than any coffee, but she would never admit that.

While she was occupied with finishing her coffee, Micah laid the cord out on the ground and selected three sticks from his awareness net. Then, removing them from their positions, he broke off the carved sections and used them to gently move the cord around to the position explained by the paperwork. "Really wish Caroline were here," he muttered as he concentrated.

"Miss her already?"

He rolled his eyes. "I could use her delicate touch right now, is all."

"Are you two...?"

Micah closed his eyes and let out a deep sigh before staring directly at her. "We are not currently involved, no."

"Not currently as in you'd like to be in the future?" Trish pressed.

"Not currently as in we were involved in the past." Micah's tone said the subject was closed, and he bent over the cords.

Trish popped up at his elbow, and he started. Luckily, his arms moved upwards to a defensive posture and didn't mess up the infinity knot. "Any luck?"

"Yep, I think I got it." He checked and double-checked the paperwork against the knot he had made. He got up and reached both arms above his head. *Pop-pop-pop* went his shoulders, and he groaned quietly.

"What's next?"

As he dug around in the box, Micah answered, "We have to attach that knot to the top of the box that will hold the containers of oil once they're processed." He extracted a wooden box, shiny with polish, whose contents *clinked* merrily. "Here."

"Oh, a box in a box," Trish exclaimed. "I love those."

Micah chuckled and opened the wooden lid. "From the instructions, we have to place the infinity knot on the lid. You can see the faint indents carved for it, then we cover it in this silver embroidered white cloth and tie the corners together underneath."

"Seems complicated."

"It only gets worse from here," Micah said. "There *is* a reason people don't attempt this often."

They struggled to lift the complex infinity knot onto the box lid for over an hour before Micah solved the problem by digging a hole next to where it lay and fitting the wooden box lid inside it. They then slid the knot sideways and into its spot. Dealing with the white fabric was easier, and soon after, the wooden box was ready to receive its first contents.

"Juniper oil and lots of it," Micah replied when she asked what came next.

"We'll have to keep hiking then," she responded after thinking for a moment. "If we hurry, we can get to another campsite tonight that is a short distance from a massive juniper grove."

They chatted amiably as they walked. Micah loosened up significantly, and though the box was still heavy, it didn't seem to bother him as he followed her.

"Don't you think it is strange that all the materials you need for this ... ritual are found in the desert?" Trish asked, looking back as they meandered up a dried streambed.

Micah rocked his head back and forth as he thought about it. "Not really. Do you know anything that fights for survival harder than a desert plant?"

Trish laughed as lore, facts, and stories ran through her mind, and had to agree. "I know juniper can help with digestive upset and skin issues. Why do you think it is the carrier oil for this?"

"It doesn't rot or go bad," Micah replied. "It will keep everything else fresh. Also, it has a calming effect."

"Where'd you learn that?" Trish asked, pleased to add another tidbit to her store of knowledge.

"Caroline."

Then they were back to her. "Why did you two break up?" Trish asked bravely, turning her gaze forward. She ignored the feeling of warmth spreading across her cheeks and kept her head resolutely straight. She could feel Micah's gaze on her back, though.

"It's not a very interesting story," he finally said resignedly.

Trish nodded her head but didn't say anything, hoping he would continue. Her hair fell forward out of her ponytail as he did.

"We were friends first," he began. "She helped save my life once and is solely responsible for saving it at least one other time. The romance began when I rented a room from her for six months. We were together most of the time, and things just progressed."

"Why did you split up?" Trish asked.

"Time and distance, really," Micah answered, fiddling with his cufflinks. "During those six months, it became very apparent that demons are drawn to me. No, I don't know why," he added as if everyone asked that question. "Even with all of Caroline's skill of masking auras, they still attacked. I needed to leave the area and haven't stayed in one place very long since. I can't ask her to wait for me for months on end, nor can I ask her to live under that kind of threat. With her lineage, she has enough of that to deal with."

Trish tried and failed to tuck her hair behind her ears before asking, "Lineage?"

Instead of answering, Micah asked his own question, "Did you mean to cut your hair that short?"

"Not at all," Trish said, accepting the subject change. "I cut it last week, and it is driving me nuts."

"Hold up a moment then." Micah walked up to her and tugged the tie out of her hair. The blond locks swung forward, and he gently, though a little stiffly, ran his fingers through them. Goosebumps ran over Trish's arms as his nails delicately scratched her scalp while he gathered up a portion of hair near the crown of her head. Working rapidly and smoothly, he plaited it down the back of her head. She stood frozen while he worked and sighed when his hands fell away.

"Sorry," he muttered. "It's crooked."

"I don't mind," Trish said too quickly. She cleared her throat and said, "Thanks." She kept walking, very grateful he couldn't see her bright red face.

Thirteen

"Why are you panicking?" Rebecca asked.

It had been nearly a full day since Caroline discovered Micah's absence. She still strode the floors alternating between wringing her hands and running her fingers through her hair. As a result, her hands were red and irritated, and her hair was a disaster. Nevertheless, her flat was spotless, and potions scheduled for the day were already heated, cooled, and re-bottled. She'd barely slept and didn't seem to hear the question.

"Caroline," Rebecca said, drawing out each syllable. "Why are you panicking? It's like you've never been apart."

"It's not the being apart," Caroline said. "It's the fact that he didn't say goodbye." She blinked rapidly to clear the sudden tears from her eyes. "He always said goodbye. Even when he left in the middle of the night or was only going to be gone a few hours, he always said goodbye to me."

"He'll come back," Rebecca said bracingly. "Now stop pacing before you ruin the floors. Turn your mind to something useful, and it won't seem so bad. How about this?" She held out some of the paperwork on the ritual they were all preparing for. "How are we going to make this?"

Distractedly, Caroline looked at the paper. It showed sketches of an ornate amulet the size of two closed fists. It was vaguely heart-shaped with three interior chambers and a spiral of tiny pipes to distribute liquid. "We're not going to make this," she said.

Rebecca looked puzzled. "Isn't this a major item here?"

"Oh, it is," Caroline replied. "We can't do anything without it."

"Then why aren't we going to make one?"

"I'm calling in my sister. She's better than I at this kind of work."

"Really?" Rebecca said skeptically.

"She focused on metallurgy," Caroline said with a shrug. "I focused on botany. Different interests; different strengths."

"Seems like botany is just memorization. Memorization and facts," Rebecca muttered.

Caroline gave her a long-suffering look and sighed. "Watch." She got a bit of chalk out of one of her drawers and drew a small square on her table. Next, she retrieved a bundle of fresh sage leaves from her windowsill and placed one leaf at each corner of the square. Satisfied, she told Rebecca to wait. Trudging up the stairs, Caroline rubbed her face to clear away the exhaustion of the sleepless night and grabbed a small bottle of purified water. Yawning, she selected her favorite thread and headed back down the stairs.

"Watch," she said again as she spun the thread into a small circular knot and placed it in the chalk square. "Feel the twisted energy?" Rebecca nodded, and Caroline dripped a couple of drops of purified water onto the knot. "Feel the difference?"

"I do," Rebecca said. "It seems calmer now."

"Correct. Anyone can make something this simple; would you agree?" Caroline asked. Rebecca nodded. "Now watch this." Caroline removed the sage leaves and wet thread but left the chalk square the same. Taking four new sage leaves, she carefully folded each one at an angle and placed them just so at the corners of the square. Making a new knot with the thread, she repeated the experiment with the purified water.

"I can't sense anything," Rebecca said in a frustrated voice a minute later, spinning her bracelet in irritation. "Why can't I get through?"

Caroline smiled at her. "With basic knowledge of botany, you can put up a wall like the first time we did this, but walls have gaps and weak points. So energy leaks out, and you can sense what is going on behind the wall. With advanced knowledge," she gestured at the current setup, "you can make something more delicate. Anything that tries to see inside now just gets spun around back to itself, and the interior is kept contained."

"How does that work?"

"It has to do with the angle of the folds on the sage leaves and the angle they meet with the corners of the chalk square," Caroline said, yawning. "But all that is useless if you don't know the basic facts and memorization."

"So, how are we going to reach your sister?" Rebecca changed the subject and fiddled with the sage leaves. "Where does she live anyway?"

"We are first going to contact the Witches Council," Caroline answered. "Clarice can patch me into a communication web, and I'll talk to Carmen directly. Hopefully, I can even see her."

Rebecca scratched her head in confusion. "They can just do that! Talk to anyone wherever they are?"

"No, but Carmen has an unusual communication mirror. They can reach her anytime."

"How much did that cost?" Rebecca sounded a bit surly.

Caroline took a deep breath and forced herself to relax. The fatigue was making her shoulders creep up to her ears. "She has done enough work for the Council that they awarded it to her. So, the cost was years of time and effort."

Clarice from the Council was pleased to help them and wheedled a report on their progress from Caroline as she set up the link.

"How may I help you today?" said a warm, professional, female voice once the connection was established.

"Sister, I need you," Caroline said, jokingly drawing out the words.

"Sister!" The voice jumped up to a pleasant girlish pitch.

"How soon can you get to Canyon Town?" Caroline asked.

"That sounds serious," Carmen answered, sobering somewhat. "Do you need help with your love life?"

"The nonexistence of my love life has long been established," Caroline said with a laugh. "Seriously, how soon can you get here with your equipment? I need you to make an amulet for me."

"How complicated?"

"Very," Caroline sighed. "Two liquids, three chambers, emulsifier plate, high purity."

"Sounds very exciting, but Canyon Town is quite far away. Even if I weren't reduced to waddling, it would take several trips of several days to get everything to you. That's not even considering making the amulet."

After pondering for several seconds, Caroline came to a decision. "Hire a coach; I'll pay for it. Just get here as soon as you can."

"Sister," Carmen said, shocked. "What is going on over there?"

"I'll explain when you get here. Just get here fast."

"Caroline, for the price of the coach to Canyon Town, you could buy a house," Carmen said, all frivolity gone from her voice. "You could live off that money for years. Are you sure?"

"I'm sure." Caroline took a deep breath and shakily let it out. "Handle the arrangements, and I'll cover whatever the cost."

Carmen was clearly troubled as she said goodbye, but she agreed to hire the coach.

"Clarice, are you still listening?" Caroline asked once Carmen had gone.

"I'm here," came the response.

"Grab a witness so I can sign over control of my money to you. Then get the funds to Carmen as soon as possible and get that coach moving."

"You truly think you are going to succeed, don't you?"

"I do. Now how do we get those funds to my sister?"

Caroline grumbled as she pushed her dining table and chairs out of the way, once again, to make room for mapping out the ritual. It was the following morning, and after further studying the notes, she wasn't sure if her living area was big enough. "I give up," she said, exasperated. "Rebecca, help me move the furniture downstairs."

They struggled with the heavy couch for nearly half an hour before getting it down the stairs. "You know," Rebecca said, wiping sweat off her face, "Micah is much stronger than I gave him credit for. He moved this thing without issue."

Caroline chuckled and stretched her back, "You wouldn't think a frame like his could contain so much power. Come on, let's get the dining chairs."

They decided to take a break once they got all the furniture out of Caroline's living room. She and Rebecca had barely settled down for a lesson on color theory, specifically how yellow-dominant green reacted differently from blue-dominant green when some customers entered the shop. Caroline went to help them and was slightly dismayed when they fell in love with her couch. The couple purchased the couch on the spot and scheduled to return the following day for pickup.

"They bought my couch," Caroline said as she plopped back down at the table where Rebecca sat, surrounded by pages of drawings and notes.

"Good for them," Rebecca said distractedly. "It was kind of ugly."

"But it was my couch."

"Aren't you only renting this place short-term anyway?"

"Well, yes," Caroline admitted. "I'd forgotten about that. I'll include the price of the couch in next month's rent and write to the owner. I doubt she'll mind."

Rebecca closed her eyes for a moment and tilted her head in confusion. "You cared enough about the couch, which is not even yours, to complain that someone bought it, but you don't think the actual owner will care?"

"It's not often that we get attached to things," Caroline said, leaning her elbows on the table. "When I rented this place, the owner told me she wants to retire and downsize soon. There were strong hints that she would sell me the place if I asked. She'll probably thank me for getting a good price on the couch," she added thoughtfully.

"Speaking of price," Rebecca said, putting aside her notes, "will it really cost that much to bring Carmen here?"

"Probably," Caroline answered. "I've never traveled by coach before, but she has once or twice."

"Was it for…?"

"Yeah, it was for stuff like this. It must be difficult to be the prodigy in a family of geniuses." Caroline said airily and laughed.

Rebecca just rolled her eyes. "When is the coach due?"

"Anytime this evening." Caroline began fidgeting with the cuff of her sleeve. "I hope she hasn't had any difficulties."

"Break downs and whatnot?"

"Yes, those too." Worrying at her bottom lip with her teeth, Caroline stood and tried to pace. Fatigue hit her, and her hip popped, shooting pain down her entire leg. She stumbled and grabbed onto the arm of a recliner before shaking out her leg, walking around the furniture, and answering the question. "I don't think you quite understand how high profile my family is."

"So, explain it. You're getting better at that."

Ignoring the barb, Caroline kept pacing. The movement was more manageable now. "The demons know who we are. Anywhere we settle for long periods is watched and targeted."

"There haven't been any around here," Rebecca interrupted.

Caroline shook her head. "That's because I never really claimed this space. Look." She showed Rebecca slender silver and white charms hanging in every corner of every room. They were easy to overlook even when pointed out. "These charms are permanently cleansing the shop and the rooms upstairs. My presence is constantly stripped away, so they don't realize I'm here."

She paused and swallowed before adding, "It's why Micah was safe here too. Anyway, Carmen has lived in the same house ever since she got married. The demons know where she lives and will follow her here. The fact that she is near the end of her pregnancy will only make their interest more…" She paused, looking for the right word, and shivered slightly. "Intense."

Rebecca stared at her for a long moment before saying, in a tone of complete seriousness, "You're scared for her, aren't you?"

Sighing, Caroline let her shoulders slump and looked at the floor. "I would never forgive myself if something happened to her or the baby because I called her here." Then, wiping her face, she added, "Come on. We need to start measuring."

They spent the rest of the day working on the layout of the ritual circle.

When it arrived safely that evening, the carriage was a loud, monstrous three-wheeled thing, belching smoke and steam. The driver wore black slacks and was swathed against the wind in a deep purple blanket. He skillfully steered the machine down the street and cut power to the steam engine from his cushioned perch in front of the black lacquered cabin. It rumbled up to Caroline's shop with no less than ten demons racing after it and stopped with a piercing whistle in a cloud of dust. The lush, purple curtains at the windows twitched, but the driver called out, "Wait!"

After checking several dials, pulling levers, and listening to the clicks and clacks of the cooling machine, he indicated it was safe to disembark. Proving his own words, he swung down and began efficiently unloading a heavy trunk and two large bags. As he carried the luggage inside the shop, the carriage door opened, and Caroline's sister, Carmen, gingerly stepped out.

Framed by the luxurious interior of the carriage, she had long caramel-colored hair that glinted gold with braided metallic charms woven through her tresses. She was tall and possessed an athletic figure, which made the large bump of her pregnancy even more distracting. Blinking eyes, the same color and shape as Caroline's, she waved and began awkwardly making her way to the door.

Caroline waved back but eyed the demons and stayed inside the ring of protective charms in her shop. Carmen seemed to understand this and checked behind her as she crossed into the sunlight between the carriage's shadow and the shop front. The direct sunlight lit up the gold and silver threads draped across her belly, entwined through her hair, and wrapped around her wrists.

"Hey, lady!" She held out her arms as she crossed the shop's threshold, and Caroline rushed to hug her.

"I've missed you so much," Caroline breathed, laying her head against her sister's shoulder.

"Don't you dare cry," Carmen warned, but then she sniffled. "I'll have to cry with you."

"No tears, I promise," Caroline replied and hugged tighter.

After a few seconds of silently processing the emotions of being together again, the two sisters broke apart. Then, spying Rebecca, Carmen joked, "Is this the romantic rival that made you call for my experienced help?"

Rebecca sputtered and blushed bright red, but Caroline laughed and said, "I told you my love life is nonexistent."

"But it doesn't have to be," Carmen persisted.

"Maybe once the work is done, you can play at matchmaker," Caroline said to appease her.

"I don't play at matchmaker; I am a matchmaker."

They retired upstairs, but then Caroline remembered that there was no furniture in the living room. Embarrassed, Caroline explained the situation while she pulled the pillows off her bed and set them up to support Carmen as she sat on the floor.

"Just don't expect me to get up anytime soon," Carmen said and took the rest in stride.

Rebecca excused herself right after dinner, saying she had the opening shift at the chocolate shop the following day. The mood shifted immediately after she left, and Carmen said, "Sister, what are you doing?" She pointed to the diagrams and descriptions from the Council paperwork that were spread all around her on the floor, as well as all the chalk marks on the floor.

Caroline tensed. "You said you would help me," she said defensively.

"I want to, but why are you doing this?"

"I told you," Caroline said, stalking over to the kitchen. "Machinery in hell freezing over; demons invading our plane, and so on."

"Yes, I get that, but why *you*?" Carmen put a gentle emphasis on the last word. "There are plenty of ways to help besides being the caster for this kind of ritual."

"It's for Micah."

"Micah," Carmen stared at her from her throne of pillows as she searched her memory.

"Your ex? The scrawny guy who worked security at Daddy's funeral. That Micah?"

Caroline took a deep breath and mentally prepared herself to reveal the extent of her relationship with Micah and admit something she'd never said out loud. "Micah, my best friend of twenty years, who got his back ripped open at daddy's funeral saving Mama from that anxiety demon with abnormally long claws. Micah, who kept the demons off me for two months after that while I grieved for Daddy. And yes," she added in response to Carmen's upraised eyebrows, "Micah, my ex." Here came the admission. "The person I would do anything for."

"Sounds like you love him."

Caroline shrugged and reached into a cupboard for some chocolate. Carmen, however, wouldn't let it go. "Does he know? Does he feel the same way?"

"Whether he does or not is completely irrelevant," Caroline said, biting into the salted caramel-filled chocolate bar. The sugar helped salve the bitterness she felt at saying the words. "He can't settle down anywhere. He has to keep moving."

"Why?"

"Demons are attracted to him even more than Daddy or Jay. They don't ever try and manipulate him, though. They just watch him and call in reinforcements until they attack." Caroline grimaced and stared down at the chocolate in her hands. "Sometimes, it only takes one day." She exhaled a puff of breath and shook her head, trying to fight back the tears as she whispered. "The Mistress of hell knows his name."

Carmen sat bolt upright at that. "I'll start on the amulet now."

They stayed up for hours, going through the diagrams, discussing, sketching, and reevaluating. Eventually, Carmen yawned so wide, her jaw cracked.

"Bedtime," Caroline mumbled around her own yawn. "You take the bed."

"I'm not taking your bed," Carmen protested.

"If your husband hears that I made you sleep on the floor, he will have my head. Distance or not. Just leave the pillows."

Carmen grumbled but heaved herself up and waddled into the bedroom. Caroline carefully did not laugh out loud at the sight.

The campsite for the second night beckoned Trish and Micah from afar. It was a flat clearing ringed by logs a short walk from a merry little stream offset nicely by the afternoon sun.

"Home sweet home, for the next week or so," Trish said as she swung off her bag. "See over there?" She pointed across the stream. "That is where the fir trees grow, and about mile that way," she gestured upstream, "are the junipers."

Micah nodded and put down the box. It felt glorious. He checked on the contents and withdrew the papers to figure out their next move. "We need to get the purified water going, find ripe juniper berries, and ..." he trailed off with a sigh of exasperation. "Each container has to be sealed with a six-strand braid. Three white, two silver, and one black. Why did it have to be six?"

"Seems oddly specific," Trish commented.

"Six is a multiplier," Micah tried to explain. "It means that the oil will be more potent—I think. In either case, I am horrible at six-strand braids."

"White usually stands for purity, right?" Trish asked, staying on subject but trying to distract him. "Why aren't all the strands white?"

"White is brittle. It wouldn't be viable by itself."

"Oh," Trish said like she understood what he meant. "Where do we start?"

In answer, Micah pulled out the small copper purifier and set it up. It was a simple apparatus consisting of a tripod with notches to hold a medium bowl about halfway up. On top of the tripod balanced a larger metal bowl with a lip running around near the inside edge. The lip extended to a small spout on one side, to which Micah attached a short length of copper pipe. He yawned as he worked and longed for a good night's sleep. At length, he handed Trish the medium-size copper bowl. "Fill that with water for me?"

She did, and he placed the bowl on the tripod. Now they could turn their attention to the juniper berries.

The trail was rocky but not unpleasant as they strode uphill toward the juniper grove. It was easy to be peaceful out here, and Trish was excellent company. But Micah found his mood souring as he caught sight of an anxiety demon following them. It hopped and skittered about, mimicking Trish as she walked. He wasn't sure if it was the same one from Trish's house the day they left. It had the same bright blue veins shimmering in a green and gold body and the same two horns jutting out from the top of its head, but it had no distinguishing characteristics from other anxiety demons.

"Any additional instructions?" Trish asked, half-joking as they reached the trees.

"Ripe berries," Micah answered. "They can't have any green on them."

They worked in silence for half an hour or so, gently plucking the ripe berries from the trees. The small sack Trish brought was bulging with them when they decided to go back to the campsite. Trish picked up the sack and turned, but her foot caught the edge of a rock sticking up from the ground. She fell and flung out her arms to catch herself. The sack went flying, the berries scattered everywhere as she landed hard on her hands and knees.

In the space of a breath, she assessed herself for damage, realized she'd dumped the sack, and started hyperventilating. "I'm sorry. I'm sorry," she wheezed between gasps of air.

The anxiety demon rushed her gleefully. Micah took three long steps to intersect it and caught it by one of the horns. It swung up crazily as he lifted it, and he grabbed the other horn, neatly snapping it with a barely audible *crunch*. Then, holding onto its remaining horn, Micah twisted the demon hard sideways and snapped its neck. Letting the demon's body whither into dust, Micah strode over to Trish, asking, "Are you okay?"

"Don't be mad," Trish piped up immediately, now curling into a ball on the ground.

"I'm not," Micah said in a quiet, soothing voice. He settled himself down in the dirt by Trish and calmly placed one hand over hers. His other hand picked up the half-empty sack and put it in his pocket.

It took several minutes for Trish to master herself and regulate her breathing, during which Micah did nothing but sit and hold her hand. When she looked up at last and tried to speak, Micah shook his head. Drawing her up, he kept hold of her hand and began walking back toward the campsite.

"Thank you," she said as they walked, "for not getting angry."

"It was an accident," Micah said, squeezing her hand.

"But I wasted all that time and effort." Her breathing began to accelerate again.

"It was an accident," Micah repeated. He paused before asking delicately, "Do you get anxiety attacks often?"

Her shoulders slumped. "Not often, but being around Kane makes it worse, and he usually comes with me out here." She sighed. "He would have been furious."

"The anger demon would have affected him so," Micah gently corrected her. "The anxiety demon attacking you would have heightened your stress, and both demons would have been happy."

"Th-there's a demon on me??" she stammered and tried to yank her hand away. Her other hand began running up and down her body as if she could brush the demon away.

Micah didn't let go and drew her body toward his. Wrapping his free arm around her shoulders, he said, "It's gone. I disposed of it before it got to you." She shuddered and rested her head against his shoulder.

"Will it come after me again?" she whispered.

"We all have a weakness," Micah said. "Demons…" He trailed off and rubbed his hand up and down her arm as he gathered his thoughts. "Everyone has trouble with one kind of demon. We can't see them for what they are, and they can influence us before we realize it. Anxiety seems to be that weakness for you. So yes, they will come after you again, but …," he added quickly as she shivered violently, "I'll help you."

"What's your weakness?"

"Despair."

"Who helps you with it?"

"No one right now." He loosened his hold now that she was okay, but her arm snaked around his waist and gripped his shirt while he continued. "Despair drives you away from emotional contact. It is isolating. Close friends and loved ones seem suddenly behind a wall, and no matter what, you can't bring it down." His mouth quirked up into a crooked smile, and he added, "Strangers don't count."

"I guess I'm still a stranger then?" she asked.

"For now," he said and smiled.

They banked the fire and set the remaining juniper berries in the copper bowl with the stream water to boil overnight. Micah explained that the steam would condense on the inside of the upper bowl and drip down through the little copper tube and into a jar he set beneath it. The sun burned the sky red and gold as they sat in silence.

Micah woke up after the moon set and opened his eyes in the darkness. The stars glimmered slightly but did not give enough illumination to see past the edge of their campsite. He took a deep breath and looked around. The campfire embers were dark and covered in ash, and the trees were quiet. He closed his eyes and relaxed. *There*, he thought as his senses picked up on the demon skirting the fire opposite him.

Gently, he reached out to Trish and shook her leg. She jerked and woke up. "Wha—?

"Be still," Micah said. She froze and looked at him, her wide eyes reflecting a couple of stars. He nodded, though he doubted she could see, and palmed his smaller knife from where it lay next to him. His arm snaked out, and the blade flew silently through the air. The tip buried itself in the dirt next to the demon stalking him, and it fled. "It's gone," he said, sitting up.

"What was it?" Trish asked. She flinched as Micah raked the coals of the fire and exposed the glowing embers. Their light flickered over her frightened face.

"Another demon."

She shivered and looked around nervously. "How often does that happen to you?"

Content with the state of the fire, Micah rose and went to retrieve his knife. "Always."

"Why?"

"I wish I knew." He started as vivid memory surfaced, and suddenly he was years younger and far away.

Laying on Caroline's bed with his head pillowed in her lap and her fingers casually drifting over his scalp and through his hair, Micah felt sleepy and at peace.

"You are one of a kind, do you know that?" Caroline asked as she looked through an old book of myths and legends.

"Why is that?" He reached up to grasp her hand gently, brought it to his lips, and placed a kiss on her palm.

Her fingertips trailed along his jaw as she said, "You shine." He raised an eyebrow, and she felt the motion even though her gaze was still on the book. "Your aura," she paused and looked down at him. "My father says that darkness seeks out the light because only in darkness will the lights shine."

He blinked and found himself back at the campsite. Sighing, he said, "Rest now if you can. There is something about me that draws them, but I'll stay awake." As he said it, he felt the familiar pang of sadness. Someone near him was afraid, and it was his fault.

Trish looked at him with kindness, then came and sat beside him. She leaned her head against his shoulder and stayed there until she drifted off to sleep.

Fourteen

The next day, immediately after breakfast, which Caroline had waiting, Carmen opened her trunk. It was neatly compartmentalized and full to bursting.

"I'm surprised that one guy could carry all this," Caroline said, remarking on the carriage driver. "He wasn't that big."

"It's lighter than it looks," Carmen said.

"That doesn't mean much when it looks heavier than anything has a right to be," Caroline retorted.

Carmen chuckled and said, "Have you got any kind of elevated work surface? I'll work on the floor if I must, but then I have to get up, and that's not fun. Plus, the little one gets cranky when I hunch over too much and takes it out on my ribs."

Caroline retrieved a small corner desk from the shop and carted it up the stairs. "Where is a man when you need one?" She huffed as she set the desk down. "I got spoiled."

"Just another reason to settle down," Carmen said.

"Don't start," Caroline warned as she headed back downstairs for a chair. "I am not in the mood."

"Of course, you're not," Carmen retorted, undeterred, "but I don't care. What are you going to do about Micah?"

"Nothing," Caroline reappeared in the living room clutching a little four-legged stool. "I am going to do nothing, because I want nothing to change. I am happy the way things are." Caroline suppressed a surge of pain over their last few interactions as she said the words.

"Your loss," Carmen sniffed as she began laying out items on the desk. "Can I get that chair?"

They worked through the morning: Carmen on the final sketches and design of the amulet and Caroline on the layout of the ritual circle. Then Carmen shooed Caroline away from her corner and got out a large lump of grey wax. She hummed quietly as she worked and occasionally broke into song. The soft lullabies were relaxing, and Caroline found herself seated on the floor in the corner, drowsing as she listened.

Rebecca ruined the mood by entering the flat around noon. She stomped up the stairs and interrupted the last verse about following a loved one down a river to the sea. "You both look productive," she snapped.

Carmen raised an eyebrow but didn't look up from her work. The lump of grey wax was now split into two halves, and she was working on making them exact mirror images of each other. "Productivity is not easily measured," she said simply.

Rebecca scowled at her, but Caroline asked, "What happened to you?"

"Do you remember that athletic guy with brown hair that Trish brought around?"

"Vaguely," Caroline said as she stood and walked toward Rebecca. "I was more focused on the anger demon on his back."

"Well, apparently, he is Trish's cousin. She has vanished without a word, and he blames us. He cornered me on the way here and shouted at me for ten minutes as people hurried past." Emotion crept into Rebecca's voice as she went on. "I don't know where she is, and the anger demon has grown."

Cautiously, Caroline reached out a hand and rested it on Rebecca's back. "Deep breath," she said calmly. "Anger demons are frightening to us all when they get that powerful."

Rebecca hung her head and shivered. "It was so happy it had a target."

"That's how they operate," Carmen said seriously. She had made her way to Rebecca's other side and now placed a soothing hand on her arm. "They take everything negative their host is feeling and throw it at other people. They delight in targeting those who do not deserve it. Let its influence drain away from you."

"Its influence?" Rebecca asked.

"It was priming you and making you vulnerable to others like itself," Carmen explained. "Let that go."

Rebecca took several deep breaths but eventually relaxed and tried to shake off the incident. "I don't understand. Demons never do that to me. They either avoid me or attack. They never try to influence me. It doesn't work."

Carmen took a couple of steps back from Rebecca and reflectively scraped one thumbnail across her lower lip as she studied the younger woman. "You really think you're that powerful?" she asked.

Rebecca shrugged and said, "Why else would they never manipulate me?"

Instead of answering, Carmen withdrew a finger-length, slim, metal stylus from her sleeve. One end tapered down into a needlepoint while the other was rounded with a small clip to hold it to the cuff of her shirt. She pricked the middle finger of her right hand and began drawing the blood down scars etched into the side of her finger.

"Are you doing the same creepy sight thing as Caroline?" Rebecca asked nervously.

"It's part of the family heritage," Caroline said dryly.

Having finished with the blood, Carmen wiped off the stylus before returning it to her sleeve. She held her hand up in front of her face and waved it while speaking. The gesture and the words exactly mirroring her sister. Rebecca shivered uncomfortably as that gaze fell on her.

Carmen's eyes were grey and pale with all the color drained away. After several silent moments, the gaze flickered to Caroline, who stiffened momentarily then smiled.

Carmen shook her head, vibrant green returning to her eyes, and wiped the blood off her hand, exchanging a look with Caroline.

"What?" Rebecca asked.

"Your aura is powerful," Carmen admitted. "But it is transient. It is like burning papers. They explode in a bright blaze, but there is no staying power, no backbone to it." She raised her hands to hold off any argument and added briskly, "You are strong, but you are also brittle. Life has not tempered you yet with trials." She waved her hands gently and continued.

"I'm not saying you've had it easy or dismissing anything you have endured. Life has simply not yet finished its work with you. You are quick to anger. I'll guess you're also quick to judge, and you *are* vulnerable. If I can figure that out after a moment of observation, the demons can too. It looks like they are finally taking a genuine interest in you."

"They've shown *interest* in me before," Rebecca snapped, mocking Carmen's words. "It doesn't mean I'm vulnerable."

"All of us are," Caroline interrupted. "Every single person is vulnerable to one kind of demon or another."

"Even you?" Rebecca sneered.

"Of course," Caroline said with exaggerated patience. "Depression from loneliness."

Rebecca faltered slightly at the open admission and cast around to continue the argument. "Even Micah?"

Caroline jerked as if she'd received a small electric shock. "I'm sure he is," she said in a quiet voice. "He's just never discussed it with me." Her gaze softened, and tears gathered at the corners of her eyes. "But I know it is some flavor of depression or despair."

"How do you know that?" Rebecca asked.

Caroline looked up, the sadness in her eyes replaced with anger directed at what haunted her friend. "I've seen the marks it left behind: punctures from great, curving fangs and thick, black bruises." She sighed. "Depression demons force their prey to put walls between themselves and the people they care about. All we can do from the outside is hold out compassion and understanding and trust they will find a gap in the wall to accept it."

She leaned back with a sigh and wiped a hand across her eyes. "Micah spends so much time alone. So much time hunting demons without support. His mental and emotional fortitude is immense to be able to handle that, but that is already a type of wall, and depression and despair thrive in isolation." She closed her eyes and seemed to slump in upon herself.

"What about you?" Rebecca asked Carmen awkwardly, giving Caroline a moment to pull herself together.

"Fear," she said, her hands curling about her belly. "For my children, and…," she looked at Caroline, "my family."

Caroline walked over to her younger sister and gave her a gentle hug. They both sniffed a little as they broke apart.

"I don't know if I feel better or worse now," Rebecca admitted.

"Go with better," Caroline advised. "You can always feel worse later." She wiped her eyes again and took a deep breath. "Shall we start today's lesson?"

"I know it's only early afternoon," Rebecca said, "but can I get a drink?"

Carmen laughed, but Caroline only offered a wry smile and said, "I don't keep alcohol in residence."

"Really?" Rebecca asked. "You don't drink at all?"

Caroline shrugged. "Depression and drinking alone are not good bedfellows."

"So, what does it mean exactly to be vulnerable to one kind of demon?" Rebecca asked uncertainly.

"It means," Caroline broke off and looked away for several seconds, gathering her thoughts. "It means I can't sense the demon for what it is. I can't always separate it from normal emotions. So it sneaks up on me."

"Is it the same for you?" Rebecca asked Carmen.

She nodded. "Fear comes in all shapes and sizes. I often need my husband to help me when it gets to me. It's worse when I'm pregnant."

A sudden idea struck Rebecca, and she felt the emotional blow like a fist to her chest. "This is what Gegan meant, isn't it?" She said, mainly to herself. "This is what he was talking about when he said I would need help."

Carmen didn't answer but went back to her desk. Caroline let the realization sink for a minute before quizzing Rebecca on color theory. Then she checked her measurements from the day before and set Rebecca up with a small embroidery hoop. Caroline told her to practice her stitching. "Because we need to get you started on concealing charms." Rebecca grumbled and quickly lost interest in the monotonous task as Carmen began humming again.

She was gently coating the wax sculptures in a slurry of some kind. Slowly, so as not to disturb her work, she used her fingers to prod the slurry into every crevice and surround the wax in a shell-like casing. Once complete, she set the misshapen sphere aside and stretched. Immediately she flinched as her shoulders popped.

"You sound worse than I do," Caroline joked, getting up to make some tea. Her skirt swished over the floor, picking up some dust from the slurry that had dribbled off the desk.

"Part one, step one is now complete," Carmen said back. "Little one is jumping for joy."

"What will you do next?" Rebecca asked.

"Size and shape the pipes," Carmen responded. She rose to her feet and began massaging her low back. "In just a minute." She sighed in pleasure and stretched again before noticing Rebecca staring at her workspace. This time, only one shoulder popped once. "Want to help?"

Rebecca eyed her skeptically. "How?"

"Dig out my sizing board, mandrel, and my notes on emulsion plates." Carmen gestured at the trunk.

"I don't know what any of those are," Rebecca declared, but she stood and walked over to the trunk.

Carmen chuckled. "It's a hazard of field expertise. You develop your own sub-language. Notes will be in one of the drawers on the left side of the trunk. Just flip through the pages until you get to the letter 'E'."

"What does an emulsion plate do?" Rebecca asked as she knelt and began digging into the trunk.

"It forces flowing liquids through a series of tiny holes. This allows them to mix uniformly." Carmen accepted some pages from Rebecca and declared they were the ones she wanted.

The sizing board turned out to be a large board folded in thirds with a series of holes drilled through it. The holes ranged in size but were neatly organized in rows of descending circumference from the top left to the bottom right. Carmen directed Rebecca to set up on her workspace and to find a short length of copper pipe.

"What does the mandrel look like?" Rebecca asked, correctly remembering the final piece of gear.

"Not important," Carmen said. "Because right now, I need spicy curry."

Rebecca stared at her as Caroline let out a peal of laughter from the kitchen. "I'll see what I can do, sister," she said as she took the kettle off the stove. "Check the icebox?"

Carmen happily wandered over and opened the door. As her eyes sifted through all the objects, she gave a cry of glee. "You still have some pickled garlic!"

Caroline snorted with laughter and spilled tea leaves across the counter.

"My daughter broke my jar last month, and I haven't gotten the replacement yet," Carmen said to the room at large. She pulled the thick glass jar out of the fridge, uncapped it, and held it up to her nose. "This smells amazing." She pulled a jealous face at her sister. "Yours is spicier than mine."

"Pickled…garlic?" Rebecca asked. "What is it with your family and pickled garlic?"

Caroline bent over the counter, completely overcome by silent laughter as Carmen began enumerating the benefits of the pickled garlic to Rebecca.

After their late lunch, which Caroline refused to make as spicy as Carmen wanted, but was very garlicky, she checked on Rebecca's needlework. It was not good. Caroline took a deep breath and verbally reminded herself that no one started out with embroidery well.

"It is pointless to stitch in straight lines," Rebecca griped under her breath.

"Straight lines are the foundation of proper…" Caroline started, but then she just gave up. Everything seemed to close in on her, and she put her face in her hands and wept.

Rebecca sat there stunned while Carmen dropped what she was doing and waddled over. Standing next to her sister and supported by the countertop, she gently pulled one of Caroline's hands into her own.

"Sorry," Caroline hiccupped.

"Stress," Carmen said sagely and instantly gave vent to her motherly impulses. "Sit down on the pillows and take some time." Caroline tried to refuse but gave in to her sister's gently worded insistence that she would work with Rebecca while Caroline got herself together.

After settling Caroline down with a cup of tea, a bar of chocolate, and a blanket, Carmen took a look at Rebecca's work. "Your disdain is obvious," she said, handing back the embroidery hoop.

Rebecca frowned. "It's hard to see the point. Nothing I'll ever make will be straight lines."

Carmen shrugged and grabbed a pencil. "Follow this then," she said and drew (freehand) a curving, faintly floral design on the fabric Rebecca was practicing on. She made sure she drew it outside the embroidery hoop so Rebecca would be forced to adjust it.

Leaving Rebecca to her challenge, Carmen went back to her own work. Carefully, she pushed her desk over next to the stove, added her mandrel to the workspace, and reset her sizing board. Next, she turned on the stove and set one of the pieces of copper pipe on the burner to heat. Humming tunefully, she returned to her trunk and removed a heavy leather apron. Passing the strap over her head, she wrapped the extended waist ties twice around her torso and tied them.

Assured that her unborn child was safe while performing the next task, she extracted an exquisitely made pair of gloves from a special drawer in the trunk. They were made of a charcoal grey material and covered in symbols and charms, stitched using sparkling silver thread. When she pulled them on, they covered her hands, wrists, and half her forearms. Carmen flexed her fingers and adjusted the lay of the fabric across her palms.

Next, she pulled a second set of gloves from the trunk. These were made of metal and looked skeletal with their small plates connected by chains. She slid these over the grey gloves, so the plates lay precisely over the bones in her hands and clasped the chains about her wrists.

The pipe on the stove was now ready. Without hesitation, Carmen picked the glowing metal up in her gloved hands and began plying it through the biggest hole on the sizing board.

Singing quietly, another lullaby, she played the red-hot metal like an instrument. Her fingers tapped the tube through each hole in the sizing board, providing a percussion accompaniment to her soft alto voice. The pipe became longer with every verse as the metal was forced through smaller and smaller holes. Again and again, she played the pipe as her face started dripping sweat and the material of her grey gloves became saturated with the same.

At last, she reached the encore. Reheating the tube one last time, she picked up the mandrel and curved the, now long and thin, pipe around it as quickly and easily as if it had been made of wax. She lovingly crafted a spiral with three full turns before turning the pipe around, repeating the pattern exactly. The result was nothing less than a stunning piece of art.

Carmen laid her creation down on a metal sheet tray to cool and blew sweat off her nose. She sighed in satisfaction and leaned back in her chair. The outside world filtered back in, and she noted Rebecca staring at her. "Yes?"

"Nothing," Rebecca said as a pink tinge appeared in her cheeks. She quickly bent over her embroidery, but Carmen noticed she hadn't even completed one new stitch.

Caroline rose and tried to hand Carmen a glass of water, but she refused, explaining she needed to take off her gloves first. Unhooking the chains of the outer pair gave her momentary trouble, but soon the metal *clinked* merrily as it was laid on the sheet tray next to the piping. Gently peeling off the fabric gloves, Carmen turned them inside out and left them to dry.

"Now I would love that drink," she said as she untied the apron. "Don't touch anything," she added to the room as an afterthought. "It'll be hot for some time."

"Your voice is as lovely as ever," Caroline complimented her while she drank.

Carmen smiled. "My children know not to come barreling into my workspace when I'm singing. It was the easiest way to avoid burns to little fingers."

Fifteen

"It's easy to find a routine in all this," Rebecca thought as she headed to Caroline's place again after a morning shift at the chocolate shop. Her heart rate kicked up slightly as she passed the spot where Kane had yelled at her, but she refused to pick up her *pace*. Because she kept her pace slow and even, she was able to distinguish a single wolf track in the dust.

She felt satisfied that she had completed Carmen's embroidery challenge, staying up until 2:30 a.m. notwithstanding, and grudgingly admitted that all the lessons were mentally stimulating. They had moved on to blended color theory now that she had a grasp on the basics. Caroline had added in practical elements too. She was distracted and couldn't help thinking: *Where is the wolf now?* Still, seeing the paw print was comforting and exciting at the same time.

Thoughtfully looking down the street and to the scenery outside Canyon Town, it took a moment for Rebecca to register what she was seeing. Her embroidery landed in the dust as she took off sprinting toward the dark-haired figure desperately running in from a distance.

"Derek!" she yelled once she was close enough, "What happened?"

He was gasping for breath, mouth open like a fish, and clutching something to his ribs with one arm as he ran. Sweat poured down his face into his wild eyes and dripped off the ends of his hair. "It's Gegan," he managed, reaching forward desperately with one bloodied hand. "Needs help."

She wrapped one arm around him and helped him stumble the last few feet into Caroline's shop. Both the sisters were downstairs chatting but fell silent as they entered.

"Gegan needs help," Derek cried before doubling over and trying to get his breath back.

"Where?" Caroline said business-like.

"How?" Carmen asked.

"Red rocks…four miles out…leopard demon." Derek managed between heaving breaths. "He's injured."

Before he got the final words out, Caroline was moving. She retrieved her worn leather satchel from behind the counter and made for the door. "Look after him, Sister," she called over her shoulder. "Rebecca, let's go."

They hurried out the door and were quickly eating up the ground with long strides. Rebecca soon pulled ahead but paused until Caroline shouted at her not to wait. She ran and kept running even when her legs started to burn. Keeping her mouth wide open and her arms pumping, Rebecca sped up. Her mind was a haze; *the leopard demon must be something terrible.* The thought swam up to the surface of her mind. Then she wondered what would become of the person the demon was attached to.

She was flagging badly, her black hair sticking to her forehead and neck, when she saw the red rocks off to the side of the road. Clearly, a struggle had happened on the road because there were scuff marks and a fine spatter of blood droplets dried in the dust. Off to the side, she saw where someone had fallen and clawed their way to their feet, leaving bloody furrows in the dirt. She looked all around but could see neither Gegan nor the demon.

Rebecca wiped the sweat off her face and ripped two hairs off her head. Then, winding them around the fingers of her right hand in a familiar intricate fashion, she spread her fingers wide and formed a small window through the black strands.

Caroline came huffing up as she held the window over some of the blood on the road and locked onto the aura signature. Rebecca held her hands up to her face, her eye staring through the small window created by the hair wound around her fingers and searched. "There!" she yelled, clenching her fist and gesturing off toward the rocks. "Gegan's over there!" Caroline didn't question her, and a fresh wave of adrenaline seemed to give Rebecca wings as she tore off toward the tower of red rocks.

There he was—off in the distance. Gegan stood with his back to a blood-red boulder. His monk's robes were shredded across one arm and shoulder, and one side of his trousers stuck to his leg with blood. He brandished his hands as though wielding some kind of weapon, but she couldn't see what.

The leopard demon stalked back and forth across from him on all fours. Rebecca could see it was waiting for its prey to weaken before it would finish the job. It limped slightly from a deep puncture wound to one of its legs, and it broke rhythm to glance at her. Clearly dismissing her for the moment, the demon turned its attention back to Gegan and rose on two legs to attack.

"It's not attached to a person," Rebecca thought, her hands automatically going to the braided belt about her waist. A fierce smile split her face as she flicked away the tracking window to free her fingers. Unhooking the belt on the run, Rebecca attached one end to her bracelet in a move practiced thousands of times. As she approached the fight, she saw Gegan's eyes widen as he recognized her.

Rebecca skidded in the dirt a mere few yards from the leopard demon and let the belt fly as if it were a whip. The braided strand came loose, and the belt tripled in length as the tip struck the demon on the shoulder. It let loose a high keening wail right on the edge of hearing as a circular chunk of its shoulder and upper torso turned to dust.

Gegan let out a roar and lunged to distract the demon as it turned to face this new threat. Rebecca continued forward, gripping the belt in both hands as she leaped up and looped it around the demon's neck as if trying to garrot it. She drew her knees up to her chest, so they rested on the demon's back, squeezed her elbows into her ribcage, and set every muscle in her body into pulling the demon over backward by the throat.

It tried to claw at her with its good arm as the other flopped uselessly, only held to its body by scraps of flesh and tendon. She ducked her head down and looking through the hole she blew in its body, Rebecca saw the demon shudder as Gegan thrust a small reverse dagger up under its rib cage. It wailed again and swiped at him clumsily. Gegan avoided the blow and thrust the blade up past the hilt, burying his hand inside the demon's torso and, finally, dealing a fatal blow.

The demon turned to dust, covering them both, and Rebecca dropped hard to the ground. All the breath was knocked out of her as she lay gasping. Gegan sank to his knees next to her, still clutching his blade. She noticed a small crossbow bolt lying nearby but didn't register the significance.

Caroline was between them then. Skidding slightly in the dust, she dropped to her knees and clawed a hairpin out of her hair. Several strands of dark red hair came out with the pin. Rapidly, she pricked her finger and traced the blood down the scars on the inside of her middle finger. She waved her hand across her face to activate her enhanced vision and felt her stomach roll. "Vomit later," she told herself, turning her gaze to Gegan. "Work now; vomit later."

He did not look well. The gouges across his leg were leaking white pus as red streaks inched across his flesh. The infection to his aura extended up past his hips. Although his monk's robes and tatted charms had protected his arm and shoulder better, they were still marred with long, angry, shallow cuts.

Caroline flexed her fingers once in pure anxiety, then got to work. Her satchel had been designed to lie flat once opened, and on instinct, her hands drew out the white, silver, and purple thread needed to fight the infection. She selected one of her biggest steel pins and focused, making a charm to halt the infection.

With difficulty, she turned Gegan onto his back and drove the charm into the hard flesh of his stomach. His dark skin was flushed and poured sweat as his body valiantly tried to fight off the demonic influence. Caroline flawlessly made a second charm and placed it at the top of his unmarred leg. The infection slowed as she looked at her supplies. She couldn't place more than three charms on his body without causing side effects, but the infection had set into his system, and one more charm wouldn't be enough.

Selecting the littlest vial of purification potion she had, Caroline unscrewed the stopper, poured it into a small, wide-mouthed, copper bowl and set it aside. Next, she opened a packet of fine silver needles and dropped them into the little bowl holding the potion. Ignoring her roiling stomach, Caroline took a deep breath and selected a wet needle. With delicate accuracy, she placed it erect on Gegan's stomach. Next, she patted it into his skin using her index finger. She repeated the process, working her way up to his chest.

He sighed as the treatment began to work, and Caroline felt her shoulders unclench slightly. She worked her way through all the needles until Gegan's torso sparkled slightly in a webwork of purified silver. He sighed as the fevered flush faded from his face, but the fight was far from over. She had stopped the infection from growing but still needed to purge it from his system. She reached for another needle, but her fingers scraped the bottom of the bowl. She bit her lip and said, "This will hurt. I'm sorry."

Even as she spoke, her hands delved into the satchel and retrieved a strange hand tool. It had a central grip offset by two long silver-inlaid copper spikes, each the length of her middle finger, that tapered into wicked points. She dipped her fingers into the potion remaining in the bowl and took a deep breath to stop her hands from shaking.

Using a swift, decisive motion, she pierced Gegan's skin with one of the hand tool's spikes and dripped some purification potion into the wound.

Quickly wiping the blood off the spike, she repeated the process. Finally, the infection began to recede. Using her last large, steel needle, Caroline made a third full charm and drove it into the side of his neck.

The stress and the overstimulation overcame her then, and she turned away from him and puked. Heaving sobs wracked her for several seconds before she blinked back the tears and turned back to Gegan. His powerful aura was fighting back, and the demonic infection was receding. Reaching to her bag, Caroline pulled out her last two flasks of purification potions. She poured both out onto his injured leg then sat back as the world turned to a kaleidoscope, and she had to let her enhanced vision go. She gagged and heaved a few times as her sight faded to dull greys and blues.

Wishing she had something to rinse out her mouth, Caroline sighed and turned to Rebecca. "Are you all right?" Then she grinned and added, "That throw with the belt was amazing." Rebecca just stared, frozen. Concerned, Caroline looked back to Gegan. His color had noticeably improved, so she relaxed again. "What?" she asked Rebecca as she continued to stare.

Gegan cleared his throat, and they both jumped. "Lie still," Caroline implored. "You need more time."

"As you desire," he whispered and closed his eyes. "Wrap up my dagger without cleaning it?"

"What do we do?" Rebecca finally found her voice as Caroline ripped a strip of fabric off her shirt and wound it around the hilt and blade.

"Let him rest for now," Caroline decided. "Then we help him back."

Gegan recovered enough after a brief rest that Caroline felt comfortable removing her needles and charms. She winced slightly at the series of small puncture wounds, but Gegan assured her he would rather have those than the alternative. He struggled to his feet and wavered slightly.

"What happened?" Rebecca asked as she squirmed underneath one of his arms and draped it about her shoulders. Caroline adjusted her satchel, ensured the dagger was secure in one of the empty pockets and did the same on his other side.

"We were walking along and chatting," Gegan began. He took a deep breath, leaned on them heavily, and began limping slowly forward. "I had out my thread and shuttle and was tatting, so my hands were entangled. I sensed the demon coming and thrust my elbow into Derek's back to get him out of the way. In my haste, I sent him sprawling.

The demon launched itself at me and clawed my arm and shoulder as I dodged. Somewhere in that time, my hands freed themselves of my tatting, and I began to fight back." He gave his good shoulder a minor shrug, and Rebecca wobbled slightly underneath it. "That shuttle was a gift from a good friend. I am sorry to see it lost."

Caroline gently patted his other arm below the wounds and said, "Consider us good friends, and we will find you a new one."

Gegan smiled and continued his story. "I yelled for Derek to take the journals and run. He obeyed my orders. I take it he sent you to me?"

Both Rebecca and Caroline confirmed it, telling Gegan how panicked Derek had been.

"Did he have the journals?" Gegan asked. "Those were the entire reason for our trip."

Unembarrassed, Caroline admitted they had not stopped to check.

Gegan's laugh rumbled from deep in his chest. "Priorities."

It was late afternoon by the time they got back to the shop. Caroline and Rebecca were staggering slightly from the efforts of the afternoon, and Gegan was trying his best not to lean on them. They crashed through the door and barely made it to chairs around a handsome dark wood table.

Derek hurried down the stairs and sagged with relief when he saw them. "Carmen is working," he said to the room at large. "She said that she is in no state to go haring around the desert, but she could not endure sitting idly by. So she's got a small plate and is carefully punching holes into it. She'll call out when she's done."

"We're just going to rest here," Caroline told him, laying her head down on the table. "No need to disturb her."

"They told me of your flight," Gegan said. "Your speed helped save my life."

A muted pink blush snaked up Derek's neck as he shuffled his feet. "I was glad to help," he finally muttered. "It's nice to have people."

Caroline raised her head and stared at the young man. "Do you not usually?" she asked.

He sighed and rubbed one hand across the back of his neck. They noticed his fingertips were bandaged. However, his internal debate was cut short when Rebecca nudged a chair toward him in a silent invitation to join them. Derek took the seat next to her, gathered his thoughts, and sighed.

"I grew up here in Canyon Town, but my mother was not a pleasant woman. She was the one all the neighbors talked about behind their hands. I was the one treated to all the looks of pity. They didn't want their children to play with me because my mother screamed and yelled at them when they passed by our house. Those children are adults now. They are starting lives and families of their own, but they still avoid me.

"The exception was always Kane. He lived across the street from me, and we would sneak out together." His face brightened but fell almost immediately. "Now that the anger demon controls him, there isn't anything here for me."

Rebecca laid one hand across his wrist and slumped over in exhaustion.

The silence was broken a short while later as Carmen called down the stairs for them. They trooped up to Caroline's nearly empty living room and found her assembling a meal out of leftover ingredients. Deftly chopping up some onions, she tossed them into a pan heating on the stove, and began adding garlic and spices. Diced potatoes and more vegetables followed before she cracked a series of eggs directly into the pan. Within minutes, they were all sitting on the floor eating the makeshift breakfast scramble.

"This is amazing," Derek said, scarfing down enormous bites.

Carmen laughed. "The secret is sprinting for your life." Caroline joined her, and together, they laughed and said, "That's the best spice of all."

"Papa said that every meal after days like today," Caroline explained, still smiling. "He said it didn't matter what mama cooked because he was happy to eat it as it contained the best seasoning of all."

Rebecca was silent, trying to absorb what had happened: seeing the wolf paw print, the mad dash to save Gegan, the fight, and what came after. Her eyes drifted to Caroline, and she admitted to herself that a grudging level of respect for the woman was building. Watching Caroline in action was a revelation to Rebecca. She was astonished at the level of skill and the array of talents Caroline possessed and had to integrate this new awareness.

"We are done!" Trish crowed as they stoppered the final bottle of infused juniper oil.

Micah sat back with a sigh of relief and fitted the bottle in with its fellows. "It's nearly dinnertime," he said. "Let's head back in the morning."

Trish agreed, and they rummaged in their nearly depleted stores for something to eat. Eventually, they settled for two of the remaining cookies. Again, Micah admitted that they were delicious, and Trish repeated her promise to get him the recipe once they returned to Canyon Town.

A soft, fluttering sensation against his face roused Micah from sleep. He blinked his eyes open and stared directly into a pair of bulbous, milky orbs. He gasped and flinched. The reaction woke Trish, and she peered out from her sleeping bag next to him.

The demon flew up and divebombed the ground with a *fwump*. Its mouth opened, and *she* appeared again. The Mistress of hell looked far worse for wear. A faint purple bruise marred one high cheekbone, and her eyes blazed beneath disheveled hair. A small portion of her skirt looked burned and caked in oozing blood. She gestured imperiously for Micah to rise, and he saw two of the fingers on her left hand were bound together as though broken.

"My darling," the Mistress drawled, "you look worse every time I see you."

Micah fingered his unshaven chin but said nothing.

From her sleeping bag, Trish gave a small, stifled cough. The Mistress immediately turned her attention to the noise. Speculatively, she turned her narrowed eyes back to Micah. "She doesn't perceive me, does she?"

"No, Mistress," Micah ground out, unable to stay silent.

The demon tapped her two seemingly broken fingers on her full, red lips. Then, she smiled, "Your signature is all over her." Micah felt his blood chill in his veins as she snapped the fingers on her other hand. Trish let out a cry of pain, and her eyes darted around in fear before latching onto the Mistress. She whimpered and scrambled up behind Micah.

The Mistress ignored Trish entirely. "Whatever your timetable is, accelerate it," she told Micah.

"Why?" he asked, highly apprehensive.

"The Baron discovered your involvement. So he is coming and bringing all his legions."

Micah stared at her for several long, terror-inducing seconds. "What could he possibly fear from me?" he finally asked.

"Darling," the Mistress cooed. "Exactly what you are, always shines through." Her image vanished as she blew him a kiss.

Micah unclenched his fists and noticed how white his knuckles were. His short nails had left indents across his palms.

"What do we do?" Trish asked fearfully as Micah began heaping dirt over their firepit.

"We leave," he told her briskly. "Soon as possible. Start packing."

It took little more than fifteen minutes to pack up their camp. The moon shone down with just enough light for them to see what they were doing, and they weren't concerned with anything other than speed. Once he had sufficiently smothered the campfire, Micah rolled up the sleeping bags and strapped them to the top of the ritual accouterments box. Trish gathered up her cooking gear, refilled their water stores, and ensured they were leaving nothing behind.

"Lead the way," Micah told her once they were ready.

Trish nervously munched on a cookie as she started walking. Micah simply shook his head when she offered him the last one and started trudging.

"Do you want to talk about it?" she asked shyly after several, long, silent minutes.

"No."

Part of Micah did want to talk about it, but that part could only scream and wail inside his mind. He could not force his mouth to say the words. Instead, he sank further into himself and his whirling thoughts.

"What's left to do?" Rebecca yawned. She'd **been** awake into the early morning hours again, replacing the charms on her belt. The tiny, silver symbols on the leather could only be used once. So after every fight, she had to cut off the last two inches of the belt. Then, she painstakingly scraped out new indents for the silver solution, pouring in the solution practically drop by drop and waiting for it to set.

Between their follow-up care for Gegan, recovery from the four-mile run, and return, explaining and dealing with the subtleties of an emulsion plate, the group hadn't had the time to discuss anything else the day before.

Caroline didn't hear Rebecca's words as she sat engrossed by the belt. "This is exquisite," she said instead of answering. Rebecca had adjusted the braiding and returned the belt to its usual shape. "How did you make this? Can I see the bracelet?"

"Sure," Rebecca said, resigned that she wouldn't get any new information until Caroline finished her examination.

"Look at this," Caroline said, showing the bracelet to her sister. "See the way the silver supplements the steel wire to increase the overall power. The lapis lazuli gemstone is masterful. It provides as much protection as is possible from such a small gem." She returned the bracelet to Rebecca and asked, "How did you make that?"

"It was a gift from Bella," Rebecca said.

"And the belt?"

"I found plans for it in one of Bella's books. Now can you please tell me what we are waiting for?"

Caroline broke off her questioning to gesture to her sister. "The field is hers for now."

Carmen was humming softly as she warmed the misshapen sphere that held the wax sculpture over the stove. The slurry had set, and now it was time to remove the wax and begin the next phase. Turning the sphere, she caught the melted wax on a metal sheet tray as it ran out of the mold.

"More waiting and watching," Rebecca groaned. She rubbed a hand across her tired eyes and walked over to rest on some pillows in the corner. Before long, Carmen's soothing voice lulled her off to sleep.

Caroline retrieved a blanket from her room, careful not to disturb Gegan as he rested on her bed and draped it across Rebecca's lap.

"Is Gegan still asleep in there?" Carmen asked.

Caroline nodded. "Need some help?"

"Just hold this steady for me." Carmen held up the warm sphere. Caroline did as directed and watched as Carmen waddled over to her trunk. Raising the lid, she removed a medium-sized pitcher tightly capped with a cork and sealed with wax, then returned to Caroline's side.

"This is my last bottle," Carmen whispered as she broke the seal. Several etched charms flared brightly across the glass as she removed the cork. Shimmering heat waves rose from the top of the pitcher as she carefully began pouring the contents into a small hole in the top of the sphere.

The molten mixture of copper and silver hissed and gurgled while winding its way into the cracks and crevices left in the hardened slurry by the melted wax. Gingerly, Carmen took the sphere and began rotating it around. Careful that none of the hot metal leaked out, she ensured it traced its way through the entire pattern she'd created. "Now," she said smiling as she copied Rebecca's words from earlier, "We wait and watch." She paused a beat before adding, "And eat curry. Is there any left?"

After consuming two bowls of leftover curry spooned over rice and vegetables, Carmen sat down and rested against the wall with a sigh, then she jumped slightly and smiled. "Little one says thank you for the food, but a full stomach cramps his style. So now, he's kicking it back into place."

Caroline chuckled and looked down at her sister while she leaned on the counter. "We've…I've asked a lot of you, Sister. Thank you for doing this."

Carmen struggled to her feet and gave Caroline an intense, sincere look. "Do you remember when I was a teenager, and that psychedelic fear demon got to me?"

"I do."

Caroline had been traveling home over twenty years ago to visit her family during a school break when she'd received word that her sister had not arrived on schedule. Their mother had contacted her in a state of near hysteria and begged Caroline to find her. Using every scrap of skill she possessed then, Caroline had designed a scrying web. It gave her a direction for everyone who shared her blood.

Unfortunately, she didn't entirely remember what she'd done in her panic and had never been able to replicate the web. It showed most of her family was heading toward their hometown, but one signature was off hidden in the surrounding forest. Caroline had raced there, grateful at twenty-five to be in the best shape of her life.

She found Carmen cowering beneath some thickly boughed pine trees. She was hyperventilating, crying silently, and shaking too hard to stand. Menacing her was a powerful demon of fear. It had three horns jutting out at strange angles from its leonine head. Six multijointed legs propelled it sideways as it tried to get closer to Carmen, but it was its coloring that nearly took her breath away. Blues, vivid purples, sickly greens, and ugly yellows banded its large body.

Without hesitation, Caroline charged the demon. It reared and lashed out with one of its front legs. The dominant claw caught Caroline on her neck and scored a wound down to the top of her breast. She grabbed the other front leg as the demon swung it toward her face and bent it sideways, dislocating two of the joints with a *snap crunch*. The demon roiled in rage and twisted its neck at an impossible angle, trying to bite her wrist. Caroline dropped its now useless front leg and leaped away. Her feet tripped on some pine roots, and she fell over backward.

The breath was knocked from her body, but she managed to bring her knees into her chest, anticipating the demon's lunge. It came at her, and she lashed out, running on pure adrenaline. Both feet connected with the demon's body and launched it away through the trees. Gasping,

Caroline managed to roll over and started crawling toward her sister.

"Carmen!" No response. Caroline got right in her face, "SISTER!"

That snapped Carmen out of her fear—then she saw the gash on Caroline's neck. She found the single bottle of purification potion Caroline had on hand and dumped it on the wound.

Clutching each other and weaving, they left the area as fast as they could manage.

"Why bring that up?" Caroline asked, coming out of her reverie.

"You were there, Sister," Carmen answered. "When I was afraid, you were there. You asked for my help this time, so I am here."

Tears sprang to Caroline's eyes, and she hugged her sister tight. "Family is more than blood," she said.

"There's Canyon Town," Trish said wearily. They'd walked the remainder of the night, and rays of sunlight were heading west toward the desert floor.

"Thanks," Micah acknowledged before sinking back into his thoughts. Being back in town meant he would see Caroline again. He was still sorting out how he felt about that. Deep down, past conscious thought and past his recent anger, he wanted to see her. He missed her touch and her voice. He missed the ease that came with being in her presence, but he was still angry. She had no right to demand he show his body to other people and no right to use him to prove a point.

A flicker of red caught his eye, and he noticed the distinctive antennae of an anger demon peeking out from behind a stone. It was a small demon, so he ignored it and kept walking past the bakery and down the road. The anger demon perked up as he passed it, and he noted the exact moment it realized who he was. It swiveled its insectoid head back and forth a few times, then left cover and began following him.

Micah was completely shocked; he nearly fell over his own feet. But when the demon made its lunge for him, he snagged it by the antenna and broke its neck. Trish looked over at him with an anxious look. "Did you see that?" he asked.

She nodded. "Kane's…" she gulped and gathered herself. "Kane's demon was a larger version. Am … am I always going to see them now?"

"I think so." Micah grimaced and felt as though twenty pounds descended onto his shoulders. "I'm so sorry. The Mistress only did that to you because you were with me."

Trish licked her lips and looked around anxiously. "Will you help me?"

"Caroline will. She's much better than I am."

"Promise?"

Sighing, Micah nodded. In the silence, his thoughts returned to his friend. The attention from the demon made him realize that he had held on to his anger too long. *Anger can be righteous,* he thought, remembering something he'd learned back at school. *But only for a time.* He decided to let the anger go.

Sixteen

"Anyone here?"

Caroline jumped at the voice from downstairs and dropped her glass. It didn't shatter upon hitting the floor, but she ignored the water that cascaded across her floorboards as she flew down the stairs.

Rebecca squawked as the water drenched the pillows she was lying on, but Carmen just started searching drawers for a towel.

There he was. Tears sprang to Caroline's eyes as she saw Micah standing in her shop. He was dusty, weary, and still wearing that huge box across his shoulders. Days of grey-infused beard hid his jaw, but underneath it, she knew he was smiling. She rushed to him and tried to throw her arms around his shoulders, but the box was in the way. She settled for wrapping her arms around his waist and burying her head in his chest.

Stiffly but warmly, he returned the hug. "We found everything you need," he whispered.

Then he heaved an enormous sigh, and a colossal weight seemed to lift.

"Don't care right now," Caroline said, squeezing tighter. "I thought you would stay away from me."

He pressed a kiss to her temple. "I was twisted up, but I'll always come back to you."

Caroline hiccupped a small laugh and remembered what her mother used to tell her father. "Don't carry your burdens alone. If they don't break you, you will twist under their weight."

They broke apart, and Micah started unbuckling the straps that kept the box secured to his back. Trish helped Caroline catch it and carry it up the stairs.

Derek (who had swung by to check on Gegan), Rebecca, and Carmen all jumped up to greet Trish and Micah. Gegan even poked his head briefly out of the bedroom. Caroline and Carmen wasted no time in opening the heavy box and examining the contents. They carefully broke the charms on the inner box and noted how the twelve jars of juniper oil were sealed and contained crystal clear viscous fluid. They were ready for infusion.

"What is that?" Trish asked, pointing to the misshapen, dirty sphere that held the amulet shell. Carmen quickly explained and said she would clean out the hardened slurry as soon as possible to begin assembling the amulet.

"Why did we need so much juniper oil then?" Trish asked. "There's no way it'll take all twelve bottles to fill that up."

"Three bottles need to be filtered through the amulet piping in preparation and for scrubbing the shell," Carmen explained. "That will ensure everything is clean and purified."

"One bottle stays pure juniper oil, and seven others need to be infused with different herbs and plants," Caroline said, then took over. "I'll start that right away," she muttered and checked the ritual paperwork, which she carried in her pocket at all times. Satisfied with what she read, she began rummaging in her cupboards.

"You sure do have a lot of stuff," Rebecca said nonplussed. She'd never looked closely inside Caroline's cabinets. They were full to bursting with neatly labeled packets, jars, bottles, and bundles.

"But that is only eleven jars," Trish said simultaneously.

"Redundancy." The answer was meant to respond to both statements. She glowed with happiness as she worked, although it took some discipline to maintain her focus while assembling the plants she'd need on the counter. Fresh sage was easy to find in the Canyon Town area, and she had picked some only two days ago. Dried damiana leaves and pressed flowers gave off a slight, pleasant floral scent as she unstopped their bottle.

Lavender was an obvious choice for its amplifying effects, and she reached for the cupboard above the icebox, where she kept it out of the way when Micah was around. The orange peel gave the air a delicious citrus tang that mixed beautifully with the damiana flowers. Her stock of thyme was with her cooking herbs, and she quickly found it among the bottles on the other shelf. Cedar and pine shavings completed the list, and she removed packets of the fragrant-smelling wood.

"Can you listen while you work?" Micah asked seriously.

"For a few minutes, then I need silence to concentrate and measure," Caroline answered as she placed thyme into a mortar and picked up her small pestle.

Micah launched into the story of the midnight visit from the Mistress. Silence reigned once he finished. Everyone stood still and quiet, deep in thought until Gegan spoke. The others jumped as they hadn't heard him come out from the bedroom.

"You are on the right path, then." He coughed and cleared his throat. "Resistance would not be deemed this threatening otherwise."

"Resistance?" Micah scoffed. "I'm one man set against a demon powerful enough to defeat the Mistress and command legions."

"One man with friends," Caroline corrected. She'd put down her tools while Micah spoke and now placed a comforting hand on his shoulder.

Micah nodded and took a deep breath. "One man with friends," he repeated, covering her hand with his own and squeezing it.

"Soon to have another friend, if this goes well," Carmen added, meaning the ritual they were undertaking and the echo they were attempting to summon.

"Don't leave us out," Derek said. "We're in this to the end now."

"Both of us," Trish added.

There was confusion until Micah explained the Mistress had given Trish the ability to see demons permanently.

Caroline, Rebecca, and Carmen immediately stated they would take Trish under their wings and help her learn to stay safe.

"After all that heartfelt stuff, we need food," Carmen declared. There was a general rumble of laughter, and all agreed that food would be good.

Caroline looked at the group gathered, enjoying the meal together, and proceeded to explain how Rebecca had severely damaged the leopard demon. Derek, Trish, and Micah stared at Rebecca, making her uncomfortable.

"What?"

Micah finally found his voice. "Well done, Rebecca. I am so proud of you!"

Rebecca nodded and looked away, embarrassed.

The sleeping arrangements for that night took some figuring out. Trish didn't want to be alone at her house, so Derek offered her the couch in his tiny, one-bedroom apartment. He lived on the other side of the canyon above a tailor's shop and paid no rent in exchange for acting as a night guard for the owner. They left plied with charms to keep them safe overnight and promised to return the following day. Rebecca departed with them and headed for her own home.

All remaining agreed that Carmen should sleep in the bed. She objected: Gegan was still recovering, she'd had the bed since she arrived, and Micah needed the rest. Her objections were ignored as the rest unanimously voted that she get the bed. Caroline decided to share with her so Micah and Gegan could have enough space and bedding to be comfortable on her living room floor.

It was the middle of the night when Carmen woke up gasping slightly. Her unborn child was playing a game, twanging her floating rib back and forth. She grimaced and rubbed her side, and the baby kicked her hand. "Little munchkin," she murmured, tickling the area. The baby kicked out again, then turned over and settled. She tried to settle back down to sleep herself, but she remembered all the remaining steps to finish the amulet and how the ritual would be held up because of her.

Sighing, she heaved herself out of bed, glanced at her older sister's peaceful sleeping face, and headed out to the main room. Micah inhaled sharply when the bedroom door creaked open and sat up while his mind began the rapid climb to consciousness. Carmen gently shushed him, as she did her young children, and guided him to his feet.

"What is attacking?" he murmured, throwing off the last shreds of sleep and unsheathing one of his daggers. Carmen hadn't even noticed him grab the belt when he got up.

"Nothing," she said in her most soothing voice. "Come lay down in here." She knew Caroline wouldn't mind waking up next to Micah, and the man was exhausted. He followed her guidance without complaint and sprawled on Caroline's comfortable bed. His breathing evened back out as Carmen shut the door.

Gegan was sitting up and watching as she reentered the main room. "I can go downstairs if I'm disturbing you," she said quickly. "I can't sleep."

"Carry on," he said in his deep, calm voice. Then he stretched and said, "I can't sleep either."

Carmen turned on the lights and got everything ready but felt awkward with Gegan watching her. His eyes glittered as if feverish, and he fidgeted. "Do you have anything to do?" she asked.

"Sadly not. My shuttle was lost to the desert."

"What's that?"

He gestured for a pencil, and she passed him one with a piece of paper. Using sure, dark strokes, he outlined an oval device, pointed at both ends made from two flat pieces connected by a center cylinder. "I wind my thread around the cylinder in the center and use the shuttle to make lace," he explained.

"I've heard of that," Carmen said. "Tatting, right?" He nodded. "I'll need a warm-up," she decided. "To clear away the cobwebs of sleep. I'll make you one, so you don't just stare at me."

"I can leave," Gegan interjected.

"It's not that. I can tell you are tense just sitting there. Working with your hands is relaxing."

"That's why you're here working in the middle of the night?"

Carmen sighed. "Partly. I don't want to be the reason for any delay. Also, I'm afraid for Caroline. She has thrown in for this completely. I worry how much of her will be left after it's over." She didn't look at Gegan for an answer but bent to her work.

It took little time to create the shuttle. She had scraps of flat copper from cutting out the emulsion plate and needed to separate the two halves of the piping anyway. She quickly shaped the scraps into pointed ovals and cut an inch out from the middle of the piping. Next, she neatly bound the pieces together using some thin cord. Then, she used her tools to imprint a unique pattern in the top metal piece before handing the shuttle to Gegan. "The charm will help strengthen anything made on this."

He thanked her, rummaged around in his pockets, and produced a ball of ultra-fine grey thread. Then, he began winding it about the shuttle.

Carmen had just begun filing the end of the first pipe to prepare it when Gegan spoke. "I've spent much time around your sister over the past weeks—"

"Don't tell me Micah is worth it," Carmen interrupted.

"Walking away from this would break her heart," Gegan continued, ignoring the interruption.

"She's going to be broken regardless!" Carmen's voice was an anger-ridden, whispered hiss. No answer came, and she tugged on her apron, needlessly adjusting the fall of the fabric. The file made a soft *rasp* as she drew it across the top of the pipe. Her goal was to carve four slits into the metal. Then she would heat the copper and peel the pieces apart, like the petals of a flower. She would then draw the petals up and form a loose cup to hold one of the small glass spheres that would act as holding chambers for the liquids in the amulet.

She hummed barely audible soothing songs as she worked and tried not to think about what was going to happen. Both pipes were soon ready for their spheres, and she set them aside to cool. The spheres were not precisely circular as each had a flattened side with a small opening to allow them to be filled with liquids. The exquisitely made glass was etched so that it would break if any shock were applied. Cautiously, she removed the glass balls from their protective cloth coverings and ensured they were unbroken. She had only one spare and breathed a sigh of relief that both were fine.

The shell called to her next, and she set to with a stiff brush and pan of water. It made a terrible mess as the casing chipped away in clods and mud, but she knew they were going to clean the floors before they could begin anyway. So she just made sure to steer well clear of the row of glass jars with their herbs infusing in the juniper oil and tried not to cover any of the marks on the floor completely.

"Oh no!" Carmen said, staring as the soft, wetted cloth she'd been using to polish the amulet shell fluttered gently to the ground. The distraction made her realize dawn light was filtering in through the windows. She chanced a look at Gegan, but he had drifted off again, his new tatting shuttle clutched gently in his hands and his belongings within reach. Carmen whined quietly, then got to her feet. She started the awkward shuffle to try and reach down and grab the cloth but quickly gave up. Reaching the floor without resorting to hands and knees was beyond her.

Luckily, Caroline emerged from her bedroom shortly afterward. Seeing Carmen awake, she frowned and said tartly, "I do not appreciate you interfering in my love life."

"What? No," Carmen hurried to justify herself. "I wanted to work, and he needed the rest."

Caroline gave her a highly suspicious look but then noticed the cloth on the floor. Picking it up with an ease that made Carmen insanely jealous, she set it on the table and checked the infusing jars.

"These are coming along. Look how the pine one is starting to change color, and the orange peel is plumping up exactly like it is supposed to." Next, she checked on the small, purified water apparatus that stayed in its permanent spot in the corner of her countertop, started one batch heating, and began scrounging for breakfast. "I need to go shopping," she said absently. Then she noticed the mess on the floor and gave Carmen an exasperated look.

"Sorry," Carmen said sheepishly.

From his pallet on the floor, Gegan coughed and cleared his throat. "Caroline?" he asked. "It's time." He held out the wrapped dagger.

She froze, holding a carton of eggs halfway between the counter and the icebox. "Are you sure?" she swallowed and went pale. "You won't recover on your own?"

Gegan shook his head. "I know the difference."

Rebecca strode jauntily into the room, carrying a box that smelled like melted butter and citrus. "What's going on?" she asked, reading the room and quickly sobering.

"The leopard demon was too powerful," Caroline explained slowly. "We need to exorcise Gegan."

"Shouldn't the exorcist do that?" Rebecca asked, gesturing to Micah, who was standing in the bedroom doorway looking rumpled.

"Don't know how," Micah said and yawned. "I'm usually the one who needs the exorcism in this situation." He didn't mention he'd only had this done once, and it had failed. The infection of the Mistress was not to be exorcised completely until he paid his debt. Shaking his head to clear away the thought, he noticed Caroline biting her lip and agitatedly fidgeting with the eggs. "Are you okay?" he asked.

"No!" Caroline snapped. She took a deep breath and said, "I'm sorry. I haven't done this in years, and the last time didn't go so well."

"You're talking about our brother Jay, aren't you?" Carmen asked. "That wasn't your fault. His—"

"That was completely my fault!" Caroline interrupted. "And you know his knee never recovered."

"This is different," Carmen countered.

"How?"

Gesturing at the dagger Gegan still held extended, Carmen answered, "This time, you have the material you need. Last time…"

Caroline shook her violently. "Don't talk about it. I'll lose my nerve." She continued to look doubtful, but she accepted the dagger still wrapped in the piece of her shirt.

"How come you didn't need this…or did you?" Rebecca asked Micah to break the tension between the sisters. "The leopard demon injured you too, right?"

"I didn't kill it," Micah explained, pouring a glass of water. He drank half of it and added, "The demon dust got into the wounds it inflicted. Only exceptionally dangerous demons cause this kind of aftereffect. Most of the time, the dust that gets in the injuries is processed and purged by the person's aura."

While Micah was explaining, Caroline had repositioned Gegan. He now lay flat in the middle of the room with his hands clasped over his chest and legs outstretched. She pulled his robes aside to expose his injured shoulder and pulled up the leg of his pants past his knee. They all observed the angry scabs across his calf.

Caroline took a deep breath and activated her enhanced vision with the prick of a finger and some tracing, then checked his shoulder. "This looks fine," she said slowly. "At least it's only your leg." Gegan grunted in response. "What color do you use?" Caroline asked as she shook away her vision, rose, and walked to retrieve her extensive collection of thread and embroidery floss.

"Vivid turquoise."

Caroline selected three bundles of thread labeled turquoise, and Gegan indicated the one on the left. She began measuring off lengths and gestured for the others to choose a color. Micah chose his customary grey blue. He took a portion of the turquoise and some silvery grey Caroline handed him and began braiding the strands together. Carmen decided on a muted forest green and Rebecca, after some slight indecision, took dark crimson. They copied Micah and quickly produced three lengths of braid.

"Can we help?" Trish asked hesitantly.

Caroline smiled briefly and gestured them to stand to the side as she answered, "Thank you, but no. This ritual falls apart with too many participants, and this combination gives me the best chance of success."

"How so?" Trish asked as she and Derek moved to stand by the kitchen counter.

"I have a deep rapport and trust with Carmen and Micah," Caroline began as she collected the braids. "And Rebecca commands exceptional power. Someday, we will need you two, and I love that you want to, but that day has not yet come."

Seeing Trish and Derek were satisfied with that explanation, Caroline turned her focus back to the ritual at hand. "Choose your contributions," she said. She positioned Carmen, Micah, and Rebecca around Gegan and began laying out the braids. Each one formed a semicircle with the open end facing Gegan and the person who made it standing within. Around all of this, Caroline ran one unbroken, twisted length of turquoise thread.

"Contributions?" Rebecca whispered to Carmen while she watched Caroline work.

"Choose something imbued with your aura and power," Carmen told her, unhooking one of the glittering metal charms from her hair. She laid it down in the open space between herself and Gegan. Caroline adjusted the way it pointed as she passed by. "You are essentially giving him a piece of yourself to help boost his aura and drive out the effects of the demon. Don't worry," Carmen added as an afterthought. "It won't hurt your item."

Rebecca nodded and slipped off her bracelet. Her wrist felt bare without it, and she rubbed her fingers over the lighter patch of skin on her arm. Micah laid his long dagger on the ground with a faint *clatter* and turned the hilt toward Gegan.

Caroline checked her surroundings a second time out of anxiety and knelt by Gegan's side. "Ready?"

"Yes."

Hefting Gegan's dagger in slightly trembling fingers, Caroline unwrapped the fabric covering. The keen blade lay beneath a layer of dust created from the leopard demon. Carefully placing her fingers around the hilt, she began tracing a series of tiny hatch marks around the claw wounds in Gegan's leg with the tip of the blade.

Delicately, she lined up the marks to coincide with the contributions from Micah, Carmen, and Rebecca. The traces of dust on the dagger, mixed with the energy and support of their friends, attacked the infection in Gegan's aura. He gave a mighty sigh and drifted into a short nap as the battle was won and the exorcism completed.

Despite the success, Caroline seemed subdued as they cleaned up and prepared to eat the lemon pastries Rebecca had brought. Carmen couldn't enjoy her flaky, buttery deliciousness with her sister moping and finally confronted her.

"It was not your fault!" she said firmly. "I don't know if Jay ever told you, but his friend, one of the people who contributed something to the ritual last time, was a liar. He was desperately in love with Jay's wife and wanted the ritual to fail. His false contribution screwed everything up, and it was not your fault."

"Why didn't anyone ever tell me that?" Caroline asked, shocked.

"We only found out recently," Carmen answered. Saucily, she added, "And I tried to before, but you cut me off."

"Sorry," Caroline mumbled. "What happened?"

"Someone found a series of unsent love letters to Jay's wife in the man's home. I'm sure there was more to it, but tiny ears were listening when they told me. So, bringing the conversation back on track, it was not your fault."

Caroline processed this for several seconds, stunned at the news. Once she recovered, she grabbed a pastry and eagerly bit into it. "This pastry is delectable. Are there any more?"

"What do we do now?" Micah asked once everyone had licked their fingers and washed down the pastries with cold milk from the icebox.

"Gegan and Rebecca can help me," Carmen offered. She meant to say, "We need to unbind the journals from the Gegan echo and prepare the pages," but her mouth faltered on the "Gegan echo" part, and she said, "Gecko." Not realizing what she'd done, she continued, "I'll instruct them while I work with the final chamber in the amulet."

Everyone laughed at the mishap, and Carmen firmly blamed her pregnancy brain for the slip. Nevertheless, they decided to keep the Gecko nickname until the ritual was complete, and they could ask the Gegan's echo how he wanted to be addressed.

"Micah, you're with me, then," Caroline said after they laughed themselves out and regained their focus. "I need your help making the circle."

"Is that what those are for?" Micah asked, gesturing to the plethora of chalk marks strewn across the floor.

"I think we'll get out of your space," Derek said awkwardly as he and Trish shuffled around and failed to find a place to stand out of the way.

"Thank you, and I'm sorry the space isn't bigger," Caroline said. "We'll send someone to get you as soon as we finish with this."

They nodded and left.

"Yup, here we go." Caroline began preparing the floor for the following stage of the ritual. First, she addressed the dust and clumps of dirt courtesy of Carmen's amulet shell. Instead of properly sweeping it up and potentially erasing one of the chalk marks, she "dry swept" it to a corner and said darkly, "Your time will come." Next, she checked her notes and painstakingly measured the chalk marks against each other one last time.

Refocusing, she positioned Micah near the middle of the room and began playing out a ball of obnoxiously yellow yarn around him. She made one hourglass-shaped loop then paused to check a knot made in the yarn. "This is the innermost section of the spiral. When we do it for real, it'll be comprised of an eight-strand braid." Micah grimaced. "Oh, it gets better," Caroline said as she laid a second hourglass shape outside the first. "Seven-strand braid too, and it gets even better."

After ten minutes of adjusting and double-checking the knotted yarn, Micah found himself in the center of a connected eight-layer spiral. "Each layer is interconnected," Caroline explained. "We'll have to lay out the spiral as you go and watch you line it up with the marks on the floor." She took up the yarn and laid it out in long lines across the floor.

"Here we go," she said as she began measuring a ball of Micah's blue-grey thread against the yarn. "You start with a single strand for the outer layer, add a second strand of my color, and twist them together for the second. The third layer and on is braids adding alternating strands of your and my colors."

Micah managed a strained smile as he contemplated the floor. "Why the hourglass shape?"

"I stand in the other side at the climax of the ritual. When I'm done with my part, I'll place the amulet on the ground between us, and you need to pick it up. Once it enters your aura, assuming everything works, the Gecko will manifest a form beside to you."

"What kind of a form?"

Caroline shrugged. "It differs. The echo of the Gegan will merge with some kind of animal spirit and take its form. The animal varies depending on the personality of the echo and is there to stabilize the echo."

"Let's get started on these braids then," Micah said, making a vain attempt to sound excited.

"It's all you," Caroline said apologetically. "No one else can help."

"Really?"

"Really."

"I don't know how to do a five or a seven-strand braid," Micah complained. "And I have long since given up on six and eight-strand."

"We'll work it out," Caroline said encouragingly. "Get to that point first."

Micah gave her a look of exasperation, sighed, and sat down on the mark in the center of the ritual spiral.

Carmen surreptitiously kept an eye on Micah as Caroline measured and handed him lengthy cuttings of thread. Rebecca and Gegan needed little supervision to take apart the old journals, and she was a master of paying attention to multiple things. It was evident from the start that the bickering between her sister and Micah wasn't serious, and she tried not to laugh as she cleaned and polished the final chamber of the amulet with some of the juniper oil.

"Watch the tension on that twist," Caroline said. "We're only on layer two, and if you're having issues now, we're doomed."

"Expect doom then," came the muttered reply.

"What was that?"

"Nothing," Micah said airily. "Nothing at all."

Meanwhile, Rebecca and Gegan successfully unbound the journal pages and began tearing them into fine shreds.

Caroline scolded, "You double twisted that part. Take it out and try again."

"I did not!" Micah replied.

"You totally did. Even if you didn't, listen to me and do it again." Caroline pointed one finger at him.

"Four strand braids were never my forte," Micah grumbled a few minutes later.

Rebecca couldn't resist chiming in as she and Gegan filled the final amulet chamber with the scraps of paper from the journals. "Aren't four-strand braids pretty basic? Caroline told me so."

Micah glared at her, though the menace was offset by the upward curl on one side of his mouth. "I dispose of demons. I don't do complicated things like this."

"I told you advanced braiding would be important," Caroline said smugly.

"Erroneous on all charges!" Micah retorted. Everyone laughed.

"Fire," Carmen called out by habit as Rebecca held a small flame up to the paper crammed into the third amulet chamber. They needed the pages to be reduced to fine ash to mix correctly with the liquids coming into the chamber through the emulsion plate.

Micah jumped slightly at her voice, and Caroline groaned. "You disturbed it! Straighten out the curve behind you before you go on."

"So, I'm at the point where I need to transition to the five-strand plait," Micah announced as he tied the fifth thread, another blue-grey, into the braid.

"Okay," Caroline said patiently. "Here is what you do. Take the leftmost strand, number one, and pass it over strand two and under strand three. Strand one should now be in the middle."

"Counting from the left to the right?"

"Naturally. Okay, next, you'll take strand five and pass it over four and under one. Once you've got that down, just keep going. Always work from the outside in and alternate sides."

"This one isn't so bad," Micah said, relieved, as he continued plaiting.

"Odd numbers are always easier," Caroline said darkly.

Carmen used the moments of silence that followed to screw the ash-filled chamber for the amulet into the emulsion plate. Once it was secure, she fixed the piping systems in place on the inside of the shell and clicked the sides closed. The amulet was now ready. The shell was clean and smooth and extended to cover half of the glass spheres. She breathed a sigh of relief and felt slightly lightheaded with tension release as she turned her attention back to Micah and Caroline.

"I loathe six-strand braids," Micah said as he started that part over again.

"It's not beyond you," Caroline said soothingly.

"Just let me take a break. I don't want to do this anymore."

"Don't you dare drop that!" Caroline said. "You are committed at this point. Just follow my directions."

Micah whined again.

"You're going to do this," Caroline said sternly, hands on hips. "It's just a matter of how painful you make it for the room."

They went back and forth like that before Caroline grabbed the yellow yarn they'd used to measure everything out. She cut six pieces and snapped at Gegan to hold them still against the wall. He complied, and she walked Micah through the six-strand braid step-by-step for nearly fifteen minutes before he got the hang of it.

Carmen, Gegan, and Rebecca all had sandwiches during the seven-strand tutorial and were getting restless by the time Micah was ready to begin the final layer of the spiral.

"This is the last time I will say this," Caroline joked. "But I told you so! You should've learned this the first four times I tried to teach you, but you said you'd never need it."

Micah stuck his tongue out at her while he concentrated.

"Well, you need it now!" she cackled.

"Finally, done," Micah said as he placed the end of the eight-strand plait on the mark at his feet.

He straightened from his hunched-over position, stretched his back with a *crunch,* and looked around.

"Stay there!" Caroline hurried to say. "I told you, you are committed. Don't leave the spiral, or you'll have to start over again.

"Wait, what?" Micah looked forlornly at the sandwich Caroline was bolting down and said pitifully, "But I'm hungry."

Caroline stifled her laughter, nearly choked on her bite of food, and cleared her throat. "I just need a few minutes to fill the spheres in the amulet, and we'll begin."

"Why didn't you tell me this was it? I thought this was a trial run," Micah pouted.

"I didn't think the amulet would be ready," Caroline said around her last bite of sandwich. "I thought this would be a dry run."

Seventeen

Filling the first little sphere was easy. Caroline consulted the instructions and carefully measured off the amounts needed from the row of glass jars. After that, she gave the liquid a gentle swirl to mix the components properly. Next, Caroline gathered four white candles with silver-colored wicks in clear glass jars and matches. She took a deep breath and ignored the confusion on everyone's faces. (She could practically hear them wondering what the second sphere was for.)

After taking a moment to steady herself, she began to walk the spiral. In the space between the second and third layers, she started with the candles. Each one was aligned to a cardinal point and lit with a match. The energy in the room shifted when she lit the fourth candle, and the ritual was underway.

Once at the center of the spiral, she gave Micah's shoulder a quick squeeze and took her position. Holding the amulet firm in her left hand, she withdrew a small, shiny, silver knife from her pocket. No one else had laid eyes on this piece for the ritual, since she'd secreted it away that day the materials arrived with the couriers. A quick slash near her elbow tainted the metal with blood, and she shifted position to hold the empty sphere up to the dripping blood. Micah started violently, nearly disrupting the spiral, and Carmen turned her head away as the blood filled the small glass sphere.

Taking a shaky but determined breath, Caroline leaned down and sharply tapped the amulet on the ground between her and Micah. The gentle *tinkle* of breaking glass sounded. Everyone gasped as the temperature in the room rose fifteen degrees in the space of half as many seconds. The air seemed to shimmer before the sensation concentrated at the outside edge of the spiral and began moving inward. The candles flared brightly as the shimmering moved past them and around the channels between the braided thread.

Caroline knelt and placed the amulet on the ground at Micah's feet. Finally bringing herself to look into his face, she flinched. Micah was livid. Every muscle in his body was taut with rage, and his face was flushed a bright red. Teeth clenched, he glared down at her. For one painful moment, Caroline thought he wouldn't pick up the amulet. Bracing herself, she glared back with an expression that clearly said, "It's done. Don't waste it."

She could hear Micah's teeth grinding together as he bent and snatched up the amulet.

Then, the shimmering sensation around them burst and made the air opaque.

Several heart-wrenching seconds later, the air cleared, revealing Micah holding the amulet with a large four-legged creature at his side. Caroline exhaled and bent forward onto her hands. "We did it."

"WHAT WERE YOU THINKING?" Micah thundered.

"It's done!" Caroline said, rising to her feet and refusing to be intimidated.

"Why didn't you tell me?" Micah demanded. "And not right now!" he added in the direction of the animal at his feet.

"It. Is. Done," Caroline repeated and stalked out of the spiral. The door closed behind her as she left the apartment.

Micah collapsed to his knees in the middle of the spiral with a yell of impotent rage. Scraping his hands over his face, he took several deep breaths and managed to master himself, barely. The effort was only successful due to years of carefully handling his emotions. "What did you say?" he asked the creature, desperate for any distraction.

Rebecca looked around, confused, and whispered to Carmen. "It worked. Why is he so upset?"

"It was the blood," Carmen murmured back.

"And? I've seen blood used before," Rebecca countered. "You and Caroline both do that weird vision thing, and she cut Gegan when we exorcised him of the leopard demon."

"The blood left her aura," Carmen said, struggling to explain. "It was used on something else… Something, *not* Caroline."

"Yeah?"

Carmen sighed. "Ever seen that done before?"

"No," Rebecca answered, "but we've established my education was fairly specialized."

Biting her lip and tapping her belly in agitation, Carmen finally said it plainly. "Blood is the carrier for the soul. Caroline gave a piece of her soul to be the base for the Gecko." She expected a gasp of revelation, or maybe an exclamation of horror, but she was disappointed. Rebecca looked just as confused as before.

Gegan intervened, and Carmen sent him a grateful look. "Breaking the soul is a wound that never heals," he said gently. "Think of water flowing from an upturned cup. There is no way to return the water, nor is there a way to right the cup. Eventually, there is nothing left."

"What happens then?" Rebecca asked wide-eyed as the reality of Caroline's sacrifice settled in.

"Her heart will still beat, and she'll still breathe," Carmen whispered, tears forming in her eyes. "But everything that made Caroline self-aware and able to interact with the world will be gone. Like Gegan said, 'She'll be an empty cup.'"

"How long?" Micah rasped.

Carmen and Rebecca flinched. Turning to stare at Micah, they realized he'd been listening to their conversation.

"She wouldn't tell me," Carmen answered honestly. "But I don't think it's more than a few years."

Micah nodded shakily and let one hand rest on the creature the ritual had summoned. It chittered to him, and he smiled.

"What kind of animal is that?" Rebecca asked, finally taking a closer look. It was about the size of a large dog with grey and light brown fur over its back, leading to a pale-yellow underbelly and darkly furred legs. The paws were large for the animal's size with wicked-looking claws. Its head had a short muzzle covered in dark fur with pale stripes running over its eyes and up the center of its forehead.

"He's a badger," Micah answered.

"I thought badgers had white faces with black bands over the eyes," Rebecca said slowly. "This guy has almost the reverse."

The badger snorted delicately through its nose and barked several times.

"He says you are thinking of a different kind of badger," Micah interpreted. "That kind is more well-known because they live in large family groups. This kind," he gestured down at the animal, "is solitary and far more vicious."

The badger smiled.

"What do we call him, uh you?" Rebecca foundered and looked around helplessly.

The badger grunted. "Ricardo," Micah said. "He was a Gegan, but he wants to use his old name while he is here with us."

"A pleasure," Rebecca said. She knelt and held out one hand.

Ricardo sniffed her hand briefly, smiled, and raised one paw carefully. Rebecca clasped the claws gently. The badger stared up at her appraisingly with its black eyes, and he barked once.

"Passionate," Micah translated.

The badger strolled around a confused Rebecca and approached Carmen. He waved a paw when she tried to crouch down, and instead of shaking her hand, he sniffed her ankles and grunted.

"Loved," Micah said.

"Thank you, Ricardo," Carmen answered, understanding that the badger was giving them a gift with his words.

Ricardo acknowledged her with a bob of his striped head and swung his gaze to Gegan. Several seconds of silence followed as they sized each other up. Finally, Ricardo snorted.

"Becalmed," Micah said quietly.

Having made his rounds and his pronouncements, Ricardo began chittering away madly.

"Wait," Rebecca called. "What did you think of Micah?"

The badger bared its teeth and hissed.

Micah flushed slightly but didn't say anything. Rebecca and Carmen both had to cajole him into answering, "Fierce."

"Really?" Rebecca asked. "You seem too laid-back for that to be your defining characteristic."

Ricardo took issue with this and chittered at Rebecca while swinging his gaze back and forth between her and Micah. After several seconds he gave a short bark to emphasize his point and nodded his head sharply.

"He says," Micah translated, "that unrestrained violence is not the same thing as fierceness. Those who act the part, who doubt in themselves and turn all their energy into convincing others are prideful, deceptive, or delusional." Micah made a face and paused, but Ricardo barked at him. "He says that people like me do not need to prove what we are."

"Hey—you—sorry…," Rebecca tried again and addressed the badger directly. "You gathered all that from a glance?"

Micah translated the barks as, "Studying people was his interest in life, and he lived long enough to trust his instincts."

"And me?" came a quiet voice from the doorway. Everyone looked and saw Caroline framed there. Her expression gave nothing away as she knelt and proffered her hand to Ricardo. "Welcome," she said seriously. "Make this place your own."

Ricardo gave her hand a shake and grunted in Micah's direction. He started and said, "You can't be serious."

Ricardo growled at him, and Micah backed down. "Content," he said through gritted teeth. "He says you are content."

Rebecca broke the stewing tension by clapping her hands and saying, "Let's get this cleaned up so we can bring back in the furniture." She bent and gathered up several loops of the yarn spiral. When the sections crossed each other, the excess energy from the ritual reacted and engulfed the room in grey smoke.

"Eek! It singed me!" Rebecca said as she dropped the thread and started feeling her way to the door down to the shop.

"Open the window!" Carmen shouted.

"Why does the smoke smell like vanilla?"

"That's not vanilla. It's caramel sugar."

"Why didn't you tell me?" Micah asked quietly as he stroked Ricardo's broad head. The badger growled low and deep in his sleep, almost like a cat's purr as he lay sprawled on the arm of the couch.

Caroline sighed and looked around her refurnished living space—anywhere but at Micah. They were alone now that Gegan had informed Rebecca he needed her help to get groceries. Carmen was lying down in the bedroom. As she sat beside Micah, she idly missed her old couch. "What difference would it make?"

"Did you tell anyone?" Micah pressed.

"Only Carmen. She needed to know blood was the other liquid in the amulet." Caroline's eyes darted to the small pouch containing the item at Micah's belt. He shifted uncomfortably but stayed next to her.

"How long?"

Caroline hedged. "It's not an exact thing."

"Don't." Micah touched her chin and gently turned her head, looked directly into her eyes, and leaned in. "How long?"

"Five years, at most," Caroline relented and shook her chin free of his grip. "The amount of blood wasn't much, but the ritual pulled a large piece of my soul away."

Micah's other hand clenched briefly in Ricardo's rough fur. "And him?"

"A few weeks usually, but no one knows what will happen when you cross over into hell."

"We'll do that as soon as possible then," Micah decided. "That way, he'll be at his strongest, and maybe the Baron won't be quite ready for us."

Caroline closed her eyes against the tears that welled up. Her throat felt clogged, and she had to clear it before speaking again. "I know it has to be done." She felt his strong arm wrap around her shoulders, and it was enough for the tears to flow. "So, you'll leave again." She felt him tense and hurried to cut off any words. "It's okay."

"No, it's not—but..." he faltered and fell silent.

Caroline kindly slipped from his embrace, excusing herself to wash her face and take a private moment to calm down.

Micah sighed and looked down. He noticed then that Ricardo had woken up and was staring at him with his dark, intelligent eyes. "Sorry!" Micah quickly removed his hand from the badger's fur.

Ricardo stretched and yawned. "Do not apologize for seeking comfort through physical contact."

Micah could distinctly hear the barking noises issuing from the badger's throat, but he could also hear the words spoken in a calm man's voice. He didn't have a deep rumble like Gegan but possessed a pleasant, middle-toned voice with a rich accent. Accepting the comment, Micah changed the subject. "You did not seem surprised to be called back."

"Knowing I succeeded, I'm not. My order also took measures before I left for hell so that I might be of service again at a later date."

"Why you?"

"I might ask the same," Ricardo countered.

Micah cringed. "I owe the Mistress a favor. She has been deposed and demands I restore her position. Restarting the machinery is a tangent mission to repaying that favor. I have to do the first, but I *am* going to do both."

"I met the Mistress," Ricardo mused. "It was near the end, and I was so very cold, but I recall her laughing and saying she'd wanted something shiny of her own, but I was already too damaged, and I barely sparkled. It all gets pretty fuzzy after that."

"Shiny?" The word stirred a memory of Micah's time with the Mistress, and he said, "That's what she called *me*. Think it means anything?"

Ricardo chittered quietly. "Ask your witches."

Gegan limped into the living room through the door to the shop staircase, cutting off further conversation. Accompanying him, and each carrying some packages that emitted mouth-watering scents, were Rebecca, Derek, Trish, and surprisingly Nathaniel.

"We met these two in the market," Rebecca explained, gesturing to Trish and Derek. "Then we stopped at the chocolate shop so I could tell Elaine why I won't be coming in for a few days. Nathaniel overheard me and demanded to come with us."

"What did Elaine say to this?" Micah asked.

Rebecca sighed, "She cried, but she didn't tell him no."

Caroline and Carmen entered into the discussion by protesting immediately.

Nathaniel was not ready.

He wasn't trained.

He was too young.

He couldn't see the demons.

"I don't care!" Nathaniel shouted over them. "I'll stand at the back and hand you things; I'll carry the bags. I'll do anything."

Micah gestured for the sisters to fall silent and put his arm around Nathaniel's shoulders in a brotherly fashion. "Why do you really want to do this?" he asked. Then Micah noticed Nathaniel was wearing the small silver hoop earrings he had enchanted before leaving to get the juniper oil.

"I remember my father before he changed," Nathaniel said quietly, looking Micah straight in the eye. "My mom too. I don't need another reason."

"He is too young!" Carmen exclaimed again. "We don't know how bad this is going to be, and his mother—"

"How old were you the first time you followed your father into a situation like this?" Micah shot back.

Carmen flushed and held her hands protectively over her stomach. She'd been younger than Nathaniel and didn't want to admit it.

Micah nodded and forestalled any other arguments. "He comes. Caroline, do you have any more vials of potion that will allow him to see demons temporarily?"

Unhappily, Caroline nodded and started rummaging in her cupboards.

"This isn't going to be fun," Micah murmured to Nathaniel.

The young man nodded. "I know." His voice took on a rhythmic cadence as if he were speaking lines from a song or poem. "If to defend your heart's desire, you'll always march to war." He paused and added, "My mom's favorite poem."

"She is very wise," Micah said kindly. "She'll be proud of you. Now let's eat."

Ricardo walked up and eyed the newcomers as everyone turned their attention to unpacking the food. Micah translated his sharp barks directed at Derek and Trish as "Daring" and "Persevering," respectively. Analyzing Nathaniel took much longer. Micah watched as Ricardo circled the young man, sniffed his shoes, and looked him up and down before turning and emitting one sharp bark, "Shiny." The badger's lips peeled back from his teeth in a vicious-looking smile.

Micah started violently and upset his glass of water, "What?"

Ricardo chittered at him and raised one paw to point at him and then at Nathaniel. "If any of them make it through this, it'll probably be him. He is just like you. Give him time and training, and he might be even better."

Micah closed his eyes briefly and looked around to see everyone staring at him. "You'll be fine," he told Nathaniel.

Ricardo growled slightly. "Why didn't you tell them what I said?"

Micah waved a hand to indicate they would discuss it later.

"When are we doing this thing?" Nathaniel said into the awkward silence.

"Tomorrow," Caroline said as she put a stack of plates next to the piles of pastries, assorted fresh bread, cheeses, and chocolates. "We go down the canyon tomorrow." She retrieved some sliced meats and a mostly empty jar of pesto spread from the icebox.

"Making our way down the path will not be simple," Gegan said thoughtfully as he assembled a sandwich. "Particularly if we are contested."

"Take the steps," Derek mumbled around a mouth full of pastry.

"The what?" Gegan asked.

"The steps," Derek repeated and swallowed. He cleared his throat and said, "Trish knows more about them."

"Sure," Trish said, pausing in making her sandwich to take up the explanation. "The first people who lived in this region kept their homes here on top of the canyon. However, they needed water from the river down at the base. So, they carved steps into the canyon walls so they could climb up and down. The steps are still there if you know where to look."

"Why make a path if there are these steps?" Micah asked and popped a chocolate into his mouth.

"The steps are not for the faint of heart," Derek explained, brushing crumbs off his hands. "They are more like slight depressions in the rock than actual stairs. The first people made them just barely deep enough to avoid sliding down the canyon walls, and erosion has not helped. You feel like a spider clinging to the rocks."

"That sounds terrifying," Caroline said with a shudder.

"But it's fast," Derek countered.

After dinner, Rebecca was the first to stand. "I'm off," she said. "I want a good night's rest before tomorrow."

Carmen and Caroline looked at each other. "You're not leaving," Caroline said. "No one is."

"Why not?" Rebecca demanded. "I'm tired, and I want to go to bed."

"Haven't you noticed all the demon attention outside?" Carmen asked. "They have been congregating since you all arrived back with Gegan. And they know we're in here. Anyone who leaves becomes a target."

"Will they attack tonight?" Trish asked. She tried to hide her anxiety, but her hands shook, and her mouth filled with a sour taste.

Carmen and Caroline wavered long enough for everyone to become nervous before Caroline said, "We doubt it."

Rebecca shivered slightly but didn't argue. Caroline dug out every blanket she owned and pulled the cushions off some of the couches from the shop. She and Carmen took the bed, after being outvoted that Micah should take it as he needed the rest more than anyone. Everyone else settled down in the cramped living room.

Trish, being the shortest, curled up on the loveseat. Rebecca claimed the space between the coffee table and the corner by the door. Gegan and Derek sprawled in the central area after shoving the kitchen table and chairs into a corner while Nathaniel blocked the bedroom door and slept uneasily on his side. Micah lay next to the kitchen cabinets, listening to everyone's breath even out and the *drip plop* of Caroline's distilling potions.

Ricardo waddled over, stretched, and curled himself into a ball right next to Micah's head. "Why didn't you tell them?" he growled quietly, bringing up his words about Nathaniel.

"What were you doing when you were his age?" Micah whispered.

"I was halfway through an apprenticeship on being a carriage mechanic. Why?"

"I was sleeping on the streets and thinking I was crazy for seeing the demons," Micah said instead of answering. "Rebecca's parents had abandoned her. Gegan was training with the order, and Caroline was healing her family on battlefields. Which adolescence would you want?"

"I can see your point," Ricardo snorted.

"Nathaniel spends his days thinking up hot chocolate recipes. His mother loves him, and they survived together. I don't want him to think he needs to take up my mantle because his aura reads like mine." His point made; Micah changed the subject. "How did you end up a Gegan if you trained as a mechanic?"

"I was in the right place to prevent something," Ricardo chittered. "I was working late one night because of misfiled paperwork, and I heard a disturbance. One of my coworkers had snuck in and was attempting to sabotage a carriage. I learned later he was supposed to be the driver for someone on the Witches Council and had been overtaken by the demons. Never knew what kind.

"He tried to disconnect an overpressure release valve. Without that valve, the entire system would over-pressurize and catastrophically fail. No one would survive."

Ricardo paused and yelped quietly—a heartbreaking sound. "He was a friend, and he attacked me. I've been in my share of brawls, and that is the only reason I survived. He didn't. He just wouldn't stop coming at me." Ricardo paused for several seconds to collect himself.

"Anyway, the Witches Council learned what happened, and they sent me to the order to heal. It was weeks before I could walk without a limp and months before my head was on straight enough to be alone. I took their classes, learned their techniques, and eventually started seeing the demons on my own." He twitched his front paws. "They even made me armored gloves to wear. I was hopeless at all conventional weapons."

"Did you volunteer to go to hell?" Micah murmured.

"In a way. There was no one else with mechanical experience, and we didn't know what happened to the machinery before." Ricardo reflected for a moment. "It seems like the demons just stopped it this time. Nothing is actually broken?"

"That's my impression," Micah replied.

"In a way, that is even more troubling," Ricardo said. "The machinery came from *our* plane. The demons shouldn't be able to manipulate it."

"Really?" Micah said loudly. He flinched and checked to see everyone else was sleeping. Returning to a whisper, he said, "I never knew that."

"The order is one of the oldest," Ricardo said. "The knowledge accumulated there is beyond imagining."

"Has the Mistress ever been dethroned before? Has she ever called on a human for a favor like this?"

The badger shook his striped head. "If she had, the effects of the failure would've been long felt."

"That's harsh," Micah said. "Assuming we will fail."

Ricardo stared at him—mouth open in disbelief. "You have no idea what you are, do you?"

Micah stayed silent but raised one eyebrow.

"You stepped out of legend, Micah."

Eighteen

Dawn was just breaking over the desert in a wash of pink and gold when Micah woke up with a cry of pain. It felt as if someone passed a flame over the scar the Mistress had given him all those years ago. Everyone jumped out of their makeshift beds, and Caroline and Carmen threw open the door to the bedroom. Then, he heard her voice. From far away and said with great pain, the Mistress whispered, "We're here."

The statement was heard by all, save Nathaniel, and sparked an immediate frenzy of activity. Caroline, Carmen, and Rebecca conferred rapidly and decided to burnish a leftover metal plate from Carmen's trunk. Rebecca would use it to set up a scrying charm and see what was happening on the canyon floor. Gegan sank to his knees with a slight grunt of pain and entered a meditative state to refuel the charges on his armor. Trish and Derek explained to Nathaniel what happened as they stood awkwardly by the wall while Ricardo observed the scene.

Micah watched everyone around him in a slight haze, but his eyes lingered on Nathaniel. He thought back to the previous evening and Ricardo's pronouncement about the young man before shrugging off the thoughts and getting to work sharpening his daggers. Ricardo gave him a few pointers, and he broke off for a moment to shove a few judicious items in an old backpack.

"Come here," Carmen gestured to Trish as she and Caroline relinquished the plate to Rebecca. "I'll start with you." She had Derek drag a chair over to her trunk, and she settled herself down and began rummaging around the very bottom. "Here it is." She withdrew a clay pot from the trunk, covered in inscribed symbols and charms.

"Oh," Caroline said excitedly, "I can't wait to see what that looks like."

Carmen smiled and broke open the seal. The coil of wire she fished out sparkled in the dim light with multicolored flashes. "This will help keep your hands from getting infected while you are fighting," she explained. "My mom enchanted it decades ago, and it has been fermenting ever since."

Carmen took Trish's wrist and began weaving a web of wire across the back of her hand and around the bases of her fingers. "Listen, I know you don't have the training, but you will be fighting." Derek inched forward and hung on every word. "If in doubt of what to do," Carmen continued, winding the wire around Trish's wrist, "Go for the throat. Nails, knives, teeth, whatever you have left. If a demon gets close to you, go for the throat."

Trish paled slightly at this sinister advice and looked to Derek. He was about to answer when Carmen said, "Other hand."

"Derek, over here," Caroline called at the same time. She threw a black crocheted duster over his shoulders and studied the effect.

"Where did this come from?" he asked, fingering the soft yarn.

"I made it years ago," Caroline said distractedly. "I was up for an hour last night searching through my closet for it." She adjusted the lay of the duster, fastened the three Dorset buttons, and tied the belt with a complicated knot. "It's a bit shorter than it should be, but it'll still provide some protection for you."

"What about you?" Derek asked.

Caroline smiled and patted the younger man's shoulder. "I have enough charms sewn into my clothes that I don't need it. See?" She ran his hand up one black-clad arm, and he felt the raised bumps of black stitching. Her long sleeve-shirt, dark leather knee boots, layered short skirt, leggings, and light coat were all covered in similar patterns.

"Why did you stop using this?" Derek asked, gesturing to the duster.

"I didn't want it to wear out," Caroline explained. "It's too delicate for everyday wear."

"Could you make another?" he asked.

Caroline gave him an incredulous look. "It took me two years to make that. Never again. I switched to embroidery after that."

"That should do it," Carmen said as she finished braiding Trish's hair. "I've spun charms and protections through that plait. That is all I can do for you." For Derek, she quickly fashioned narrow bracelets from the remainder of the sparkling wire.

He gave her a smile of thanks and stepped to the side with Trish. She leaned on him and made extra focused attempts to keep her breathing steady.

"Rebecca, you're next," Carmen called. "Let me braid back that hair so it stays out of your face."

"Don't interrupt my scrying," Rebecca said from the corner where she was staring at the burnished plate. Carmen moved behind her and awkwardly bent down.

While her sister attacked Rebecca's mane of tangled back hair, Caroline examined her worn leather satchel. She'd been given the bag many years ago, and it had never let her down. First, she checked her stores of purification potions, topped up the bottles, added more white and grey thread, and tossed out two bent silver pins. Next, she retrieved a belt from her bedroom.

A series of sheaths marched across the wide leather straight as soldiers. Inside each was tucked a fragile, tempered glass vial. One by one, Caroline removed the vials, inspected each for dust or cracks, then filled them with purification potions from her stock. She started with the highest purity at her left hip and worked her way around until she ran out of vials.

Then, checking her remaining potion stocks while she braided her hair down on her left side, she calculated it would be months before she replaced everything. Satisfied, she reached for her final piece of equipment and drew a stiletto blade with a needlepoint from a slitted pocket behind the row of vials. It was as sharp as ever. She returned it to its pocket, and all that remained was to don the satchel and belt when they left.

Gegan was messing with the sleeve of his robes, still deep in thought, and Micah was working on his second blade when she looked up again.

Finally, Caroline turned her attention to Nathaniel. "Let's get you set."

"I don't have anything," Nathaniel said. His voice cracked, and he squirmed slightly in embarrassment.

"I bet one of Micah's shirts would fit you," Caroline mused. "We'd have to roll up the sleeves, though." She made another quick trip to the bedroom.

Gegan looked up from where he sat on the floor and attached a newly completed tatted strip of lace to the shoulder of his robes. "The shuttle you made me is fantastic," he remarked to Carmen.

"How are you all so calm?" Trish said. Her hands shook a little as they curled around each other in their skeletal wire gloves. "We're about to become targets."

"That's why we're taking these precautions," Micah said, sheathing his daggers and adjusting his belt. "Few people have gone to battle with the demons this well protected."

"We need to decide now what route to take," Caroline said. "Do we take the steps?"

"Bad idea," Rebecca said sharply. "Look at this." She grabbed a leftover piece of chalk and started drawing on the floor. "Here is the canyon and the portal." She drew two squiggly lines and a large X between them. "We are here." She used a Z to show their current location in reference to the portal. "This is the demon activity."

She scribbled all around the X inside the canyon walls. "There are two strong presences here near the portal," she drew two Ds. "The horde is moving toward us, but there are so many, they are clogging up the canyon." Sitting back after drawing arrows to express her point further, Rebecca wiped the sweat from her face. "If we take the steps, it will only take one demon attacking at the wrong moment for everything to be over."

"You can't go down the path," Carmen said. "You'll be overwhelmed."

"But not killed," Micah said. He crouched and tapped the Ds on Rebecca's map. "These must be the Baron and the Mistress. If he brought her, then he won't allow us to die at the hands of his horde."

"You can't know that," Rebecca argued.

"He brought the Mistress," Micah repeated. "He brought his vanquished enemy to see the final stage of his victory. He's going to face me directly because as long as I'm around, the Mistress has a chance."

"That doesn't mean you'll be fit for combat when his minions bring you down there," Caroline interjected. "Facing you directly and a fair fight are far, very far, from the same thing."

Micah acknowledged her point and fell silent. He sat back on his heels and let his eyes wander around the room as he thought. As his gaze fell on Nathaniel, who was now draped in one of his old shirts, the idea flashed, fully formed into his mind. "We use you," he said, pointing to the young man. "Ricardo and I go down the steps while the rest of you take Nathaniel down the path. The demons will focus on you, and they won't be looking for me."

Nathaniel blanched. "Why would they do that?"

"Micah, there is no way the demons will think Nathanial is you," Caroline said gently.

"You don't understand," Micah said. For a moment he looked to Ricardo to back him up, but then he remembered that no one else understood the badger. "Nathaniel is just like me."

"Really?" Asked Rebecca in a tone of pure skepticism. "No offense," she added to Nathaniel.

"Look at him," Micah said, staring hard at Caroline. "No, *really* look at him."

Caroline sighed and humored him by pricking her finger and activating her enhanced vision. As soon as her colorless eyes trained on Nathaniel, she gasped. "He is!"

"He's what?" Rebecca asked. Nathaniel seemed embarrassed into silence.

"It's just like yours," Caroline remarked to Micah. She could scarcely believe it. Here was another person with a two-layer aura. Additionally, the upper layer was the same glowing cage of energy. Caroline looked harder to try and see what was contained beneath the shimmering strands, but it was hidden. She shook off the enhanced vision and remembered that many people did not come into their own until they were older than Nathaniel was now.

Carmen stared at her sister in unbridled disbelief. "You can't be bringing that up right now."

"What?" Rebecca asked.

Ricardo chittered at Gegan, overriding the argument between the sisters, and Micah translated quickly. "He says you can explain about the shining auras."

Gegan obliged. "Supposedly, long before humans had the ability to perceive demons, the demons were opposed by beings with shining auras. So the demons acted as darkness to the other's light. But when the demons got too close to the shining beings, they were burned as moths to a flame."

"The darkness was drawn to the light but could not consume it," Caroline quoted.

"That is a myth!" Carmen shouted and raised shaking fists to her face. "Do not do this now. Do not plant myths and false tales in their heads. Right now, we need to do everything in our power, so you all come back out of that canyon."

"Just look at them," Caroline pleaded. "This could work."

Carmen closed her eyes and pressed her fingers to her forehead. "Then we drop this?"

Caroline nodded, and Carmen withdrew her metal stylus and activated her enhanced vision. She glanced between Micah and Nathaniel before grinding out, "It could work," from between clenched teeth.

"Switch shirts," Caroline demanded to Micah. "We need him to wear the one you usually do."

"I'm l-lost," Nathaniel stammered. He looked pale and a bit shaky, so Micah helped him sit on the loveseat.

Gegan immediately distracted Caroline and Carmen with a request for a brace for his wounded leg. Rebecca read the room and started explaining some finer points of demon-fighting to Trish and Derek as she adjusted her belt.

"Why are they saying I'm like you?" Nathaniel whispered as he pulled off the extra shirt draped about his shoulders.

Micah unsnapped his cufflinks as he thought about what to say. "If you decided this kind of life is the one you want," he waved at the room and started unbuttoning his shirt, "demons won't attack you like they do others. They can sense the kind of person you are. I'm the same kind."

"How do you know that?" Nathaniel held out the old shirt.

"It's obvious," Micah said with a small smile. "You kept your mom safe from the demons all this time."

"But my dad—"

"Was not your fault," Micah said, stripping out of his shirt and handing the warm material over.

Nathaniel gaped at Micah's thin, scarred torso, but the second shirt quickly covered it again. His strong hands rapidly did up the buttons and settled the fabric across his shoulders.

"Caroline," Micah called. "I need a silver chain and your kit." The room fell silent as he ripped a few hairs out and used them to bind a bracelet around Nathaniel's wrist.

"It won't be enough," Caroline said after looking Nathaniel up and down. "We need something completely imbued with your aura."

"Hammer," Micah said and held out a hand to Carmen.

Puzzled, she handed him a small jeweler's hammer from her trunk. Micah placed his compass on the table and, without hesitation, brought the hammer down on the first link in the chain. The solid steel held up to the blow, but the top of the watch casing was not so strong. It snapped under the blow, and a small gear rolled away and spun down to lay flat on the table.

Micah left the compass on the table and turned to Nathaniel. "This has rarely left my person in decades," he said quietly. "If anything will make them think you are me, it is this." He lifted Nathaniel's sleeve and saw that the young man's forearms were corded with muscle. Then he pushed Nathaniel's sleeve up higher, bound the chain just above his elbow, and faced the room.

Everyone was staring at the compass which had sprung open. The red arrow quivered facing the direction of the portal, the demon horde, the Baron, and the Mistress, but the silver arrow pointed directly at the pair of them.

"What's left?" Carmen asked finally, looking around at them all.

Micah buttoned his cuffs with the aura suppression Dorset cufflinks and settled his vest around his shoulders. He placed the compass in his pocket, and his hands faltered as they searched for the chain in a reflex action. He chuckled and reached for the bottle of purified water to activate the cufflinks. "Time to go."

Ricardo nodded, and Derek stepped forward. "I'll take you to the steps."

They turned toward the door, but Micah paused. He took a deep breath and faced Caroline. "Until next time, goodbye."

"Until then," she whispered.

They left without a word, exited the shop at a lope, and ran through the demons watching the shop without a backward glance.

Caroline took a slow deep breath, and her body shook as she released it. "It's time," she said and held out a small bottle to Nathaniel. "Drink this: you will see."

Nathaniel downed the liquid in one shot and shook his head like a dog with water in its ears. He stayed at the back as everyone filed down the stairs and out the door. Heads up and gazes forward, they started toward the path. The demons stiffened as the group passed them by, and several took off hurriedly for the canyon walls. The rest began to shadow the group at a distance.

"Are those what made my dad...?" Nathaniel trailed off as he watched one lime-green, cockroach-like demon flutter its wings.

"I don't know," Caroline answered truthfully. "I wasn't there, but from what Micah told me, the demon that got to your father was bigger, stronger, and far more vicious."

"When this is over, will you make it permanent?" Nathaniel asked. "I want to see them always."

Caroline started, and her skirt swished around her knees. "Why?"

"I'm never letting one of those things near my mom again."

At that moment, even without her enhanced vision, Caroline saw the resemblance between the young man before her and the older one racing away.

They reached the edge of the canyon, and Nathaniel leaned over to look down. He shuddered at the mass of roiling, swirling, creeping, wriggling technicolor climbing up the walls. "We're going into that?" The view and the surge of dread caused a wave of vertigo, and he backed up quickly.

"Indeed," Caroline said and turned onto the descending canyon path.

Gegan and Rebecca quickly passed her and took the lead. Trish, Nathaniel, and Derek tried to project the same confidence as they walked as a group in the center, and Caroline brought up the rear. Gegan began chanting in a low soothing rumble. His armor flickered into sight and glittered in the sunlight until they passed into the shadows of the canyon.

"What does that do?" Trish asked.

"It makes me feel better," Caroline said, thinking she meant the chanting. "What it does for him, I couldn't say."

They quickly dropped into the morning shadows of the deep canyon and kept their pace as hurried as possible. Within an hour, Caroline could make out characteristics of individual demons. Flailing limbs, flashing eyes, tails, claws, and teeth stood out in stark relief for a moment before being replaced by more of the same.

Rebecca lashed out with her whip-like belt and struck a demon attempting to dive into the group, and the battle was joined. An advance guard of the demons sprang up the walls and rushed sideways across the banded rock. Gegan defeated three with quick slashes from his small knife. One launched itself at Trish, and she threw up her arms. It collided with the charmed wire gloves and burst into dust.

Derek appeared out of nowhere, grabbed one, and wrenched its neck sideways. He flinched when it dissolved into dust in his hands but quickly regained his composure and said, "They're away."

A moment's clarity settled on Caroline, and she felt entirely at ease with her choices—from the moment Micah first stumbled through her door to the present battle. Had she had the chance, she would not change a single thing.

The next wave of demons swung high above them on the canyon walls and fell upon them. Gegan threw his hands up and roared. Then, a vast surge of energy rippled out from him and decimated the entire group. The dust sifting down on them coated everyone and added years to their faces.

The demons didn't pause. They clawed their way through the dust over the rocks and sprinted up the path with disturbing speed. Gegan expended another two double charges of energy, but they kept coming. Finally, his charges spent, he raised his knife and prepared for hand-to-hand.

They were surrounded. The waves of demons crested over them and crashed. One neon pink demon with extended claws raked Trish across the shoulder before Gegan dispatched it. Caroline grabbed one of her lower potency vials and smashed it over Trish's wound. She gasped at the cold liquid, and Caroline propelled her forward. "Keep going!"

Rebecca had doubled up her belt and was using it as a noose. Gegan was impaling the demons as fast as she caught them. Combined with kicks, vicious thrown elbows, and wrenching motions, they were clearing the path ahead.

Trish let out a wail and collapsed. An anxiety demon slipped through her defenses and curled its claws about her throat. Several other anxiety demons ganged up on her as she froze in fear. Their effects forced her to hyperventilate until she passed out. Caroline and Derek fought their way to her and scattered the demons. Derek caught the last one and squeezed its neck until the demon burst into dust. Trish moaned and began to stir.

Heaving, his muscled forearms bulging and bloody, Derek pulled her upright, nodded to Caroline, and reentered the fray. Claws caught at his duster, and he lunged out with a right hook. His fist passed through the demon's face and the claws withered away.

Rebecca screamed in rage and pain as an anger demon climbed her slim frame and sunk its pointed fangs into her neck. Caroline shoved two demons off the path and fought her way over. Her stiletto blade slid free from her belt and passed under its ribcage in two fluid motions.

Caroline caught Rebecca as she collapsed and held her fast. Her free hand drew the vial at her left hip, and she ripped the stopper out with her teeth. Pouring the contents on Rebecca's wound, she tore off a chunk of her skirt and pressed the charmed fabric onto the wound.

The charms worked and slowed the blood flow. Rebecca tried to stand, keeping one hand pressed to her neck, but her legs gave out, and she slumped to the ground. Grunting, she grabbed one demon and ripped its throat out with her teeth!

Through a lull, Caroline saw two massive demons wading through the rabble. They stood a full eight feet tall and were covered in grey hair with three curving horns. Their teeth stuck out of their misshapen jaws as they smiled down at their prey. Gegan appeared in their path and set his feet for a fight. The first demon reached for him, and his hand flashed upwards with a glint of metal.

The demon howled, an eerie echoing sound in the silence of the rest of the battle, as three of its fingers flew away and dissolved. It lunged at Gegan and hit him bodily at the waist. Gegan reversed his dagger's grip as the punch bowled him over and drove it down into the demon's back. He plunged the small blade into the demon's low back until it broke away. The second demon launched a viciously powerful kick and struck his injured knee as Gegan tried to regain his feet.

Gegan screamed in pain and lurched sideways. Both demons raked him, and pieces of shredded lace flew through the air mixed with blood, chains, and small metal plates. The uninjured demon grabbed Gegan roughly around the waist, lifted him full into the air, and jumped off the side of the path.

Derek gaped in disbelief, and the remaining enormous demon—despite its injuries—landed a solid punch into his stomach. Derek doubled over, gasping, and the demon grabbed him. Then, following its fellow, it pulled its prey down into the depths of the canyon.

Caroline fought on, but a horde of small demons quickly mobbed her. Her thoughts began to fragment as she was overwhelmed. Pain bloomed in her chest, and she belatedly realized the demons were piling on her chest and restricting her breath. Everything became fuzzy as she caught sight of Nathaniel. He was fighting against more of the enormous, furred demons, but one of them hoisted him up onto its shoulders. Blackness descended.

Nineteen

"Not for the faint of heart," Micah muttered as he reached his left foot down and searched for the next indent in the vertical cliff face. "Understatement. Epic understatement."

"Two steps until the next rest," Ricardo reported. The badger hung from the back of Micah's waistcoat, and it was a struggle to counterbalance his weight with the backpack.

His feet now on level ground, Micah shook out his arms and flexed his fingers to get rid of the tingling sensation. He wasn't sure if it was due to fear, adrenaline, or both. Looking back up, Micah marveled at the people brave enough to carve these slight depressions in the rock. Made for a human gait, the steps were too far apart for Ricardo to manage on his own, and only by splaying his fingers across the rock as he descended could Micah keep control.

"We're almost there," Ricardo said, poking his nose over the edge of the small rock outcropping they stood on. "One more rest area, then we are at the bottom. Where do you think the others are?"

Micah shrugged and rolled his shoulders. A faint roar echoed through the canyon, and he flinched. Only a human voice, a deep voice raised in righteous rage, could make a sound like that. "Let's go. Which foot do I start with this time?"

"Left," Ricardo answered promptly. "Derek said, 'Right, right, left, left, left, right and down.'"

Micah started down and felt thankful for Derek's knowledge. "You have to start each section on the correct foot," he'd explained. "Otherwise, you'll hit a gap step and be stuck." His foot slipped, and Micah clung to the rock as a cold feeling of dread rolled up his spine. "Focus," he told himself. "Focus and get through this."

They reached the canyon floor, and Micah took two breaths bent over with his hands on his knees. Ricardo unhooked his claws and scampered down to the ground. "Which way?" he asked, looking up at the impressive rock walls surrounding them.

Micah fished his compass out of his pocket and tried to open it. The damage required him to dig his thumbnail into the top of the case, and after a few tries, it sprang open on both sides. The hands of the clock had permanently stopped, but the red arrow pointed to his left.

Consciousness returned to Caroline with the subtlety of an earthquake. She groaned and tried to roll over. It felt as if metal bands wrapped around her chest, and she couldn't get a deep breath. Gasping, she laid her cheek on the cold rock beneath her and opened her eyes.

Deep shadows covered the canyon floor, but everything was bathed in purple light. A pulse of red suffused the purple, and Caroline realized the demons had surrounded her. Their eyes and teeth glistened, and she closed her eyes, anticipating the pain, but it didn't come.

Slowly, she blinked and struggled to stand. The effort brought surges of stinging pain to her chest, and she gasped for breath as tears gathered at the corners of her eyes. Around her, she could make out bodies lying amongst the demons. Everything was lit eerily by the double-door-sized portal glittering just above the ground nearby.

Silver veins surged with energy and stood out starkly against the glass-like surface of the portal while black veins bled inky trails into the light surrounding them. A faint mist hung about the portal as the spine-chilling cold condensed moisture out of the air.

"Why, I have a much larger audience than anticipated. How *delightful.*" The mob of demons parted, and Caroline let out an involuntary whimper as she saw what approached.

Seven feet tall and unnaturally thin, the demon walked on four stick-like legs. Its head was triangular with two bulging, bulbous eyes above a saw-edged mandible. Its arms curled up close to its chest and rubbed against each other with a grating noise. Translucent wings fluttered slightly against its abdomen as it swayed toward Caroline. The whole effect was one of a giant praying mantis colored in vivid green shot through with gold.

Power rolled off the demon in waves and nearly obscured the other demon limping behind him. This one was female-shaped and resembled a magenta wasp. An ugly cut marred her forehead, and blood crusted her bell-like lower half in several places. She held one arm stiffly against her chest, and her fingers were taped together.

The Baron and the Mistress, Caroline realized as the demons walked past her without further acknowledgment. She gasped as she saw what they were circling.

"How is this pathetic example of humanity your champion?" the Baron asked. He flicked out one long arm and grazed the side of Nathaniel's cheek. The young man jerked and nearly fell but kept his feet. His eyes darted around in panic, and tears coursed down his face.

While Nathaniel diverted the Baron's attention, the Mistress stepped away from him. Standing near the edge of the canyon, where the purple light didn't pierce the shadows, she revealed her fangs. "Your advance attacks are as nothing now," she spat. "You were deceived." Then, stepping aside, she exposed Micah.

Caroline gaped as she saw Micah stride forward into the arena. Even without her enhanced vision, she could see strings of glittering energy emitting from him. And underneath that, his aura crackled at the edge of sight like grey-blue lightening. He drew his daggers and bared his teeth.

A flash of movement caught the corner of Caroline's attention. She flicked her eyes in that direction and saw Ricardo tugging on Nathaniel's sleeve and pulling the shaking young man toward the canyon wall. An angry hiss pulled her attention back to the confrontation in front of her.

"You," hissed the Baron, slinking forward. "You disturbed my plans before. Years I waited. I planned to kill my enemy with utmost precision, and you stepped in. Thanks to you, my assassin wound at *her* feet, and the Mistress destroyed it." He shot the Mistress a hateful look.

Micah's only response was to switch his long dagger into a reverse grip and take a defensive stance.

"You forced me to endure years of the shrieking." The Baron lunged out with its left arm. The saw-edged ridges glanced off Micah's blade as he flicked it up to block. "Wailing…" Its right arm flashed toward Micah's face, and he ducked. "Deafening, piercing, moaning…" The Baron punctuated each word with another lightning-quick attack. "Keening…" Its claw grated against the top of the long dagger, curled unnaturally, and wrapped around Micah's forearm. "WIND!" The Baron roared as it ripped its arm back.

Micah's shirt mitigated most of the cutting force. The charms sewn through the fabric flared silver bright as they tore under the pressure. Instead of losing his hand and wrist, Micah was left with a burning cut that ringed the middle of his forearm. He curled his lip at the injury and flicked away the blood.

He juked left and tried to get behind the Baron, but the demon's triangular head rotated on its thorax and followed him. He kept circling, and the demon's entire thorax spun to keep him in sight, its arms raised and ready.

"I worked on that young witch for years," the Baron hissed, weaving and rotating its abdomen to face Micah fully. "She finally relented and started the process to bring us fully to the human plane. My advisors barely made it through with the ritual she prepared." It snapped its mandibles and advanced on Micah. "But you interfered. You found the ritual, and that witch ran for the demon plane before everything was ready for me. I missed escaping the horrid wind because you interfered— AGAIN!"

Instead of circling or blocking the advance, Micah dropped his shoulder and lunged forward. He dived between the saw-edged arms and rolled as the Baron tried to skewer him. The demon swung its thorax around and lashed out again as Micah scrambled to his feet behind it. He brought one dagger down onto its abdomen, but the demon's armored wings prevented any damage. The dagger tip *clanged* slightly as it ricocheted off.

The Baron screeched. It flailed wildly for a moment and kicked Micah with one spindly leg. He tumbled away, narrowly avoiding a second kick.

"It wasn't even enough that you ruined the ritual. You followed her to hell." The Baron pointed at Micah and began stalking closer. "My advisors ripped her to pieces, but you fought. You struggled and would not submit until, of course, *she* arrived. Then you dropped to your knees, and she kept you. My advisors brought me the pieces of the witch—and I ate them." A gruesome pink tongue emerged from the mandibles and licked the air. "Never have I tasted something so sweet. So, you see, I ended up victorious in the end." It turned and kept Micah in its sight as he circled again. "I absorbed her power and stopped the machinery myself!"

Micah kept his focus solely on the battle. He didn't dwell on the horrible fate Devon met all those years ago, and he refused to glance at the human forms lying on the canyon floor beyond the arena in which he stood. When the Baron shifted its weight to turn its abdomen toward him, Micah took two steps and launched himself at the demon. One leg had just lifted off the ground, and he severed it at the knee with his short dagger.

The Baron slashed at him as it staggered, and Micah took two long cuts across his chest. His shirt and waistcoat flapped open, but he managed an off-balance jump and landed on the demon's back. Micah wrapped his knees around the base of the demon's thorax and jabbed his short blade into its body to anchor himself. Then, he drew the long dagger across its thorax just below the head. His arm rotated awkwardly to bring the sharp edge of the dagger in contact with the demon, so the slice lacked finesse and power. The long blade glanced off the hardened thorax jarring his hand, but the short dagger sunk in the demon's body just beside the wing joint.

Clinging to the Baron with all his strength, Micah felt the demon's body thrashing and writhing beneath him. It spun its thorax in an attempt to unseat him, and Micah wrapped one arm around its thorax and clung on. He gripped his short dagger with all his strength and dug it deeper into the demon's body. The Baron twisted viciously, and Micah lost his grip. His knees flew sideways off the demon's body, but his short dagger remained embedded. Micah wrenched it across the demon's body, severed its wings, and drew a deep slash across its abdomen as he flew off and landed hard on the dust.

The wings glittered in the harsh purple light of the portal as they floated gently to the ground. Surging to his feet, Micah charged the demon, now twitching and shrieking with pain. One thrashing leg caught his hip and twisted his body awkwardly. Instead of body slamming the demon to the ground, he flopped onto it sideways.

Adapting instantly, Micah braced his arm against the injured abdomen, leaped, and brought the hilt of his long dagger cracking down on the back of the demon's head. The slender thorax wasn't strong enough to hold up Micah's total weight, and they crashed to the ground. The demon's legs pinwheeled wildly through the air as

Micah held its head down in the dirt. He bashed the back of its skull with his short dagger and leaned all his weight onto the demon's head. Then, positioning his short blade, he drove one vicious, smooth thrust into the base of the demon's skull.

It stilled. The body ceased twitching and thrashing, but it did not turn to dust. Instead, it lay there and bled until it seemed to deflate.

Micah rested his head on his forearm as he lay face down in the dirt next to the body and tried to release his grip on his daggers. They were sticky with blood, and he was too tired to pry his fingers loose.

"My champion," cooed the Mistress' soft buzzing voice. "My wonderful, shiny, glittering, darling champion. I have not seen such a fight since the days of old. Truly."

"I'm not yours," Micah grunted, raising his head and glaring at the Mistress. "Our deal is complete."

"That it is, darling." The Mistress reached down with her uninjured hand and ran her fingers over his shoulder. He felt a tug deep in his chest, and a small warmth of blood seeped onto his ruined shirt. The Mistress stood with one long ebony hair clutched in her fingers.

"Away, my demons," she called in a ringing voice. "Away to hell. Be quick, darling," she added to Micah. "Now that it is known humans can be devoured, you will be intensely pursued. The demons will reform soon, so be quick, and you do look entirely *delicious*." She strode through the portal, pausing only to blow Micah a kiss as the mass of demons packing the canyon floor dissolved into dust.

Micah took a deep breath and felt tears prick the corners of his eyes. It was done. Gentle hands turned him over, and he stared into Nathaniel's terrified chocolate brown eyes. Behind him, Ricardo was tugging the small backpack toward the portal, and Caroline was tending to Rebecca. Straining his eyes, Micah could make out Rebecca's chest rising and falling.

Ricardo deposited the backpack, waddled over, and dug his nose under Micah's hand. He didn't say anything but grunted quietly and sniffled.

"Help Caroline," Micah rasped at Nathaniel. He leaned heavily on the young man and made it to his feet, sheathing his daggers. His hands made small sucking sounds as he pried them loose from the hilts.

"But. I…" Nathaniel trailed off, staring open-mouthed as Micah limped toward the portal.

"Caroline," he called as he wrapped the straps of the backpack around one hand. "Goodbye."

For one instant, he stood framed by the portal with Ricardo at his side, but before she could answer or acknowledge him in any way, he was gone.

Tears blurred Caroline's vision as she ripped another layer from her skirt and doubled up the fabric over Rebecca's neck wound. The demon's teeth had sunk into her upper trapezius, but no major arteries had been damaged.

Her other injuries showed signs of infection, and Caroline quickly created charms to support her aura and expel the demonic influence. Her vision went fuzzy at the corners as she worked, and she couldn't take a breath without pain radiating throughout her chest.

Neither Trish nor Nathaniel had any significant injuries, and they helped her turn Gegan onto his back, re-splint his leg, and douse his many injuries in purification potions. However, Caroline was concerned because of the large bruise forming on his temple, visible despite his dark skin. He regained consciousness slowly and didn't recognize where he was at first. They forced him to lie still and waited to see how bad the injury to his head was.

Derek whimpered and clutched his left hand when they roused him. Two metacarpal bones jutted through the skin, and the entire hand was swollen and bruised. "What do we do?" he panted.

Caroline steeled herself as she doused his hand in purification potions and wrapped it. He paled, and she spoke quickly to try and distract him from the pain. "Carmen contacted the Witches Council as soon as we left. They should be sending healers as quickly as possible. Unfortunately, none of us can make it out of the canyon on our own power, so we wait." She gulped and felt the tears splash down her cheeks. "There is one more thing we have to do. Trish, Nathaniel, help me." She walked slowly toward the portal.

The portal flushed black and silver as she approached and shrank to the size of a dinner plate.

"What are we doing?" Trish asked as Caroline pulled off her satchel and unrolled it on the ground.

"We're closing the portal," Caroline said solemnly.

"But," she blanched as she said, "what about Micah and Ricardo? Won't they need this to come back?" Caroline didn't respond and just began sorting through her things. "He's coming back," Trish said, her voice rising in pitch. "He has to come back!" Her breathing quickened, and she started to cry.

Caroline slumped slightly. "He came back from hell once before. That's already more than anyone else."

Epilogue

"So that is the machinery?" Micah asked into the eerie silence, dropping the backpack. His fingertips were blue, and his breath came out in painful gasps. Being in hell again brought back a host of horrible memories, and he shivered from more than the cold.

"That's it. I thought it wasn't very impressive the first time either," Ricardo said as he limped closer, "but from this angle, I have to say I feel differently. It is small but mightier for it." He shook, and pieces of his fur fell out, leaving bald patches of bright red skin.

"How does it work?"

"What you see here is the control box." Ricardo sneezed and pointed a claw to the hole in the ground the machinery occupied. "Down there are the pipes, the fans, and the gears. When it's working, the fans force air through the pipes and blow it all over hell."

"I never knew the winds of hell were caused by this," Micah said.

"No one else does," Ricardo admitted. "I figured it out before when I descended into the belly of the machinery. The winds keep the temperature just enough above freezing to prevent ice buildup." He gasped for breath, swayed slightly, and lay down.

"What's wrong with it?" Micah knelt by the backpack and began fumbling with the clasp. Ricardo struggled to his feet and edged forward. He chittered to himself as he examined the gears, levers, and pipes.

"It's frosted over," Ricardo said a short time later. His eyes were glazing over, and his body was convulsing. "There is nothing broken. The gears were stopped and held manually long enough to freeze. So to get it started, all we have to do is warm everything up."

"Warm sounds nice," Micah said. He shivered and almost dropped the jar of cooking oil he'd stolen from Caroline's kitchen as pain rippled through his frame. Popping the top off, he poured the oil on the machinery. It bubbled and slithered down over the cold metal.

"Ready?" Ricardo asked in a whisper and collapsed.

"Yes, I could do with some warmth." Focusing through his tears, Micah steadied his hands just long enough to strike a match. He flicked it onto the oil pooling around the base of the machinery, and it went up in flames. The metal groaned and whined as the flames licked, and above them, in the populated portions of hell, Micah thought he heard the sighing of the wind.

The End

Acknowledgments

There are many people without whom this story would never have been possible.

To Patrick for your endless patience, support, and love. I wouldn't be the person I am today without you. From the day I woke up and said, "I dreamed a novel," to this day, you have been my rock. I love you.

To my dad, John, you have always supported the turns I made in life and have given me the confidence to pursue my dreams. On to the next adventure!

To Betsy for your input, time, and research. Without you, there would be no pickled garlic in my life, and I would not know where the auditory apparatus of a praying mantis is. You give my life flair, laughter, and joy.

To Raven for you time and expertise. You have improved this story immeasurably. Thank you for all your efforts on my behalf, lending me your skills with commas, and inspiring book two.

To Jenn, your skills lie in venues I have never visited. Thank you for your beautiful cover art ideas, your explanations about ISBNs, and your marketing skills.

About the Author

Erin Evans has led a life full of left hand turns. She has competed as an international level athlete, served as a nuclear electrician's mate in the Navy, trained as a massage therapist, and taught herself SOLIDWORKS.

Currently living in Phoenix, she is a stay-at-home mom to a beautiful son, an engineering consultant on calorimeters, and a knitter, creating overly complicated things for fun.

Throughout all the twists and turns of life, stories have written themselves through her mind. This debut novel is the first of many, across a range of genres, waiting to be written.

Contact Page

To contact Erin, please email:

Erinevans204@yahoo.com

Paperback and Kindle version:

www.amazon.com

Made in the USA
Las Vegas, NV
16 June 2022